Nothing Burns

IN

HELL

PHILIP JOSÉ FARMER

TOR®

A TOM DOHERTY ASSOCIATES BOOK
NEW YORK

This is a work of fiction. All the characters and events portrayed in this book are either products of the author's imagination or are used fictitiously.

NOTHING BURNS IN HELL

Copyright © 1998 by Philip José Farmer

A Tor Book
Published by Tom Doherty Associates, LLC
175 Fifth Avenue
New York, NY 10010

www.tor.com

Tor® is a registered trademark of Tom Doherty Associates, LLC.

ISBN: 0-812-56495-2
Library of Congress Catalog Card Number: 98-10259

First edition: May 1998
First mass market edition: November 1999

Printed in the United States of America

0 9 8 7 6 5 4 3 2 1

Nothing Burns

IN

HELL

1

Nowadays, my worst nightmares are about money.

I was in the office of the president of the First Corrugated Bank. I was saying, "If you'll extend the time limit on my loan, sir, I'll shine your shoes and kiss your big, bare, and shiny bottom. Please!"

The president looked old enough to have created the Big Bang. His eyes, one of which I knew was missing, were hidden behind sky-blue sunglasses. Most of his sky-blue suit was covered by a massive white beard. On the giant ashwood desk behind which he sat was a statuette of St. Moneta, Our Lady of Black Ink. Near it was a telephone shaped like Bugs Bunny. It rang and rang, but the old man ignored it.

"There are free lunches, Mr. Corbie," the old man said, "but not for man or woman. Don't think you can tomfool your way out of this mess. This is a check-and-balance universe. Pay up!"

"Why don't you answer the phone?" I said. "It may be a reprieve from the governor."

The old man picked up the receiver, listened, then held it out to me. "For you. It's not the governor."

I awoke sweating and groggy. The real phone, my phone, was ringing, and its alert light was flashing. I sat up in bed, my heart beating hard. Had to be bad news. My father had unexpectedly died? But when I saw the number on the illuminated caller ID display, my heart beat slowed. Mimi Rootwell, my boss, would not be calling about my father. Why, then, would she wake me up at 5:08 A.M.?

I picked up the receiver and said, "Just a minute, Mimi. I'll go across the hall so I won't disturb Glinna."

I threw off the sheet, sweat-soaked despite the air-conditioning. Glinna, her bare back to me, didn't stir. I reached out for a cigarette to take with me, then remembered I'd quit three years ago.

Old habits don't die. They just circulate in the nervous system.

A moment later, I turned on the study lights. I sat down at my work station and picked up the phone receiver. "What is it?"

Mimi's voice was the sexiest I've ever heard. But the only thing she's ever gotten passionate about—as far as I know—was the agency, Andrew Bell Investigations and Security Systems. It was in bad financial shape when she inherited it from her uncle, and she had been rebuilding it ever since.

"A woman, sounds young, phoned me five minutes ago. Bless my soul, who needs sleep? If I don't, you don't. Anyway, I have a possible case for you. I don't want it, and you might not. But it could be a thousand dollars plus expenses, no receipt required, for one day's work. Your potential client is obviously desperate and in a hurry."

"A thousand? Why wouldn't I take the job?"

"Why not? Even you show good sense now and then. She wouldn't give her name. My caller ID displays the number of a public phone booth in East Peoria. She'll be transferring money to someone, wouldn't say to whom or why, wants you as a backup."

She paused. I thought it best not to speak until Herself gave permission.

"I told her my agency wouldn't accept a case which might involve something shady. I did tell her I knew a man who might take the job as a temporary freelancer. I didn't tell her you'd stepped into financial ickypoo and badly need the money or that you sometimes obeyed what you call The Higher Law. You know, Tom, your character, such as it is, is inconsistent. You're usually so tidy and orderly, almost prissy. Yet, you're very flexible in the way you operate. You contradict yourself—"

I dared to interrupt her. "I contain multitudes. I've got my mother's genes and my father's . . . never mind. You were telling me about the Mysterious Stranger, remember?"

"I didn't give her your name or phone number. She'll be calling me back about nine. Why she's waiting so long to do that when she seemed to be in such a blazing hurry, I don't know. When I hear from her—if I do—I'll notify you. Where'll you be about nine?"

"At my father's house, making my weekly visit. If she calls, hang up after you put her through to me. You don't want to know what it's all about."

"I wouldn't think of listening in."

"Sure you wouldn't, Paula Pry." I spoke too softly for her to hear me clearly.

"Oh, by the way," she said. "I may need you in a few days for an important case. Right now, I can only tell you it involves the most powerful and wealthy family in Peoria. If I give it to you, I'll expect you to handle it with velvet gloves, duck your head, doff your cap, say 'Sir' and 'My Lord.' I'm not asking you to kiss the client's ass, just be polite and discreet." She hung up.

I stood there for a moment. The most powerful and wealthy family in this city? That had to be the Alliger line, of whom

Simon Grettirson Alliger was the Alpha male, the Bull of the Woods, Old Nobodaddy.

Ninety-nine percent of the citizens of Peoria didn't know about the family because its members were very publicity-shy. They never appeared in the newspapers except in the obituaries, and these never mentioned how many money pies they had their fingers in. They seldom went out to eat; they dined mostly in the mansions of their own very select group. Mimi wasn't kidding when she said I'd have to deal with them as the very rich demanded they be dealt with.

On the way to the kitchen, I analyzed my dream in about six seconds. Nothing Freudian about that, no sexual symbolism. It sprang from my anxiety about my financial problems. My conscious mind is too happy-go-lucky to worry much during the daytime. But when I'm sleeping, I can't keep out the things that ooze from the cracks in the wall. As for the old man and the desk objects, they came in dream-twisted form from my childhood reading of Old Norse, Native American, and Jewish-Christian myths.

I got the drip coffeemaker going. The radio weathercaster reported that it was sunny now, cloudy later. Nature was going to pitch another hot sizzling ball across Earth's plate. The temperature would rise to at least ninety-one Fahrenheit, but a massive cold front was moving in.

I turned the radio off and breathed in the odor of Colombian coffee and ground French vanilla beans. It was one of the seldom failing pleasures of life. Another was the silence. That would vanish, however, when the people in the next-door apartment woke up. Two weeks ago, Sheridan Mutts and Cindi Wickling had moved into there. I didn't know them, though I'd seen Mutts a number of times at a tavern, The Last Stand. Since the first night, they'd been at It every night.

By "It" I mean they played loud country-western until two in the morning. This was punctuated by shrieks, high-decibel laughs, and the sounds coupling couples are supposed to make. Show-offs, Mutts and Wickling wanted the world to know what supersex sounded like.

My wife, Glinna Heithbarn, and I had been using earplugs when we went to bed. They made us feel as if we were deep underwater. However, the plugs and air-conditioning noise usually dampened the uproar. Not so last night.

I thought of vengeance vile and violent. Yet, I was trying to climb to a high peak of spiritual development. Though I wasn't a Catholic, my hero and role model was St. Francis of Assisi. But it seemed to me I was a pumpkin trying to change into a gilded coach in a place where midnight never came. How much free will does a pumpkin have?

For a while, I walked the saint's way with Mutts. I tried to get friendly with him before saying anything about the hellish racket. No go. Then, one evening in the apartment building parking lot, I'd politely asked him to keep the noise down to a civilized level.

He'd bellowed, "Hey, I gotta live! It's a free country, ain't it? You don't like it, Choirboy, move!"

"The name's Corbie," I said. "It's not the music per se. I even like some country-western — in small doses. It's the loudness I can't tolerate. Hear that, Woof-woof?"

His face reddened, and he clenched his hands. He said, "Call me that again, and you get your teeth knocked out. Got that?"

He was a construction worker, thirty years old, six feet and five inches tall, and weighed two hundred and eighty pounds. Fifty pounds was beer belly. His wild dirty-blond hair and wool-pile beard looked like a vulture's nest on top of a diseased oak.

I was thirty-nine, six feet three, and one hundred and ninety-six. I still had the rangy build of an all-state high-school baseball pitcher, which I once was. Yet, face to face with Mutts, I looked like a frail teenager squaring off with a professional wrestler like Hulk Hogan. I didn't want to tangle with him. One of us might get badly hurt or even killed. That one would probably be me. So, I had just laughed and turned away from him.

Other tenants besides myself had complained about the nightly din to Selinda Tuneball, the manager of the building, which I call the Rinky-dink Arms. Selinda's very curly orange hair, blanked-out eyes, and snub nose made her look like the comic-strip Little Orphan Annie. But Annie's nose wasn't red, and she'd never breathed out Ripple wine, four dollars a gallon, day and night. And Annie had guts. Selinda was too afraid of Mutts to get tough with him.

I'd asked her for the phone number of the owner, who lived in Florida far from the turmoils and troubles of his Peoria tenants.

She'd said, "Mr. Katzenwinter has an unlisted number. I'm not arthurized to give it out."

"Arthurized?"

"That's what I said. Anyway, I don't know just now where he is. I can't even get hold of him to tell him the esophagus needs fixing."

She meant the soffits.

Being the curious person I am, I'd found out that my apartment key unlocked every door in the building except the storage room. My scroogey landlord had installed identical locks he'd purchased wholesale. Of course, neither he nor the manager had mentioned to the tenants that any key could open any other tenant's door. And Selinda was never sober enough to think of putting a different lock in her own apartment door.

I hadn't waited to install a deadbolt lock on my door.

Selinda usually left the building on Wednesday at 10:30 A.M. to shop for groceries and liquor. After that, she'd be in a bar until noon or later. That day, I waited until the booze-bedeviled woman drove away to become an instant menace to the other menaces infesting our roads. Then I went down to the first floor. After unlocking her door with my key, I entered her smelly troll's cave. At the end of the narrow hall was a second bedroom, converted into an office. Its gray-steel three-drawer filecase was by her desk. An open lock was hanging on the hasp of the top drawer. In less than a minute, I'd located Katzenwinter's Miami address and unlisted phone number.

During the next week, I tried the landlord's number five times. All I got was the answering machine and an unpleasant whining voice telling me to leave my name and phone number. He'd get back to me later. Each call, I stated my name, phone number, and my complaint. Though he must have wanted to ask me how I got his number, he never replied.

So, in Tuneball's apartment again and wearing latex gloves, I used her ancient typewriter to tap out a formal letter of complaint to the landlord. I wrote that we, his tenants, would be installing our own locks as of now but would send him the bills for the work done. If he didn't reimburse us immediately, we'd get a lawyer. At the bottom of the page, I ink-stamped THE COMMITTEE. There wasn't any, but there might be. Then I ran off copies from Selinda Tuneball's copier and slid one under every tenant's door except Mutts and Wickling's. I didn't want them to know yet how easy it was to get into their premises.

The letter caused high indignation and anger among the tenants. And, of course, questions about the writer's identity. I played innocent. At least half of the tenants sent the copies to Katzenwinter's address, which I'd provided on the original letter along with his phone number. As far as I could determine, Mutts and Wickling still knew nothing about the affair.

Next steps.

Collect dog turds from the front yard of a friend who wasn't home at the time.

Enclose in a cardboard box with a lock and a key just like those Katzenwinter had provided his tenants.

Tape the box. Stick on a label with the landlord's Florida address. For the sender's name and return address, print: ORLANDO FURIOSO, 123 HIGH JUSTICE COURT, OPAQUE, IL 66669.

Drive to Pekin, a town ten miles south of Peoria and on the east bank of the Illinois river. Ship the box to my landlord via the Pekin UPS. (Never use the federal mail system for anything like this.)

Also in the box was a plastic envelope enclosing a hand-printed quotation from the Bible, the Book of Job, I believe.

"Oh, Lord! My bowels are in an uproar."

But I was still waiting for my landlord's reaction.

2

I went back to bed so I could sleep for a half hour or so. By the time I awoke, Glinna was jogging somewhere in the neighborhood. Thus, I had some time to think about the details of the surprise birthday party I'd arranged for her tonight. (She was born July 2, under the sign of Cancer. I was born April 1, hence, I was an Aries. The astrologers don't recommend that Cancer and Aries marry. However, statistics show that such marriages last as long as any others.) I'd purchased for her a foot-high bronze statuette of a Cretan snake goddess. It was now hidden in my closet. We really couldn't afford it just now, but it was, in some distorted way, my peace offering to her for having put us so deeply in debt.

Soon, Glinna, sweaty, panting, and claiming to be on a high after putting five miles behind her, would appear on the rise of the road. I thought that anybody who'd run in the high-humid heat squeezing central Illinois was crazy. Though Glinna had many excellences, she was a Greater

Kook, no rare bird nowadays. I loved her deeply, anyway.

To those who didn't know any better, our living room looked "New Age." But crystal balls and statuettes of the Antlered Man and the Great Earth Mother were around long before the fateful birth in the Bethlehem manger. Glinna says her religion is the oldest in the world, at least sixty thousand years old, perhaps a hundred thousand years old, very Old Stone Age.

The room was crowded with books and artifacts, but I tried to keep it clean and orderly. This wasn't easy since Glinna was not a neatnik. In fact, right then, I spotted a crumpled paper napkin and several large cookie crumbs on the carpet. I put them in the wastebasket, then I closed Glinna's copy of *Basic Black Magic*, which had been lying open and facedown on a sidetable.

I wished I could've ignored the litter. But I was, in this respect, too much like my mother. As soon as I saw anything needing cleaning or rearranging, I just had to do it at once.

The shelves and cases in the front room were loaded with books on astral projection, reincarnation, and other occult subjects. There were also many astrology books. "The stars govern your life. Tomorrow you'll meet your dreamboat and win the big state lottery. But don't bend over if a male Sagittarius with Mars ascendant is close behind you."

A tachyon emitter, a foot-high silvery metal cylinder, was on an oak pedestal by the hall entrance. Its radiation was supposed to tune you in to good cosmic vibrations. The truth was that tachyons were purely theoretical time-traveling particles invented by physicists for intellectual fun. But that didn't stop crooks from selling emitters to the gullible.

Near the emitter, in a wall niche, were two trophies for

state championships my high school baseball team had won. I'd been its star pitcher.

My own bookcase held many volumes, three of which were very rare and very expensive. They were why I owed so much money and why my dreams were troubling me and why I was considering the offer of the Mysterious Stranger.

Henry Miller's *Tropic of Capricorn,* illustrated by Grandma Moses. (She must have been liberated by LSD while painting these for the book. Though still primitive in style, the always scary and often phallic images seemed to have crawled out of the slimy swamp of the collective human backbrain.) Homo Erectus Press, 1969. Limited edition of a hundred copies, boxed, signed by the author. The plates were lost in a fire. $10,000.

Mark Twain's *The Mysterious Stranger,* first edition, 1916, mint. Once owned by President Franklin Delano Roosevelt. A slim volume packed with enough misery and hopelessness for fifty thick novels. I read it when I get too manic, which I certainly was not at this time. $3,000.

Irene Iddlesleigh, by Amanda Ros, the world's worst author. First edition, 1897, signed by Ros. Mint. $1,000.

These volumes were cheap at the price and a solid investment. They should have been in a box in the bank, but I couldn't bear to stick them in a dark place, and so, of course, the insurance premiums were high. I'd had to borrow $14,000 and pay for the books at once so I could beat out another would-be buyer. The loan also meant that Glinna and I had to put off saving for a down payment on a house. She wasn't at all happy about this, especially since I'd not said anything to her about the loan until after I'd purchased the books.

When I got to the kitchen, I poured coffee into my Three Stooges mug, then carried it into the spare bedroom. Spread out on a table by the computer was a printout of my astrological chart prepared by Glinna before her morning jog. I skipped the boilerplate about the zodiac, houses, aspects, and so on. The gist was that July 2 would never fade from my mind. I'd meet strangers who'd become lifelong friends. I'd make a woman very close to me ecstatically happy with a gift. This was a hint I should get a high-priced and unusual birthday present for her. But the Cretan snake goddess was already hidden in a closet. Its price deepened the financial hole we were in.

Just as I put the chart back on the table, a rumble like a volcano beginning to erupt shook the southern wall. The baboons next door were up now and listening to a love song by Cayuse Cooney. "Honey, What Your Dog Did to My Leg, I'm Achin' to Do to You."

Then my apartment door slammed. Glinna, her white T-shirt and shorts dark with sweat, stormed in denouncing our noisy neighbors. I'd never heard her that angry before except when she'd exploded about my borrowing money to buy those books.

I went down the hall to meet her.

"This is how my wonderful day starts," I said.

"I don't like to do it," she said, "but I may cast a spell on those pricks, never mind the bad vibrations coming back at me. It wouldn't be evil, not when it's for a good cause."

During this, she'd been shedding her shoes, socks, T-shirt, shorts, and panties. Of course, she'd dropped them on the floor by the sofa.

"You could shoot Mutts and Wickling," I said. "But it'd be a felony, more's the pity. However, while you're working your spell, I'll be solving the problem my own way."

"I don't want to know what it is."

"Oh, by the way," I said, "Happy Birthday!"

I *was* happy, happy I'd remembered to say that now. She would've gotten even madder if I hadn't.

"I've had my shower," I said. I started to take off my pajamas. "Your hormones are whirling around. So're mine. They need settling down. We got time. Besides which, it's been a long time."

"Four days," she said. "Is that so long? I'm sorry, the signs don't indicate an appropriate or happy union."

I was frustrated and angry, but I didn't dare say anything to her. She'd bring up the loan and God knew what else. Screw the stars, I thought. And then, better them than nothing. Our sex life wasn't what I wanted it to be, mainly because of her eccentric notions. There were, for instance, those crystal balls and pyramids she had to arrange in hexagrams under the bed so that they'd focus the most intense sexual energy on us. During the right astrological time, of course.

It got so that I couldn't drive past a crystal shop without getting a hard-on.

Glinna said, "Soon, I'm sure. After all, I want it just as much as you."

Then she smiled, kissed me on the mouth with lips maybe a trifle too thick, and headed for her shower, her long pony-tailed auburn hair swaying, her narrow hips rolling, rolling, rolling. At thirty-five, she was still beautiful, unflawed except maybe for the lips and a nose a trifle too long. She was six feet tall, slim, and narrow-waisted. Her legs seemed to be as long as Jack's beanstalk, though much more shapely, and she strode like a strip teaser. She'd financed her education at UCLA by working for several minutes just three days a week. She never told me how she got the gig, and I really didn't want to know. But she did admit that wealthy compulsives had paid her to urinate into teacups (very fine china, though), from which these men drank with both relish and gusto. Glinna got the highest pay in California for the easiest job anywhere, and her product was said to be the best on the West Coast. The connoisseurs agreed that it combined an angel's purity with a certain cheekiness and its bouquet evoked the sound of far-off silver bells ringing.

This also described Glinna's character to a P.

Glinna had had no qualms about making very good money so easily. Though she'd been raised by parents who were witches, or wiccas, as they prefer to be called, at the age of twelve she had fallen from grace. She'd left the religion of the Earth Mother and become a devout member of the Second Revised Free Will Apostolic Baptists. Just after her graduation from UCLA, she'd gone back to her natal religion. Become, as it were, a born-again witch. And then she became deeply ashamed and remorseful about having sold her urine.

I regretted this because it wouldn't have taken her long to pay off the loan, and it'd been no effort for her. However, I didn't have the nerve to ask her to resume a profession she loathed and which some might say was immoral.

Of course, her high school teacher's job résumé omitted the above facts, and she was very secretive about her religion. Central Illinois is full of people who seem to know much more about hell than they do of heaven and who mistakenly and ignorantly equate witches with Satanists. Glinna, like most wiccas, doesn't believe there is a Satan.

Just as I finished eating breakfast, the phone rang. I picked up the receiver and put a finger in my left ear to dim the roar from the wall.

"Niagara Falls observation platform."

"What?"

"Tom Corbie, Mimi."

"For God's sake, shut off that cacophony!"

"Would that I could. It's from the apartment next to mine."

"I wouldn't put up with it for a minute! Why don't you call the cops?"

"Because I don't want the fingerbone of suspicion pointing at me when I do what I have to do."

"Don't tell me what that is," Mimi said. "Here's the latest. No-name, your Mysterious Stranger, called three minutes ago. The caller ID number is for a phone booth in East Peoria, a different number from the one this morning. She's changed her mind, won't phone you. Instead, she'll meet you where she won't run into anybody who knows her. She didn't say that, but it's obvious. Pete's Midway Duck Inn at 11:40 A.M. She'll be wearing earrings shaped like Celtic crosses. I told her to look for a tall blue-eyed man with medium-length wavy red hair. He'd also have a broken nose and a winning smile. I didn't tell her about the charm you can fake when you want to unlock the client's word hoard . . ."

"Fake? I'm deeply hurt."

". . . or about your uppity mouth and your laughing at the strangest things. Let her find out for herself. But, Tom, take my advice. No matter how much you need the money, walk away from this."

"I'll certainly consider your words of wisdom. But, Mimi, as you know too well, a PI in this medium-sized city or even in Chicago usually just does tedious legwork, research, and stakeouts for lawyers and insurance companies. However, this one smells of enigma and romance, a damsel in distress, dragons nibbling at her lovely ass. I'll be cautious, but it couldn't hurt to hear her out. Call me Sir Galahad."

"How about Sir Dimwit?"

She hung up.

Glinna had to get to the high school early for her summer school special education classes. In the afternoon, she had a part-time job as a computer teacher at Illinois Central College. While "Keep Your Woman in the Corral" blasted through the wall, she kissed me, said good-bye, and was on her way to what I call Humpaduck High School. Shortly thereafter, the stereo was turned off, and the abominable twain slammed their door shut. I watched them through the French doors until they got into their vehicles in the parking lot. Then, wearing latex gloves and carrying a paper sack with the tools needed for my project, I left my apartment. After unlocking my neighbors' door with my old key, I entered the premises. I left the door slightly open so I could hear noises in the hall.

The huge entertainment-center cabinet was against the wall I shared with Mutts and Wickling. After pulling one end of the cabinet out, no easy work, I disconnected the three-prong plastic power plug. I spread out a newspaper below it and cut off its prongs with a hacksaw. The paper caught the metal dust and the severed prongs. I sandpapered the end of the plug and then cleaned the surface with a rag. After applying industrial glue to it, I put on it a tiny wooden disk I'd carved out several days ago.

When the glue had dried enough to hold the disk and plug surface together, I put glue on the open end. Then I held the surface against the outlet. When the glue was dried and the prongless plug was firmly fixed to the outlet, I put the rolled-up newspaper, the sandpaper, the bottle of glue, the brush, and the hacksaw into the sack. After which, I shoved the cabinet back against the wall.

When the stereo was turned on, it'd emit only what Glinna and I, and no doubt others, longed for. Silence. Mutts would try to troubleshoot the set himself. When he looked at the plug, he'd be sure there was no faulty connection there. But why wasn't the set getting any power? It would take some time before Mutts, the rugged independent macho, would reluctantly call in a serviceperson. That person might screw around for some time trying to locate the cause of the malfunction.

Of course, when he did find out what had happened, he'd suspect me. I was the only one who'd complained to him.

3

efore I left home, I donned blue jeans, a white short-sleeved shirt, dark-blue socks, black oxfords, and a thin dark-blue jacket. Usually, I wear a long-sleeved white shirt, a conservative tie, and a suit when I meet a new client. But I wasn't sure the Mysterious Stranger would even show up.

The sun was shining as if it wanted to nova out and destroy the solar system. The air was steadily getting warmer. Clouds here and there were scouting for places where the advancing storm could do the most damage.

I entered East High Point Road. It runs close to the edge of the bluffs, which rise a hundred and fifty feet or so in this area above the flatlands and the Illinois River. At the end of the road are millionaires' mansions overlooking the river valley. My father's house, however, was in the upper-middle-class area, mostly Republicans, and a sprinkling of Fort Apache Democrats.

Just past the first curve of the road was a small grassy plot enclosing a boulder on which was a bronze plaque. This recorded that Charles Lindbergh used to land here in his De-

Havilland biplane at Peoria's oldest airport while flying the mail (1926–1927) from St. Louis to Chicago. Glinna says that very few of her students or the young teachers know about Lindbergh's famous solo flight over the Atlantic Ocean in 1927.

I turned into the driveway of my father's house and stopped the motor. Here lived Michael H. Corbie, Ph.D., retired ex-Bradley University professor of mathematical economics. My father is well known in this field as the author of *Wall Street as the Theatre of the Absurd* and *Checks and Balances in the Jivaro Shrunken Head Market, 1890–1940*. The book he wrote under the nom de plume of Malander P. Snike, *Great Assholes in American History,* is much more widely known. Half the subjects in the book are admirals and generals, one-fourth are evangelists, and the rest are politicians.

The two-story red-brick building was not Frank Lloyd Wright-designed but looked as if it were. From its back you could see the Forest Park woods, Upper Peoria Lake, and the bottomland and bluffs across the river. Deer, coyotes, foxes, and other wild beasts, including walkers, joggers, and flashers, now abounded in the Forest Park woods and the oak forest around that. It was in these woods and along the river that I had the happiest days of my relatively happy childhood. Here I found Indian arrowheads and other artifacts, some at least ten thousand years old, and played with the neighbor kids. Sometimes, I listened to the whangdoodle, a bird which spent its life grieving, much like Poe's raven. My father had told me about it, and not until I was ten years old did I discover that the melancholy but mellifluous cry rising from the Whang-doodle Woods in the evenings was actually made by the mourning dove.

He also told me stories of Withiha, short for Withihakaka, the shape-shifting trickster, the Great White Hare of the Peoria Indian myths. He was, in appearance and character, much like Bugs Bunny. According to my father, Withiha is still around in these woods and playing his tricks on animals and humans alike.

"So, my son, don't assume that things or people are what they appear to be."

My father, at the age of seventy-six, still roamed the woods. A grove of giant oaks there, he said, was his temple. In it, he felt at peace with the world and deeply religious, even as much as in a hardware store, and there he worshiped Fred, the Great Whangdoodle. I first heard about Fred when I was twelve, and my father and I were walking through the oak grove.

"Contrary to your mother's accusations that I'm an atheist or agnostic, I believe that a creation implies or even proves the existence of a Creator. But I reject all previous religions and all their names for God. And I want a god I can feel at ease with, though I wouldn't dream of getting too personal with It. So I call It Fred, the Great Whangdoodle. I am Fred's only worshiper, and I like it that way. There won't be any heresies or wars springing from Fred's religion."

My father wasn't blaspheming or being facetious when he called the Creator Fred. He was telling me that the names for the Supreme Being, God, Yahweh, Jehovah, Allah, whatever, were important only to the group bestowing it, unasked, on the Creator.

As for my religion, I'd been a Biblical literalist until the age of reason. Then I'd become an atheist, an agnostic, and then, born again, a member of the Church of Jesus Christ Minimalist. But I'd fallen from grace. Just now, I was between deities. My only faith was that the sun would rise in the east.

Nobody answered the front door chimes, so I walked around to the side of the house and looked through a window into the garage. Mike Corbie's 1991 scarlet Mer-

cedes was inside. And Sheba had sold her Harley-Davidson a
month ago.

My father, a contrary old geezer, wouldn't give me a key to
his house, nor would he tell me why he wouldn't. I went
alongside the south side of the house until I came to the open
deck at the corner. Up the wooden steps I went, paused to
drink in the wonderful view of the green woods and the blue
river and to listen to the nearby buzzing of bees and the delightful calls of wrens, chickadees, cardinals, and bluejays. A
ruby-throated hummingbird, surely God's most exquisite and
beautiful creation, was dipping its long beak into a wine-
colored feeder, its wings a blur.

As I expected, the sliding screen and the sliding glass door
were locked. I looked inside at the living room. No father. No
Sheba.

If my dead mother could have seen the mess, she would
have died again. The scattered clothes, accumulation of mail,
newspapers, coffee mugs, a half-empty bottle of bourbon,
dirty breakfast plates and bowls on the coffee table, a half-full
sack of potato chips, a bowl of greenish dip, and other items
made it look like a teenager's bedroom. Or as if, despite the el-
egant furniture and French impressionist paintings, it was a
crackhouse.

Even a gorilla, which fouls its own nest, would have been
disgusted.

If my mother were here, she'd have kept the room clean
and orderly. Too much so because it would somehow have
given an impression of a sterile operating room. But her neu-
rotic horror of dirt and disarrangement was preferable to this
yahoo's cave.

Mom sprang from the womb with a scrub brush clamped
between her gums, her chubby little hands groping for
a broom, a dustpan, a bucket, a mop, all the weapons needed

to battle for life against a disorderly and filthy universe.

I've seen her, dressed to go to a formal party, head for the door, then stop because she saw on the hall table what no one else could, a dust fleck gleaming like a crystallized turd. Despite my father's thundering at her that they were late, get her ass in gear, she'd walk to the kitchen, come back with a rag, kneel down, and wipe off the minuscule offender.

As my father said, "The cosmic battle is not between evil and good. It's between dust and duster."

My mother! My father! No wonder I have so many warring elements in my character. She, so quiet, so tidy, so religious, so temperate, so hopeful, so unread. He, so gabby, so sloppy, so pagan, so wild, so cynical, so drunk (should I say, crazed?) with learning.

What had made them meet and why had they ever gotten married?

They ran into each other, literally. He was speeding on a state route east of the river and close to Morton, the Pumpkin Capital of the World, when he drove into the village of Holy Flats, and her car broadsided his.

I'm not kidding about the name of her native village. Originally, it was Hurley-Fflots, named after the two men who came to this area in the early 1800s to trade whiskey with the Indians for furs. The name became Holy Flats when Pennsylvania Germans of the Church of Gadrine settled in the area in 1847. (A.C. Gadrine, a Swiss preacher, founded the sect, a spin-off from the Church of the Teutonic Christ, in 1690 in southern Germany.) According to my father, they all had been and still were shrewd, tight-fisted, bigoted, prudish, hypocritical, self-righteous, and patriarchal.

My eighteen-year-old Gadrine mother was taking her first solo drive that June day when she ran her father's 1935 Ford into the side of Mike Corbie's brand-new 1955 Chevrolet. Both were at fault, and that state continued in their marriage.

I suppose nothing romantic would've grown out of that encounter if my mother hadn't been as beautiful as a fairy-tale princess. Seeing her, thirty-five-year-old Mike Corbie, Ph.D., forgot in a microsecond his anger about his wrecked car. One thing led to another (it always does, doesn't it?), and he courted her until she said she'd become his wife. Her parents were very much against her marrying out of the church, especially to a non-Republican agnostic boozing radical whose morals were undoubtedly tainted. And, horrors, he went to movies and dances and listened to the radio.

For once, ever-subservient daughter Rose Sharon disobeyed her father. She really loved Mike Corbie and was fascinated by him. Hormones win most of the time, temporarily, anyway. One big thing affecting her decision was that she couldn't stand the drab and ugly clothes her church demanded that its women wear. This policy was intended to keep the women from being sexually attractive except to the men of the church (their standards were low). My mother was an exception, a barnyard hen who longed to be a bird of paradise.

Her father gave in, and the family attended the wedding in Peoria, though they must have been uneasy in a Methodist church. And, as my father admitted, Rose's folks were basically nice people if you overlooked their pennypinching, narrow-mindedness, and general ignorance of things not agricultural or Scriptural, and their ingrown souls. Which, of course, he never did overlook.

I, the only child, was delivered on April 1, 1957, at Peoria Methodist Hospital.

Mom wanted my middle name to be her family surname.

"For God's sake!" Mike had cried. "Why in the world did I take unto me a wife from the benighted boobs of the Bible Belt? Schnarsch! Schnarsch! Is that a surname or a pig with diarrhea farting? It sounds like a toothless dog gumming his chow! Schnarsch! Schnarsch! Schnarsch! You want his playmates and schoolmates making fun of him? Barking 'Schnarsch! Schnarsch, Schnarsch!' at him, making his life miserable! You want him to put that name down when he applies for college, put it down on a job résumé? Shit, shinola, and sugar, woman!

"No, it'll be Thomas Gresham. After Thomas Gresham, died 1579, financial adviser to Queen Elizabeth the First. He originated an unquestioned truism in the field of economics. Bad money drives out good. Carve that in granite. Bad money drives out good."

"I don't like it, it's ill-omened," my mother had said. "It makes it seem as if our child is the bad money."

"Ill omen! Superstitious rot! What the hell does Schnarsch mean in German? Simpleton?"

I thank God that my father had prevailed.

In 1986, I was a private investigator in Los Angeles. I had a degree from UCLA in criminology, five years on the LAPD, and three years as a PI. Then my father summoned me home to help him take care of my mother. She, he said, had been suffering with cancer of the liver. But they had decided not to tell me about it until it was certain that chemotherapy and radiation weren't going to stop the thing eating her up. Though she should be in the hospital, she'd insisted on dying in her own house. For once, he gave in to her. But he couldn't nurse her without help, and it was time they dropped their concern for my peace of mind.

I felt like telling him I should've been told at once and why didn't he ram his concern up his colon. But I didn't say it. Not until I drove into Peoria did I quit being angry at him. It was a harrowing time, though Mom was usually half-dead with morphine and didn't complain. To do so was against her nature and her religion.

One day, my father went to the grocery store. I was sitting in a chair in my mother's room and holding her hand. Then she opened her eyes and whispered that she had something to say to me. I got out of the chair and leaned over close to her mouth. Her breath was foul with medicine and death.

"What is it, Mom?" I said.

She spoke so weakly I could barely make out her words.

"What if they're wrong?"

And she died, her eyes and mouth open. No more sight. No more words. No more cleaning and dusting.

Much later, my father said, "Tom, what did she mean? 'What if they're wrong?' Was she thinking about a recipe for fried broccoli, some method of preparing food?"

"I'm not sure," I said. "But I think she meant that maybe the preachers didn't know that what they preached was non-sense. Maybe she wasn't going to heaven after all. Maybe she'd just be dead, a nothing. She worried about that, really fretted, you know."

"No, I didn't know," he said. "Why'd she tell you and not me?"

"You never really listened to her. You always made fun of her. I did listen. Most of the time, anyway."

That hit him hard. But it was too late to make amends.

After we buried my mother, I decided to quit the agency in LA and be a PI in Peoria. Shortly after that, I met Glinna.

So, here I was on the side porch of this house and won-dering where my father was. I decided that he was down in the valley forest and communing with Fred. But where was Sheba Peece, his ex-hippie, ex-anarchist live-in? She must be home because she loathed, among many other things, walking.

I went around to the other side of the house. The main-floor bedroom louvers were shut. When I stood close to a window, I could hear Sheba cursing shrilly. Then she began beating on the bedroom door and calling out for my father to unlock it.

She and my father had had another verbal combat about who knows what. Sometimes, she caught him in a room and locked the door on him, and sometimes he locked her in. I didn't know why they didn't carry keys to the rooms. It would've been so easy. But they didn't, so keys must be forbidden by the rules of the sick game they played.

When he did return, he'd unlock the bedroom door. Sheba and he would continue screaming at each other or reconcile by going to bed. He was a cadaverish seventy-six and she was a scrawny beat-up sixty. The clang of bones on bones would be like glass chimes in a windstorm.

As I drove away from the house, my pocket phone rang.

"Tom Corbie speaking."

The Mysterious Stranger's voice made me think of nightingales and ripe apples. This is not a thought a wary private investigator working on a case should have.

"I changed my mind about not phoning you again. I want to make absolutely sure you'll be at our meeting place at the appointed time."

"Unless the Norns decree otherwise," I said.

"The nuns?"

"No, Norns, the three Viking Fates. Originally, there was only one—"

"Fates, shmates! Be there!" And she clicked off.

4

pring Bay Road was a two-lane paved highway running
along and relatively near to the east shore of Upper Peoria Lake, Pimiteoui, Fat Lake. The bottomland farms along here
grew the best melons, corn, and tomatoes I've ever tasted. I
longed for them while I lived in Los Angeles.

I drove off the highway into the gravelly parking lot of the
Duck Inn. Black clouds racing from the west had locked up
the sun. Their shadows had sped toward an assignation with
me as I'd crossed the McClugage Bridge to get to the east side
of the river.

A bad omen? Not to unsuperstitious me. I just have a poetic
turn of mind.

The Duck Inn was an unpretentious one-story white
wooden building. Though it was out in the country and on a
lightly traveled road, its reputation was wide and its business
good. Long ago, Al Capone had stopped here to eat and drink
after shooting (for a change) ducks. But the most interesting
customer during the early 30s was Frankie McErlane, the

gangster who invented the "one-way ride." Called the most vicious killer in Chicago, he murdered his wife, her two dogs, and, at the very least, eight well-known hoods and only God knew how many lesser hoods. Once, he shot it out with gunmen while he lay in a hospital bed with a cast on his broken leg. Near the end of his career, he went crazy and fired at imaginary enemies in empty streets.

Across a gravel road from the Duck Inn was a bronze plaque set in a pillar of rocks cemented together. It commemorated the slaughter of thirty defenseless women, children, and old men of the Potawatomi tribe in 1812 near this place. Warriors of this tribe had taken part in the Fort Dearborn massacre (in what later became Chicago). They'd killed, scalped, mutilated and tortured white men, women, and children. Both sides claimed to be justified.

Few Peorians, I'm sorry to say, express genuine regret for the Spring Bay incident. They reason that, after all, the red man was not only a born loser but had failed to develop the land properly. Therefore, anything that happened to the Indian was his own fault. However, one week during October, the annual Potawatomi Massacre Repentance Festival is held here, and everybody has a good time.

Most of the patrons of the inn were local stumpjumpers, good farm people. The others were hunters during duck season and city dwellers who came here to enjoy the fried food, fatty gravies, beer, and raucous companions. Today, a weekday, only two cars and two pickup trucks were on the lot in the front of the inn.

I wrote down the license plate numbers of the parked vehicles and their year, make, and color.

By now, I could hear the rumbling and see the flashing in the clouds above the hills across the river. It looked like one hell of a soup Mother Nature was stirring in her big energy-kettle. Pieces of paper, loose twigs, and leaves were flying around, and cigarette stubs were rolling along the ground. I had to press down on my hat to keep it from blowing off. The air was somewhat cooler, though.

I returned to my car for the raincoat I'd forgotten to take out of the trunk. With it draped over my left arm, I walked around behind the building. I wanted to make sure that no cars were hidden there. After all, my prospective client would know that I could track her down through the DMV. Except for the Duck Inn owner's car, which I recognized, of course, there were none.

A minute later, I was walking in a rain so heavy I felt as if Noah's Flood was dumping on me. Thunder and a nearby flash of lightning made me sprint to the front of the building. A wooden ramp rose to the front door above the low porch. I passed two low, thin, horizontal metal bars secured to uprights on each side of the ramp. Farmers and duck hunters were supposed to use these bars to scrape the mud off their boots before entering. By the door was a sign: NO DOGS OR GUNS ALLOWED INSIDE.

Soaked, wishing I'd been smart enough to put the raincoat on sooner, I stepped into the building. The air-conditioning should have felt good, but I shivered with cold.

Before me was a large room enclosing a bar to my right and, elsewhere, wall booths and tables. Not more than a dozen customers were there. The decor was Early Primitive Barndance. The heavy but savory odor was Rural Chow à la Cholesterol. Three men on stools and clutching bottles of beer sat there, their eyes fixed on the TV on the wall. This week, a local station was featuring a Tab Hunter festival. One of the men on the stools turned around—a commercial had just come on—and smiled.

He bellowed, his voice audible above the thunder, "How they hanging, Corbie?"

Since everyone had heard him, the woman sitting in a booth at the far end of the room had no trouble identifying me. No more than I had knowing she was the Mysterious Stranger. I didn't even need the big Celtic crosses hanging from her ears. She had a face that said she was $350 per bottle of wine and a light salad, easy on the dressing. But that didn't mean a thing as far as her character and intentions went.

I walked toward her. She did not have a handbag. But a genuine leather briefcase was on the seat between her and the wall. She looked up at me through huge sunglasses from under a wide-brimmed straw hat. Maybe she thought that the hat would make her look as if she were one of the rustic customers.

"Right?" I said, pointing at her.

"Right. Please sit down."

The voice was the one I'd heard over the phone.

I slid along the seat until I was facing her. We were silent for a moment while we sized each other up.

She wore no makeup. Her skin was creamy white and smooth. No sun-worshiper, she. No wrinkled leathery skin or skin cancer when she got old.

What I could see of her long pony-tailed hair was a beautiful blue-black, but I didn't know if that was its natural color or if it was a wig. Its color and texture, however, and her lightly pigmented skin made it likely the hair had once belonged to an Asiatic woman or was dyed.

Her forehead was hidden by the drooping brim of the hat. The dark glasses concealed her eyes and eyebrows.

Age: anywhere from twenty-five to near forty. Nowadays, what with plastic surgery, who knows how old a woman is?

On the seat by her was a dark-blue expensive-looking raincoat, maybe a Burberry. Her figure and legs were hidden under a large blue cotton man's shirt, neck open but not to the cleavage, and very baggy jeans. Her shoes were purple Reeboks. I didn't think she was accustomed to wearing the outfit. Anyway, this was T-shirt and shorts weather.

She lifted the big mug of black coffee with her slim left hand. Her nails were well-manicured; the polish, clear. No rings. No white bands on her fingers indicating she'd recently taken off rings. The sleeves of her raincoat hid any wrist-watch or pale band of skin where a watch could have been worn.

After she sipped the coffee twice, she said, "Would you like something to drink? Or to eat?"

"No, thanks. Might as well get the business over with. I know you won't ID yourself. Mimi Rootwell told you I'll make up my mind about taking the case after I get all the facts or what you say are the facts."

"My, aren't we brusque?" she said, a teasing note in her voice.

I gave her my deeply serious and soulfully empathetic look. Sometimes, it works. Sometimes, it doesn't.

"I can be unbrusque if we have enough time for it. Do we?"

"No," she said.

For the first time, her voice hinted of desperation. But maybe that was to fool me. As it was, she looked at her left wrist, caught herself, and lowered the mug. I assumed that she'd concealed her watch under the sleeve because it might give me some clue to her background. A genuine Rolex, for instance, meant she had no money problem. Unless she'd stolen it. Few things are certain.

"There's this man," she said slowly. "He's got something on me, blackmailing me, trying to, anyway. I haven't committed a crime, but he knows something I don't want revealed to certain persons. I stand to lose a lot, too much, if I don't pay him off."

"How much is the payoff?"

"Not much. Ten thousand dollars. But as soon as the money's blown, he'll be back for more. I'll deal with that when it happens."

Ten grand wasn't much?

"You want me to kill him?" I said.

She started, then leaned forward and placed a slim cool hand on my warm bear's paw.

"Would you do that?"

"Do you want me to? For a price?"

She took the hand away and straightened up. "No. But I had to know what kind of a man I'm dealing with."

I shrugged. I didn't tell her I wouldn't kill a human being except in self-defense or defense of another person. It was better to be an uncertain quality.

"What do you want me to do?" I said.

"This man is psychotic. He hates me so much he might kill me even if he'd lose future payments. I want you to be near enough to take action if he attacks me while I'm giving him the money. But you must conceal yourself while I'm doing that."

"I'd have to know the layout of the meeting place."

"I don't know yet where it is. At or around one o'clock I'll get instructions in a public phone booth. I have to leave soon. I'll phone you when it's time."

Cloak and dagger stuff. Next, she'd be having me rescue the Prisoner of Zenda or the Man in the Iron Mask. But this kind of thing did happen sometimes in real life.

"Give me your word," she said, "that you won't follow me until I meet him."

"No problem," I said. "If I take the job."

No self-respecting and ethical investigator, having only the few facts she'd given me, if they were facts, would take the case. Was she setting me up for a frame? Or was she genuinely afraid of the blackmailer? If there was one.

By then the thunder and the lightning were shaking the walls, and the rain was ramming into the windows.

"Are you carrying?" I said.

She twitched, then said, "Shooting him would mean publicity, the last thing I want!"

I didn't doubt that, but she had not answered my question.

"Well, I don't know," I drawled. "First, let me tell you what it'll cost. I usually get from sixty to seventy dollars an hour, plus expenses. In this situation— "

"That's all right," she said quickly. "Your expenses plus a bonus. One thousand dollars. Paid right now."

Instead of being an incentive, that offer made me even more suspicious. Still, a thousand!

"If I accept, it'll be half in advance."

"I'll pay the whole sum right now. I have all I'll need, all you'll need, right here."

She tapped her finger between her breasts.

This was getting even more intriguing. Maltese Falcon stuff and also a woman who carried a roll in her cleavage.

If I took this job, I'd be tormented for a long time about whether or not I should report the money to Uncle Sam. Though I try to be honest in all matters, I sometimes can't resist temptation. A thousand dollars! Probably a bagatelle to this woman, but a lot to me. It'd take a chunk out of the ten thousand dollar loan.

As for paying the IRS tax on the thousand, I'd let my conscience steer me on the right course when the time came to render unto Caesar what is Caesar's.

"If a crime is committed during this case, I have to report it to the police."

"I know that," she said. "Look! I have to know right now if

you'll accept me as your client. I don't want to go with my back unguarded. But, if I have to, I will."

Damn! I was just too curious to say no to her. And I was too eager, dangerously eager, to escape the humdrum of my usual cases. I shouldn't say yes. But . . . a thousand!

"First," I said, "I want a look inside that briefcase. Call me Perry Paranoiac, but I have only your word for what this is all about. For all I know, the briefcase is stuffed with newspapers."

She laughed, and said, "If I were in your place, I'd do the same."

She put the case on the table, unlocked it with a tiny key, turned it around, and shoved it to me. I opened it. Well, well! After I'd snapped it shut and pushed it back to her, I said, "Looks OK. New money, though. Didn't he want various denominations, nothing new, no numbers in order?"

"He doesn't care. He knows I won't set any dogs on his trail."

"OK," I said. "I'll do it."

She reached down into her shirt, pulled out a plain white bulging envelope, and handed it to me. I thought she could just as well have carried it in her raincoat pocket. Why the dramatic next-to-the-breasts stuff? Was she subtly trying to seduce me into accepting the case? But I'd already accepted. Maybe it was her peculiar way of bonding us. No. I was, as usual, getting too analytic, too psychological. Or was I?

"You can count it if you wish," she said.

"Not here. After I leave," I said. I took out my wallet, removed two dollars, and placed them on the table. "For the coffee and tip," I said. "On me."

"Too too generous," she murmured.

"I'll give you an itemized expense account when you pay my hourly rate."

"Don't bother. There's an extra two hundred in there. That should cover present expenses, wouldn't you say? But if you want more, I got it here."

She placed a finger between her breasts.

"It's far more than enough," I said.

I'd better take what I could get now. I felt that I'd never see or hear from her again after this business was over.

She slid to the end of the seat, the briefcase in her left hand and her raincoat draped over the left forearm, and stood up. I slid out, too. Standing by her, I estimated that she was approximately five feet and ten inches tall.

"I assume you'll be armed," she said.

"Correct."

"Good!" she said, smiling at the same time. Lovely.

Then she looked serious. "Don't follow me. What you do, you'll park outside the Holiday Inn in East Peoria. Wait there until I call you, or go inside if you want to. Just be ready to go, no delay."

She didn't even say good-bye or good luck while accompanying me to the door. She closed it after me but stayed inside.

After counting on the porch the one thousand and two hundred dollars, all in century notes, I dashed through the rain toward my car. I thought, It's not too late to back out. Then, am I a wimp? No, I'm not. But I wondered how many knight errants had had misgivings before they set out on the quest for the Holy Grail. And how many had started the journey while a wind howled around them and rain and thunder and lightning lashed them?

Knight errant? Me? I was no Sir Gawain, no Sir Galahad. More like the sad sack knight, loony Don Quixote.

When I got inside the car, I couldn't see more than a few feet ahead of me even with the windshield wiper thrashing at top speed and the headlights on. A mist quickly formed on the inside of the windows. I turned on the defogger. When the windows were clear, I started to ease out onto the road. No lights of approaching cars showed. That didn't mean much because the darkness and rain would sharply limit the extent to which they could be seen. But, surely, any drivers out there would be going very slowly.

Just before the car reached the edge of the road, I had to pass gas. I stopped the car to ease it out. The odor forced me to lower the window despite the downpour. Water hit my left shoulder and ran down the inside of the car. I raised the window and then started forward onto the road.

My headlights glared on a van speeding in the lane I was about to cross. I yelled with fright and slammed the brakes hard. It rocketed by, but not before I'd seen a bearded white man hunched over the steering wheel. His face was turned toward me, and his expression was probably inspired by terror. I saw it as demonic, eyes staring, his mouth in a snarl, white teeth gleaming. He looked as if he were a tormented soul hell-bent on killing me and himself.

The damn fool moron! Driving in this blackness and blinding rain without his headlights on. Hurling himself and his vehicle northward at sixty miles an hour. If my car had come onto the road a second sooner, it would've been hit broadside. I surely would've been killed or, worse, mangled and brain-damaged.

That would've been like the knight falling off his horse and breaking his neck just as he set out from the castle to slay the dragon. Tragic slapstick. Something for others to laugh at. Meaningless.

Except that I believe this is a meaningful world. I can't

prove that it is. But I've observed that those who insist this universe is meaningless always act as if it were jam-packed with significance. Behavior reveals the true belief; judge a tree by its fruits.

5

Ten minutes later, the thick rain thinned into a drizzle. The overcast just above me lightened as if the sun were about to break through it. To the south and the west, however, the lightning hammered bright-white surveying stakes into the ground. It was as if the black clouds meant to claim central Illinois forever.

Two miles before I got to the McClugage Bridge, I saw a passengerless taxicab in the opposite lane. Then I knew how my client must've made sure I'd not see her license plate. She'd taken an East Peoria taxi to the Duck Inn and would take another cab back to that city. I rejected my impulse to pull over to the side of the road and wait for the cab to return, then follow it.

The radio weatherperson said that the temperature had dropped within one hour from ninety-one F to sixty-six F. It was as certain as itching for the bathless that more storms were coming today. Many accidents were being reported. Three people had died not a mile from where I was. I shivered

when I thought that I could have been among the casualty reports.

My car phone rang. I wasn't expecting my client's voice
since I hadn't even got to East Peoria yet. She said, "He just
phoned. He said I'd have to wait in East Peoria for quite a
while. I don't know what that means, an hour or six hours. I
suggest you stop right now where you can get out of the
storm and wait for my call."

I left an answering machine message for Glinna that I might
be late for dinner, which was scheduled for 7:30 P.M., but that
she shouldn't get alarmed. Then I drove into the parking lot
of the Holiday Inn and sat in the car for an hour. Then I read
some of my favorite passages from Homer's *The Odyssey,* the
greatest adventure story ever. After which, I walked to the
hotel lobby and drank some coffee. Then, I read *The Farmer's
Almanac* until I got tired of reading, and I walked outside
during a half-hour lull in the storm.

At 4:20, I left another message for Glinna, saying I would
probably be far later for dinner than I'd expected to be. But
when I could reasonably anticipate the time of my return, I'd
call her. I was just about to try to get hold of the people in-
vited for the birthday surprise party when I got a call from my
client.

"Do you know where the Lakeside Cemetery in North
Pekin is?"

"I've been there."

"The man who's going to get the money told me to meet
him there within the next fifteen minutes. I'm to park by the
Coriell family plot. He gave me directions. Do you know
where the plot is?"

"Yes. My father and I attended Vernell Coriell's funeral. My
father was in Coriell's World War II paratrooper company."

She said, "This man probably won't show up there. If he

doesn't, I'll have to go back to another phone booth and wait for his call."

"You don't have a cellular?"

"Really, Corbie! And have you trace me through the phone company's billing records?"

"Just how smart is this guy?" I said.

"Not very, and he'll probably be drunk. He has little self-control, as I told you, and whiskey takes away much of that little."

"I'll be hidden nearby."

"I hope you'll be close enough. He won't come out into the open until he thinks I came alone. I might have to wait a long time."

"Probably," I said. "The rain and the heavy overcast make it easier for him to hide. On the other hand, it'll make it easier for me, too."

I looked at my fake Rolex wristwatch.

"Unless you've got something else to impart to me," I said, "I'm gone. Fifteen minutes is not a long time to get to the cemetery, especially now that the storm has gotten a hell of a lot worse."

Pekin (32,000 population) was on the east side of the Illinois River and about ten miles down from Peoria. When the village was laid out in 1829, a founder's wife named it after Pekin, China. She mistakenly thought that if you dug a tunnel from the village straight down through the center of the earth, you'd come out in that city.

The drizzle became slashing sheets just as I got to the Shade-Lohman Bridge. Wind gusts rocked my car. The light was as dim as that of very late dusk. Thunder rolled above me. Lightning bolts crashed close enough to make me jump. I slowed down to fifteen miles an hour. The traffic lights near the exit looked like red, yellow, and blue ghosts. I drove southward along the right lane. The familiar landscape and buildings had become darkened and distorted by the very heavy rainfall. It was as if I'd driven into another universe.

A sports car, a van, and a pickup truck, all with no headlights on, splashed my car as they passed. The drivers were demented. But who, in one way or another, isn't? After some miles had crawled behind me and I was in North Pekin, I saw on my right the veiled bulk and dim lights of the Abel Vault and Monument Company building. An entrance to the Lakeside Cemetery was just beyond it. My car eased through the gateway onto the gravel-covered one-lane road. Going two miles an hour, I drove past trees, upright gravestones, and tall monuments.

A minute later, I turned off the lights and the motor. The car's right tires were on the grass. My guess was that I was about sixty feet from the designated meeting place. I couldn't see more than three feet ahead except during lightning flashes. These illuminated my client and her car, about eighty feet ahead of me. After turning off the interior lights, I got out in the downpour and closed the door as silently as possible. Then I opened the trunk and removed my BAR .30-06 rifle from its case. I couldn't use a night scope because the lightning flashes would have blinded me. But I did attach a conventional scope. My Dan Wesson .44 Magnum revolver with a six-inch-long barrel attached was in my raincoat pocket.

Rifle in hand, guiding myself mostly by lightning, I walked on the slippery grass. A clump of trees momentarily concealed me. Now, my client and her vehicle were about forty feet from me, and I could make them out somewhat more clearly. I half-concealed myself behind the tree closest to her. Instead of the hat, she was wearing a scarf. She'd taken off her dark glasses, of course. Her car, its right wheels on the grass, had its headlights on. But the illumination, even during the flashes, was too indistinct for me to identify its make and year.

It was black or blue or some dark color. Its license plate had been removed.

She was standing by the first stone in the row of stones on the Coriell family plot. Ten feet beyond her was darkness. She waited while the wind whipped her coat hems and ballooned her scarf out. Her back to me, she stood as motionless as a marble angel on a monument.

After a weary but tense ten minutes, during which I kept looking behind me for anyone sneaking up on me, I faintly saw a glow in a southerly direction. It blinked three times, then went dark. My client took a flashlight from her raincoat pocket and pointed its beam toward the origin of the signal. Her return flashes, diffused by raindrops, fuzzily outlined her.

Presently, a figure appeared from the darkness and the rain. Lightning bolts illuminated it but were too brief and dazzling for me to see it clearly. My client directed her flashlight beam at the advancing figure. It became a short man wearing a long-billed cap and a raincoat. His legs seemed to be covered by jeans tucked into dark calf-length boots. A flashlight, turned off, was in his left hand.

A revolver was in his right hand.

He came closer, blinking in the beam directly pointed at his face. Some things were extending from around his mouth. They seemed to be long tendrils, tumorous growths. A corner of his mouth was twisted up, the result of a knife wound, I'd bet. After he said something to her, she moved the light a little to one side. His face was now a shadow except when the bolts crashed not too far away and lit it up. He jumped every time one struck. So did I. My client, however, had nerves strong as bridge cables. She did not start.

The two talked for a moment, both gesticulating wildly. I couldn't hear a word over the thunder.

She turned, walked to the rear of the car while opening the trunk lid with a key control, and took out a briefcase. By

then, I had my rifle pointed at him, my eye against the scope.
That limited my vision of the surrounding area. I lowered the
rifle an inch. For all I knew, his buddy, if he had one, was behind me. But I didn't dare to take my eyes off the two in
front of me.

She slammed the trunk lid down and handed the case to
the man. He must have said something to her. She turned and
raised the lid again. After putting the revolver in his right-
hand coat pocket, he leaned forward deep into the trunk. By
its light, he opened the case and started to count the money.

I'd never have exposed my back to my victim. Maybe the
sight of all that money blew his caution out through his ear-
holes. She didn't move, just watched him while he counted
the money twice. Then the man snapped the briefcase shut,
backed away from the trunk, and closed its lid. She walked by
him and around the car toward the driver's seat. As soon as
her back was to him, he pulled a long hunter's knife from his
belt, stepped around the rear of the car, and lifted the blade
high.

I shouted a warning to my client and aimed the rifle at the
man's ribs. The warning, however, also alerted him. Just before I squeezed the trigger, he dropped onto the gravel. My
bullet probably drove into the side of the car. She spun
around and started to draw something, a weapon, I assumed,
from her raincoat pocket. But he was on her and stabbing at
her with the knife in his right hand.

At that moment what sounded like a rifle fired from somewhere out in the darkness. She fell heavily backward, the man
on top of her. I didn't know if she'd been hit or not. Her left
hand was by now gripping his right wrist. Then she bent her
head forward and seemed to clamp her mouth against his
face. He screamed with pain while trying to wrench his knife
hand loose.

The confederate fired again. The bullet whizzed close to my

right ear. The muzzle flash came from the southeast. I jumped to my left, past the cover of the tree, got down to one knee, and fired my rifle at the area where I'd seen the flash. The woman's attacker broke her grip. His knife seemed to strike the side of her face. She screamed and then became limp. The man, holding a hand to his face, got to his feet. The knife lay where he'd dropped it.

He screamed, "That hurts! That hurts! Goddammit, that hurts!"

I fired above his head to distract him so the woman could escape, if she could move. When he heard the rifle, he stooped down, grabbed the briefcase from the gravel, and ran behind the front of the car. I regretted not having dropped him. The man in the darkness — if it was a man — shot again. This time, the flash was from the southwest. The man behind the car screamed again.

In another relative quiet between bolts, he yelled, "You dumbass! You shot *me!* You shot *me!* I already been hurt, then you . . ."

A man yelled loud enough for me to hear him distinctly. "Deak! Deak! It was an accident! I swear . . ."

Thunder drowned out the rest.

By then, the woman had rolled off the road to the grass on the left. She should've taken refuge behind or under the car, but she was probably somewhat stunned and not thinking clearly.

During another space between lightning bolts, Deak shrilled, "Almond, you goat-sucking half-wit! Don't use no names!"

Through the darkness and rain, I could see the vague shape of my client, by now crouched in front of the base of a big monument. She had been remarkably cool and self-possessed for a civilian.

Just to keep Deak nervous, I fired at the ground below the

right rear tire of her car. Then, stooping, I ran until I was almost to a gravestone large enough for cover. Almond's rifle banged, and a bullet thummed near my ears. I saw the muzzle flash, and I stopped and fired at where it had been before resuming my run.

Another lightning flash showed me the stone. DICK PIZ-ZLE//1863–1944//7 WIVES//HE REJOICED THAT THERE IS NO GIVING//IN MARRIAGE WHEN THE DEAD RISE//ST. MARK 12:25.

The flash also revealed me to Almond, though I must have seemed a dim wavery target. I felt a tug at the right shoulder of my raincoat. Also, a burning pain. I scrambled around behind the gravestone and replaced the empty four-cartridge magazine with a full one from my coat pocket.

In a brief comparative silence, Deak yelled. "Get in the truck, Almond! Wait for me! I'm coming out!"

Nice of him to announce it. Despite the shots aimed in my direction, I fired back twice at the flashes. Lightning streaks showed Deak running across the grass, headed toward Almond. I could barely make out the briefcase swinging from his left hand. As he sprinted, he held his revolver across his chest and fired it in my direction. It was a wonder he didn't shoot himself in his left shoulder. But, running as fast as he was, he couldn't be badly wounded.

I put my left hand under the arm of my shirt and felt my wound. The bullet had just touched the skin. There wasn't much blood.

Then the woman shot twice at him. In between lightning strokes, I could hear him squalling. Headlights came on about seventy feet south of the gravestone the woman was behind. They moved swiftly toward Deak. I shot once; the woman, twice. Lightning revealed a pickup truck and its bullet-shattered windshield.

That unnerved Almond, who forgot all about his rescue mission. He swung the truck off the gravel and onto the grass.

More bolts revealed that its tires were slipping on the wet grass and that it had turned three-quarters of a circle. But he backed it up fast, though the tires must have been still spinning, and he headed down the road.

Deak shouted, "Wait for me, you yellowbelly, or . . . !" Lightning smashed the rest of his words.

What he'd said was evident, though. He shot once at the truck. Almond must have heard the bullet whistle by or could see in the rearview mirror that the flash was coming from none other than Deak. His truck slid to a stop.

By then, I'd forgotten my desire to just run them off the scene. I stood up and fired at the rear tires, though they were not a clear target. My client also rose and fired three shots. Deak turned and shot back once. He had luck that he didn't deserve. The woman fell.

Deak must have scrambled into the truck. It took off, wheels spinning, gravel flying. Its headlights showed it going east, then curving northward, headed for the exit gate. I raised the rifle to expend the last cartridge in the magazine at a point just below Almond's neck, silhouetted faintly by the interior lights of the truck cab. But I lowered it. Out there, beyond the truck, made invisible by the darkness and rain, was Route 29 traffic. I couldn't take the chance that my shot would hit some innocent on the highway.

I ran to the woman. She was sitting up, her flashlight lying on top of the grave mound and its beam pointing at the calf of her left leg. The Swiss Army knife she'd used to cut off her pants leg from the knee down lay on the grass. She was holding the ends of a handkerchief tourniquet just above the wound. Not much blood was welling. What there was was being washed down her leg by the rain. She'd been very lucky. The bullet had passed through the side of her calf, and, apparently, not severed any major arteries or veins. Even so, she was going to be in pain from muscle injury. Though she had fallen at Almond's first shot, she must not have been hit then. She had dropped to the ground to make herself a smaller target. But the second shot had made a minor wound.

That she'd come armed meant she wasn't the ordinary type of blackmail victim. Or maybe she had hoped that we'd shoot the man called Deak and also whoever was with him. And then she'd shoot me. Or maybe not.

"Doesn't look too bad," I said as I knelt down by her.

"In and out, no bones hit. You go on. I'll make it."

"You should go to a hospital."

"Nothing doing!" she said. "We ... I ... have to avoid all publicity!"

She raised her head to look at me. Her left cheek was bloody from stab wounds. It wasn't that that shocked me, though. The left eye was gone, and the socket, the eyelid, and the flesh around it were a bloody mess. The eyeball had been gouged out or scooped out with Deak's knife. She had to be in excruciating pain, yet, aside from that one scream, she'd shown no sign of it. What a woman!

She said, "Go after them! I'll be OK! If you catch up with them, the money is all yours! I don't care what you do to them! If you're forced to kill them, so be it! The money's yours, what you've earned and ten thousand dollars cash!"

She began to struggle to her feet. As I helped her up, I said, "Even if I could catch up with them, what if I did? You want another shootout on the streets? The cops'd be there in a minute."

"For God's sake, quit gabbing! Go after them!"

"I will if you'll tell me where to go to get them," I said. "And their names. Otherwise ..."

The briefcase appeared in my mind like a mirage of an oasis to a man dying of thirst in the desert. With ten thousand plus the thousand she'd paid me, I'd only owe three thousand on the loan. I didn't intend to murder to get the money. But there'd be ways other than that.

I said, "If I take the money from them, that won't solve your problem. They'll be back demanding more."

"I doubt it," she said. She was swaying now. "I told Deak Mobard that this was the last payment. If he showed up again, I'd kill him or make sure he and Almond, his brother, were killed. I think that's why he attacked me, though he may have been planning that anyway."

"It doesn't seem reasonable he'd kill you. That'd be like tearing up a credit card for which you're never billed."

"For God's sake!" she said. "Every second we talk, they get farther away. Stop arguing, stupid!"

"Where are they going?"

"Goofy Ridge. You know it?"

"I used to hunt around there," I said.

"I don't know just where they live in Goofy Ridge. You'll have to . . ." She put a hand to the blood still flowing from her cheek. "I'm going now. I'll call you tomorrow, find out what happened."

She limped swiftly to her car, got in, turned the motor and the headlights on, and drove away. She was tough, so tough that I wondered why she hadn't ambushed the two men and shot them herself. Maybe it was because Almond and Deak weren't the only ones in the blackmail plot. If blackmail was what this was about.

Though I was in a hurry, I took out my flashlight from my raincoat pocket and turned it on. I went over to the place on the road where she and the man had tangled. The flashlight beam showed three objects. One looked like a headless worm but was actually a tumorous growth five inches long. She'd bitten it off from Deak's face and had spat it on the gravel. Near it were the parts of a fake-eye assemblage, a plastic sphere and a shield bearing the image of the pupil and iris. The latter had been inserted under the eyelid and over the plastic sphere. I placed the fake-eye assemblage in a plasticine envelope I always carried in my jacket pocket. I didn't see any reason to save the tumorous growth. I suppose her pain and the wounds had prevented her from looking for the plastic parts.

Once again, I thought, What a woman! And I wished her luck in getting to wherever she was going to be treated. It wouldn't be a hospital. The staff there would call the police to question her about how she got the knife and bullet wounds, and she certainly didn't want the police involved.

6

The rain lessened, and the thunder and lightning sounded more distant. The wind still blew hard enough to rock the car. I could see at least a hundred feet ahead of me. I'd left State Route 29 for the unmarked County Route 16 when I saw what I thought was the Mobards' pickup truck. I pulled up behind it long enough to make sure that the truck had no windshield and that the passenger was Deak. Then I dropped back about a half mile.

I didn't know what would happen when I caught up with Deak and Almond nor how long the business would take. I decided I'd better leave another message for Glinna and then try to get hold of the guests for tonight's party. Glinna wasn't going to take kindly to my being late for her birthday even though I couldn't help it. The storm I'd face when I did get home would make this one look like a zephyr.

And then I heard a beep-beep-beep rising up from the cellular phone. I didn't even have to look at the instrument to know what it was signaling. The battery was almost dead, and I'd forgotten to put an extra in the glove compartment. So, no more phoning home. No more phoning anybody for a while.

After the truck had put seventeen miles between it and Pekin, it slowed down even more. We'd left Tazewell County and were now in Mason County. We were going by Manito, population 1,100, a village which exists mostly to supply local farmers with groceries and machinery. In the Algonquian Indian tongues, Manito means Great Spirit. But that's the interpretation according to the white men. Actually, the Native Americans believed in a host of spirits, river spirits, rock spirits, tree spirits, and so on. The idea of one ruling spirit like our Judaeo-Christian-Muslim God was not in their religions.

Manito was the center of a sort of geological schizophrenia. Peat swamp to the north of the village. Prairies, once wetlands, to the east. Areas of blown sand to the west. Whether or not the geology of the area had an effect on the inhabitants' mentality, I didn't know. But my father claimed that the particular location and geology of my native city helps make the Peorianess of its citizens.

A moment later, I followed the truck west onto County Route 15, also unmarked. It was a lonely stretch of highway, rolling hills, farmlands, huge irrigation machines looking like Martian spiders, and an occasional house. After a few miles, I came to Sand Ridge State Forest, an area that reminded me of lakeshore Michigan. Lots of sand and pine and fir trees. During the 1930s, pines and firs, trees more at home farther north than central Illinois, were planted here, making this area even more schizophrenic. The sandy forest floor and the sand dunes had been deposited by a melting glacier 15,000 years ago. Such un-Illinois plants as sand flocks, silvery bladder pods, and prickly-pear cactuses grew here. Their nearest relatives were in the American southwest deserts. Here also lived a reptile unique to Illinois, a lizard with six yellow stripes. Like the desert plants of this area, it would be much more at home in Arizona.

After I'd gone a few miles, the rain and thunder and lightning sprang out from some hiding place. The daylight ran down a hole. The truck went more or less southward for miles, then slowed to turn right onto a two-lane paved road. On its left side was a one-story motel most of whose guests were hunters.

I could make out a familiar sign through the rain and the darkness. 1/2 MILE TO MALLARD CLUB. An arrow on the board pointed down the road. There was no sign indicating that this was the larger part of the unincorporated hamlet called Goofy Ridge.

In less than a minute, the car was on a dirt road in an area of pre-World War II and new trailers on cement blocks, Permastone cottages, pig shacks, and shanties. Some of the latter were leaning over, seeming ready to fall, so dilapidated that even the ghosts haunting them had moved out. Many outhouses, wooden crappers, stood among the residences. Weeds crowded the tiny yards. Trees surrounded the residences, all of which had been built helter-skelter, no zoning laws, no property planning. Along the road were clusters of metal mailboxes and receptacles for *The Pekin Times* newspapers. Contrary to what most Central Illinoisians believe, some Goofy Ridgians can read.

I came to a large clearing on one side of which was the Mallard Club. Six vehicles were parked in front of the one-story, rectangular, and windowless building. The pickup truck was not among them. To the west, a hundred feet away, the waters of spring-fed Lake Chautauqua, named after the New York lake, lapped at the shore of the ridge.

Though I knew it would be useless, I stopped the car at the entrances of two narrow dirt roads leading from the clearing.

I got out and looked at the deep water-filled ruts in the illumination of my car headlights. There was no way I could tell what road the truck had gone on.

I drove back past the tavern through the open gateway of a wire fence onto somewhat higher ground. On the fence was a sign declaring that this was the property of the U.S. Fish and Wildlife Service. After I parked the car near the fence, I turned off the lights and windshield wipers. I lowered the window far enough to get a good view of the clearing and the tavern, then I cut off the ignition. Since the rain was from the west, it did not enter the window. The nearby trees on the edge of the lake formed a dark screen into which my dark car would blend. I'd decided that I'd just have to take the chance that one of the Mobards had been dropped off at the tavern. If so, Deak wouldn't want to call attention to his wounds. Almond, I suspected, would be inside buying liquor to celebrate the loot they'd gotten. I was willing to invest an hour watching in the car. After that, I didn't know what I do.

If I was wrong, and I could be, I had no way of tracking the two to their trailer or shack or cave or whatever burrow they lived in.

Not a living being was in sight within the outside lights of the tavern. Though some of the trailer and shack windows nearby were lit, I could see no one in them. The silence made it seem as if everybody here had died.

I'd been here many times while on my way to one of the duck hunters' clubs nearby. Despite the bad reputation of Goofy Ridge citizens, they'd never bothered me. If you didn't insult them, you were safe from assault. But you wouldn't be accepted by them unless you worked hard and long at acting and talking like them, and maybe not then.

Their suspicion of the police was as dark and heavy as the clouds just now above them, and these were as black as a mole on the Devil's ass. When the Mason County coroner comes here, he carries a gun. County ambulance drivers venturing in here are always escorted by a squad car. According to the county sheriff's department, the population of this trashy Land of Oz, four hundred or so strong, was responsible for ninety percent of the crime in the county. Of these, however, only about ten or fifteen percent were rapists, thieves, wife and child abusers, psychopaths, self-mutilators, murderers, and other refugees from the law. Almost all, though, according to what a cop told me, were strange. Including the dogs.

It's only fair to note that many here have part-time or full-time jobs, some working as far away as Peoria.

Though Goofy Ridge was only forty miles southeast of Peoria, it was a sort of a frontier town, an Illinois Tombstone, a riverside Hole-in-the-Wall. Many crimes, usually violence by the citizens against each other, are never reported. It's only when the county police drive through the hamlet, which isn't often, that they come across the victims of these crimes.

For instance, a cop happened to look through the front window of a house while he was driving by it. He saw a body, swollen and black with corruption, lying in the front room, and he smelled a sickening stench seeping from the door and the windowpanes. Investigation showed that the man's head had been cracked open with an iron skillet and then the man was shot in the chest. Though the body could be easily seen by those driving or walking by and had been lying there for twenty-eight days, no one had reported it. The unwritten law is that you don't never tell the cops nothing.

I'd wondered while following Deak and Almond if they intended to take refuge up here. Now I knew they were in, as some unkind people call it, a poke of poachers, a freehold of freaks, a ward of weirdos. I'd get nowhere knocking on doors and asking about the Mobards. I might even get shot.

Then the tavern door opened, releasing bright lights, tobacco smoke clouds, and loud voices. A man, both arms hugging a large paper sack containing something bulky, staggered out. The outside lights of the tavern were enough to show a small man wearing a long brown raincoat and a dark baseball cap streaked with what looked like white paint. Though his features were blurred by the rain, his long gray ponytail and gray sideburns almost to his jawline were visible. Then another man stepped out from the door.

He shouted, "Thanks for the drinks, Almond!"

Almond turned. "You're welcome, Hoot!"

The fates favor every man with a pure heart and a noble soul. And sometimes they even look with kindness at me. All I had to do was to follow Almond. I waited until he had lurched onto the one-lane dirt road at the north side of the clearing. This went north for a few yards, then forked and became two roads. I got out of the car, locked the door, and put the keys in my shirt pocket. Any road he took would be wide enough for only one vehicle and hemmed in by trees. Should another car come down the road in the opposite direction, one of us would have to back away until he came to a branch road.

Slipping in the mud, I hurried as fast as I could. I saw Almond's dim figure shambling in the tunnel formed by the branches meeting over him. I stepped onto the side of the road. There, weeds gave me a steadier footing, and I could duck behind a tree if he looked back. This road became a path more than a roadway, the tire ruts separated by weed growth. Some two hundred yards or so on, it would go by the Orion Gun Club, which was usually deserted during summer.

Shortly before getting to the fence put up by the club, Almond turned left. He began climbing the six-foot-high ridge of earth along the road, erected to keep floodwaters from the road. He cursed as he slipped, and the bottles in the sack clinked. I waited. Presently, I could see his blurry silhouette on the top of the ridge. I could also see the shape of a shack roof just above the other side of the ridge.

The truck, I supposed, was in a clearing some yards to the north, a parking place for the Orion Club members.

When Almond disappeared down the other side of the ridge, I waited about three minutes and then went to it. At one time, flat stones had formed a rough stairs, but they had slid down to the bottom and were half-buried in mud. Pulling myself up by handholds of weed, I got to the top, though not without slipping back several times. I crouched for a while to check the layout.

Just below me, a little to my left, was a wooden shack, fifteen feet long and eight feet wide. Its windowless back was almost against the ridge. A stovepipe stuck out from the flat roof of corrugated iron sheets. The rain hammered on the roof. Light shone from a window on the side toward me. Its flicker indicated that it probably came from a kerosene lamp.

Oak, pine, and willow surrounded the shack except for the ridge side. Beyond it, lakeward, set in pinoaks, was the outline of a smaller building. No lights shone from it.

I could hear two loud voices, one a man's, one a woman's, and blaring laughter. I couldn't make out the words nor did the occupants pass in front of the window. After looking around for people outside the shack, I went down the stones set in the ridge on the shack side. I was slow and very cautious descending; the stones weren't secured firmly.

At the bottom, concealed by the large trunk of a hickory nut tree, I looked around again. I heard the squeak of rusty hinges. I wasn't sure if the sound was made by a shack door opening or by a door elsewhere in the woods. Say, an outhouse door.

I walked, crouching, toward a tree closer to the lakeshore and crossed a footpath on the way. From there, I could get a view of the front of the house.

Just as I got behind the tree and straightened up, I heard what sounded like the rattle of a chain. A moment later, a low whine chilled me. But the dog hadn't started barking yet. Bent over, I moved slowly away from the footpath and toward the lake. I still couldn't get a full view of the front of the shack. When I got behind a bush and peered through its leafy branches, I was chilled again.

Two short-haired black and tan dogs, massive beasts, were chained to tree stumps about ten feet outside the door. One was on the right side; one, on the left. Anybody passing between them to the house would be confined to a narrow path just out of reach of their lunges. At the front of the shack was a very small porch and one window near its far corner.

As I took the revolver from my coat pocket, I heard a faint noise behind me.

Then a man's voice spoke very close to me.

"Freeze, asshole! Move, I blow your goddam head off!"

7

He added, "Got me a 10-gauge double-barrel, peckerhead. Now . . . move slow, drop the pistol, grab for the sky, walk slow to the house. Can't miss this close."

His voice was deep and grating, and he slurred his words. He stank as if he'd not had a bath or washed his clothes since last Christmas, if then.

Arms raised high, I started for the shack. Then he said, "Stop!" I supposed he was picking up the revolver.

"OK. Walk. Don't try nothing." Then he shouted, "Hey, brother! Milly Jane! Come out! See what I got while I was coming back from the crapper! Another piece of shit!"

He laughed, choked on phlegm, and coughed violently.

The dogs were crouched, the chains attached to their collars stretched to their full length. Their wide-open mouths showed big wolfish teeth. I had expected them to bark, but they just growled. They were obviously part rottweiler. Their thick skulls could dull a jackhammer-chisel. Their jaws, capable of exerting six hundred pounds pressure plus, could rip arms off and crush the bones at the same time.

The shanty door opened. More light spilled out. A man and a woman stepped out.

I made sure to stay strictly in the narrow safety zone between the dogs. Their wet black noses were six inches from me. Suddenly, the downpour became a drizzle. The only sounds were waterdrops dripping on the leaves and the shack roof and then splopping on the ground, distant thunder, the dogs growling, and the squishing of shoes and boots pulled up from the mud. Ahead, only ten feet away, standing on the narrow porch, were Deak and Milly Jane.

"Caught me a cop," Almond said.

He'd assumed I was one of their eternal enemy, the Mason County sheriff's department.

Deak was about five feet five inches tall, weighed about one hundred and forty pounds, and looked to be around sixty plus. His shaggy eyebrows, long pony tail, and long sideburns were white. The narrow, foxish, and unshaven face was deeply incised and browned by sun and wind. The big scar at the left corner of his mouth, added to the three-to-five-inch-long tendrils around the mouth, made his face look like a very ugly Martian's. A red spot among them marked where my hellcat client had bitten a tendril off. His eyes were set close together, a common feature among those Goofy Ridgians who were inbred.

He wore a blue duck hunter's cap on the front of which were letters. UCKS UNLIMITED. The initial D was missing. A small black mallard's feather was stuck on one side of the cap. This indicated that he was a true citizen of Goofy Ridge, an insider. Also, he wore a necklace of duck bands, a local symbol of prestige, the poacher's equivalent of the Medal of Honor. A long-sleeved brown shirt, a belt with a huge silver cowboy buckle, ragged blue jeans, and rawhide cowboy boots completed his outfit.

His skinny arms cradled a .375-caliber Winchester Model

94. Since it was an expensive weapon, for him, anyway, it was probably stolen.

There was a hole in the upper arm of his shirt. A brown stain around the edges revealed where Almond's bullet had gone through and given him a slight flesh wound.

Deak's voice sounded like his brother's, including the slurring. "Know what we do to cops, cop? We shoot off their peckers and them throw 'em in the drink!"

By "the drink," he meant the nearby Illinois River.

I didn't reply.

Milly Jane laughed like a goose gabbling, then shrilled, "First, we ennertain 'em! Ain't that right, Deak!"

Her slap on his back propelled him forward a step. He howled, "You crazy fat-ass! I ain't no punchin' bag!"

I estimated that Milly Jane was between fifty and sixty years of age, was six feet tall, and weighed at least three hundred and fifty pounds. Change her gender, and she could pass for a sumo wrestler, and maybe the sex operation wasn't even needed. Under her enormous bright-yellow Mother Hubbard were gigantic breasts and a camel's-hump belly. Her feet were bare. Her long tangled hair was tobacco-brown shot with gray. Her eyes were as big and as round as UFOs and just as scary. Something wild and savage crouched in them.

Her hand, liver-spotted and big as a roast of beef, gripped the hilt of a machete.

Deak said, "Almond, take off his coat. Then frisk him."

"Put your arms down behind you," Almond said.

I obeyed. He yanked off my raincoat and threw it on the mud. The dogs snarled. At his command, I raised my arms again. One of his hands patted me all over. Then his hand came up from behind between my legs, and he squeezed my testicles. I yelped with agony, and I fell half on the porch and half on the ground. All three laughed.

When I'd recovered enough to stand up, I was told to walk

into the shanty. Almond urged me on by hitting me hard in the back with his shotgun. The blows on the kidney area hurt the most. Deak and Milly Jane backed up into the shack, where they separated, one on each side of me, the rifle pointed at me and the woman's machete raised high.

A stench of kerosene, burning wood, stale sweat, booze, tobacco, and dirty anuses sickened me.

The shack was a mess. All sorts of objects had been dropped on the unpainted and muddied wood planks: a pair of purple tablecloth-sized panties, a brown apple core, a broken whiskey bottle, several crumpled cigarette packs, and a ceramic statuette of an owl, its beak broken off.

The room contained a dirty and broken-backed sofa, several lit kerosene lamps, an old battery-operated TV set on a wooden pedestal, two wooden tables, six metal folding chairs, a metal bucket of water and a tin dipper on a narrow stand, another stand holding a chipped ceramic pitcher and a soapless soap dish, a towel rack nailed to the wall, two sleeping bags piled in a corner, and other items. On top of one of the tables were three quarts of Old Clootie whiskey and the sack Almond had been carrying. On a bare wooden wall was a framed slogan: GOD BLESS THIS HAPPY HOME.

Clothes hung from nails on two walls, Deak's raincoat among them. A hole (made by a bullet?) was in its right shoulder.

Against the west wall was an old-fashioned cast-iron woodburning stove. On top of it was a portable gas-burning camp stove. By it, hanging on nails driven into the wall, were skillets and spatulas. In the southeast corner was an incongruous object, a very large wardrobe of ornately carved mahogany. Stolen, of course. It dominated the shanty and was unexpectedly clean and polished. Milly Jane's pride and delight, probably.

One of the tables bore a chopping block on top of which

was a butchered rabbit, a bloody cleaver, and a few flies crawling on them. Milly Jane hadn't yet put the guts and dismembered parts in the bucket by the table.

Nailed to the northern wall was a gun rack holding several shotguns and rifles.

My client's briefcase wasn't in sight.

Deak dragged out a foldable metal chair into the middle of the room and opened it. He said, "Sit down."

I did so, my back to the door.

Almond stank like his brother and looked like him, including the clothes and the mallard's feather. The latter, however, was flecked with dried white paint. But his face had no tumorous growths, and he now wore rimless glasses. He went outside and returned with my coat. It was ripped and torn in many places.

"Goddam dog got to it. I coulda sold it."

"Almond, you skunk's ass!" Milly Jane shrilled. "I told you time and again, don't take the Lord's name in vain in this house! Next time, I'll flatten you!"

"Oh, damme to hell and gone!" Almond said. He was grinning. "Sorry 'bout that."

No sooner had I sat down than Deak told me to stand up. Apparently, he'd forgotten for a moment what he'd intended to do with me. No wonder. His breath stank of cheap booze.

"Take all your clothes off," he said. " 'Cept' socks. They don't count."

"All?"

"Everything. You be naked as when you was born."

I stripped down to my socks. Though it was sixty-six F outside the shanty, I was shivering. An Eskimo wouldn't think that was cold. But when you're sure to die soon, you're as chilled as if you're locked inside a meat locker.

Milly Jane guffawed, and she said, "A fine lookin' figure of a man! His prick's shriveled up from the cold, yet he puts you two punies to shame!"

"Shut your dirty mouth!" Deak said. "He'll be a fine figure when we get done with him! Anyway, if Almond and me ain't heavy hung, how come you married us?"

" 'Cause it takes two of you to make one good man!"

Deak, scowling, told me to sit down again. Almond opened the wardrobe and brought out a roll of industrial tape and several lengths of rope. From his pants pocket he took out a big jackknife to cut the tape. After securing my wrists behind me and my ankles, he bound me close to the back of the chair with rope around my stomach.

By then, the woman had gone through my clothes. My wallet, car keys, loose change, and the now unloaded revolver were on a table. Finding the thousand dollars in the envelope had so distracted her she didn't search the outside jacket pockets. Thus, she missed the plastic eyeball and the shield in the one pocket. She said, "God's good to us! This is our lucky day, Deak!" But when she read my driver's license and PI license, she shrilled, "Come here, Deak! This ain't no Mason County pig!"

Deak lipread the cards. Then he said, "He's a private dick from Peoria! Name of Thomas G. Corbie! What the hell?"

All three stared at me. Then Almond picked up from the floor what was left of my raincoat and pointed with a finger at the bullet hole in its right shoulder: "Hey! You suppose . . . ?"

I could see what was going on in their one-watt brains. Over there was the cluster of my raincoat, license, and revolver. In the opposite direction, far away but creeping closer, was the vision of what had happened at the cemetery. Eventually, the two would get close to each other, and then, like a nail and a magnet, they'd unite.

Almond said, "Harly lied again! She said she wouldn't — "

"No names!" Milly Jane said. "No names!"

"But he ain't gonna live to—"

"Shut up, I said!"

Deak chewed his lip while the tendrils around his mouth waved like sea plants in a strong current. Milly Jane's brow wrinkled as if she were trying to fold her brain around a thought. Almond was jittering around and scratching his crotch as if he had the crabs. Maybe he did.

Milly Jane smiled, and said, "It's better this way. If he was a Mason County bull, this place'd be crawling with 'em. But we gotta make sure. Like, where's his car? Does he have a carphone? He musta been just a hired gun, a backup. I bet he don't know nothing 'bout her, not even her name or what's going on. Almond, you go look for his car, take his keys along. Look first where you parked the truck. His car probably ain't there since we didn't hear none pass the shanty. Then look around the club. Soon's you find it, put your skinny ass in the car and get it back here. If it's got an alarm system, you know what to do."

Almond looked as if he were very reluctant to leave, but he did so.

Deak swore, and he said, "Hell's fire! Things always go wrong! Who'd've thought Harly was—"

"I tole you, clam up 'bout that!" Milly Jane said harshly. "Yeah, I know the dick won't be telling nobody, but what if he does get away? You never know what's going to happen. Only the Lord knows that. So say as little as possible about that. Got it?"

"Yeah," Deak said. "The Lord giveth and the Lord taketh away, as the preachers say. But He give us eleven thousand dollars, and I be damned if He's gonna take it away. Not even the Devil gonna do that if I got anything to say about it!"

"You got a mighty big mouth for such a squeakmouse. Don't tempt God. Ain't He been good to us today?"

"About time, too, after all the shit He put me through all my life," Deak said. He started toward the wardrobe. "Lemme make sure I wasn't dreaming about that money.

After opening the wardrobe doors and pulling out the bottom drawer, he picked up the briefcase. Its lock was broken. He sat down on a chair and emptied the contents on the table. He gazed reverently at the tumbled mass for a while, then removed the rubber band from a bundle. His lips moved as he started counting.

"Ain't no use doing that again," Milly Jane said.

"I ain't no good at numbers, you know that. I jes' wanna make sure. My brains're whirling, what with—"

"Far as your brains go, you're sitting on them. Forget checking the money again."

Milly Jane filled two plastic glasses with whiskey and handed one to Deak. "We really shouldn't get any drunker. But, what the hell, we deserve it."

After emptying the glasses, they began crumpling the bills into balls and throwing them at one another while whooping and shouting until they were out of breath. All around them, on the floor and under furniture, were one-hundred dollar bills.

I heard the sound of an automobile motor passing the shack on the other side of the earth ridge. Milly Jane said, "Almond. Your idiot brother took his time, though."

"He ain't no idiot!" Deak said. "He's smart as me."

"Won't argue 'bout that!"

A few minutes later, the dogs whined loudly. Almond called. "Lemme in! Got my arms full!"

Deak staggered to the door and opened it. His brother, mud dropping off his boots, entered. He bore on his back a large brown burlap sack. Deak closed the door. Almond upended the open sack. The paraphernalia taken from my car crashed onto the floor.

On the wooden floor planks was a jumble of my rifle, a

parabolic sound detector, binoculars, a tape recorder, a box of tapes, a Nikon camera, the cellular phone, and my night-vision scope.

"We sell this stuff and the car, we be even richer!" he shouted. "Oh, this is one hell of a good day!"

Maybe for you, I thought. Not for me.

My father says I'm a brainless optimist. Maybe I am, but he's a brainless pessimist. He forgot he'd told me that it was illogical to be an optimist or a pessimist. The universe was not set up to shower you with gifts or cut your legs off. It just rolled along, and what happened to you made no difference to it. However, I just can't stay down in the mouth very long. My inborn nature buoys me up like a cork in the sea. As long as I was alive, I could hope to escape. I was always sure of that.

Perhaps, I am too confident. For instance, in the Bible, Book of Genesis, the patriarch Jacob encounters an angel at a river ford. They wrestle; Jacob loses. But I knew that if I had wrestled the angel, I'd have pinned his wings to the mat, never mind that Old Testament angels didn't have wings.

8

Milly Jane pointed to my equipment. "Take that to the storage shack. Bring back potatoes 'n onions. Coffee, too. Gotta sober up."

"I ain't no workhorse," Almond mumbled. Cursing under his breath, he put the paraphernalia into the sack and staggered out, the sack slung over his shoulder. The door banged behind him.

"How'n when we gonna get rid of the dick?" Deak said, his pronunciation even more slurred. He was holding a coffee mug he had just filled with Old Clootie.

Milly Jane had lit the portable gas-burning camp stove on top of the iron stove and rolled the rabbit pieces in flour. The grease in the big skillet on top of the camp stove was smoking.

"Get the plates and stuff out," she said. "And lay off the booze. You gonna be even more useless than usual."

"In a minute. I wanna know when and how."

She said, "Ain't it occurred to you that we don't even know how Har—she—got him involved? We don't know what he

knows about her or us, neither. He's gotta be made to talk.
And we gotta get rid of his car, too."

"No problem," Deak said. "Wes Drinkentimmer up in
Bloomington'll take it off our hands."

Milly Jane slammed the edge of the cleaver into the chopping block. Deak and I jumped.

"Dummy! We wouldn't get no real money from him! He's
so tight he wouldn't give an acorn to a blind sow! Besides,
he's supposed to've gone nuts, crazy as a shithouse rat! The
car can wait. We gotta find out what the dick was up to."

For the first time, I spoke. "I have to piss."

The cold, the fear, and Almond's blows with the rifle over
the kidney area had changed my bladder's schedule.

"Yeah, sure," she said. "Deak, get him a jar or something. We
ain't untying him so he can go outside."

Though Deak grumbled, he lurched around the shack until
he found an empty mayonnaise jar. He failed to tilt the jar
down far enough, and so my urine slopped out of it. The fluid
warmed my crotch and part of my buttocks, but, a few minutes later, they got cold.

After emptying the jar outdoors, he set it by my chair.

"How about a blanket?" I said. "I'm cold."

"Not as cold as you're gonna be."

"You're a great humanitarian," I said.

He glared. "What'd you call me?"

"Look it up in your dictionary."

"Up what?"

I laughed. That was a mistake. His fist slammed me on the
jaw. My head snapped back, and my chair and I went backward and onto the floor, which banged hard against my head.
For a few seconds, I was in a sort of limbo. Voices came out
of the darkness. Ancestral voices prophesying doom? No.
Milly Jane was screaming at him to get me upright.

"And don't do that again 'less I tell you!"

Deak was dancing around, holding the hand that had struck me. "Damn, that hurts! I ought to kick the shit outa him!"

Almond walked in holding a small bulging plastic bag. Through the open doorway behind him, I heard the dogs growling. "He giving you trouble, Deak?"

"Not anymore. Here. Help me get him up."

Grunting, they lifted the chair and me to an upright position. Now, I was sitting with my right side toward the door. My head and jaw hurt. So did my hands and arms. Tied behind my back and over the back of the chair, they'd taken the first impact. Though they had softened the blow against my head, they had been made numb for a moment.

Milly Jane had peeled and sliced the potatoes and sliced the onions. The scraps had gone into the bucket on the floor. It also held the skin, head, and guts of the rabbit. She told Almond to take the bucket outside and dump it for the dogs to eat. He grumbled that he wasn't no maid, but he did as ordered.

Soon, the smoke from the skillet grease filled the room even though the door was open. My eyes burned from the fumes, and I coughed.

"For God's sake!" Deak shouted. "Cook outside!"

"Too rainy," she said.

But, shortly thereafter, cursing, she picked up the camp stove, the skillet still on it, and carried it toward the doorway. Just before she reached it, she stumbled over the mayonnaise jar, began to fall, and propelled herself forward while trying to regain her balance. She screamed as she tossed the camp stove and the skillet, filled with grease and food, straight ahead away from her. (A very strong woman, that Milly Jane.) The stove and skillet shot out through the doorway and onto the porch. The skillet turned over and dumped its grease before it struck the porch. She thundered through the entrance and onto the narrow porch. Then her bare feet slipped in the grease. Arms flailing, she slid off the porch and fell face-down in the mud.

The dogs couldn't take this, discipline be damned. They barked while lunging as far as the chains permitted. Deak and Almond were bent over, holding their sides, whooping and laughing. Milly Jane raised her head and yelled, "I'm burned! My feet hurts bad! Goddammit, Deak, get me some vaseline!" Then she rolled over on her back.

Deak staggered through the door holding a jar he'd gotten from the wardrobe. Still laughing, he bent down and handed it to Milly Jane. She grabbed his wrist, pulled him down, and slapped him in the face. He quit laughing. After he'd scraped off the mud from the bottom of her feet with a knife, he rubbed the vaseline on them. Then Deak did his best to help her stand up, but she fell with him on top of her. She punched him in the ribs.

"You're useless as balls on a baby. Whyn't I get me a real man 'stead of a puny river rat?"

Together, Almond and Deak got her halfway up before she fell down again. Her face and the front and back of her yellow Mother Hubbard were smeared with mud. At last, panting and swearing, the two raised her and helped her limp back into the shack. She lay down on the sofa, her feet sticking out over the end. She was groaning and so was the sofa under its burden. Deak applied more vaseline.

"That's good," Milly Jane said. "It helps. Now bring me my slippers and smear 'em inside with vaseline. Maybe I can walk without hurtin' then. Bring me a whiskey, too. I need it to kill the pain."

"We all do," Deak said. "Almond, fetch us two drinks."

"Didn't Lincoln free the slaves?" Almond said. But he

brought them a whiskey each and one for himself. After downing half of his glass, he went out onto the porch to urinate.

Deak gulped down the rest of his whiskey, sat down by the table, and refilled his glass. Milly Jane said, "You ain't much for sympathy, Deak. Time was, you'd a held my hand and tried to make me forget my pain."

"That was two hundred pounds ago."

"You heartless bastard! How'd you like me sittin' on your ugly face?"

"Aw, Milly Jane. Things ain't the way they was. But we can be happy now. We got all that money and won't have no trouble gettin' more when it runs out."

"Yeah, like the trouble we havin' now."

"Nothin' we can't take care of," Deak said.

"You been sayin' that all your life. Mary told me you was a fuckup from the day you was born."

"Yeah? I ain't one to put down the dead, but Mary was the one who fucked up, not me."

"And now I'm the one, huh?"

"I din't mean that," he said quickly. "What I meant, I done well. It was the others—"

"Oh, shut up!" Milly Jane said.

After several minutes of silence broken only by their whiskey slurping, she said, "Whyn't you ever talk to me?"

Deak, looking indignant, sat up in the chair. "Jesus! You just said . . . !"

She sighed, and said, "You don't know nothing 'bout women. Never mind. Make some coffee. I said we gotta sober up."

Deak started toward the doorway with a huge gray enamel coffee pot. He was going to fill it from the rain barrel, but he stopped walking when he heard a scream. All of us heard his brother's cry of distress. Then Almond charged into the house. He said, "You ain't gonna believe this! Elsie's dead!"

Milly Jane sat up. "Dead! What you talkin' 'bout?"

"The dumb bitch ate everything I gave her 'cept the rabbit's head. I noticed she couldn't quite reach it so I threw it to her. It got stuck in her throat! She choked to death!"

Milly Jane lay back down. Her voice quivered, "I can't believe it! You stupid idiot, Almond! You know better'n give 'em a rabbit's head!"

"No," Deak said, a tear running down his bristly cheek. "Ain't so. Don't try puttin' the blame on him. They eat plenty a rabbit's heads before."

Deak pointed at me. "It's him. He's brought us bad luck. You burn your feet, now Elsie dies. What next?"

He strode toward me, his face twisted, the long tumors around his mouth flapping. He grabbed my testicles and squeezed hard. I yelled with pain and toppled over backward again. The back of my head slammed once more against the floor, and I was knocked out. The only good thing about that was that I didn't feel the pain in my testicles and my head. But I did when my scattered wits managed to get together again.

While in that other world, though, the realm of the unconscious, I dreamed. I saw the face of Odin, the chief Old Norse god, the all-father of the Vikings, the being who'd been the bank president in my dream this morning. I could now see that it was actually my father's face. And then I saw my mother gliding phantom-like toward me, light shining from her in the gray mists surrounding her. She looked as she did when young, five feet and eleven inches tall, big dark-blue eyes, dark-red hair, her face not just pretty but beautiful, though her nose was perhaps a trifle too long and too curved, long slim legs, full breasts, narrow hips.

Her voice was thin and far off, truly a ghost's. "Son, I now know the answer to my deathbed question. I was wrong, and they were wrong."

"Mother! I cried. "I thought I'd never see you again! What is the answer?"

Smiling as if she were shaped out of joy, she disappeared, and I awoke to great pain.

9

Almond said, "Man, I'm gettin' tired of hoisting him and Milly Jane up."

"Look," I said. "My legs and arms're getting numb, and I won't be able to walk after a while. Why don't you tie me with ropes? Loose enough so it won't stop my blood flowing? Tie my hands behind my back, and don't bind my ankles. You know I can't run far. And give me some blankets or keep the door shut."

There was a silence while the woman thought about my proposal. During this, Almond lay down on a sleeping bag and started snoring loudly. After about three minutes, Milly said, "OK. Do what he says, Deak. I ain't no monster. I don't like to see anybody sufferin'."

"Since when?" Deak said, and he snorted. However, while the woman sat up on the sofa, aiming a rifle at me, Deak undid the tapes. I writhed on the floor in agony as the blood began to move again in my legs and arms. After a short while which seemed much longer, the pain began to ease. Then Deak tied my hands behind me but loosely. I said I had to empty my bladder again. Milly told him to take me out on the porch and let me take a piss and walk back and forth on the porch for a minute to get my blood going.

When I got to the porch, I could see the dog, Elsie, on her side, eyes glazed, the ears of the rabbit head jammed in her throat sticking out of her open mouth. The male lunged fiercely at me as if he blamed me for his mate's death. He stopped when Deak shouted, "Down, Wiggles!"

I didn't know why this hundred-and-twenty-pound killer monster was called Wiggles, but I supposed he'd been a cute pup. I wondered if I'd ever be warm again. The wind-driven drizzle hitting my bare body and the chill air seemed to form a heart-shaped icicle in my chest. I was shivering uncontrollably.

After I'd relieved myself and walked back and forth three times on the porch, I asked for a drink of water. Deak did bring me a tin cup full of water from the rain barrel at the corner of the shack. But he threw the cold water into my face, then walked away, cackling, and refilled the cup. Though I expected him to repeat his cruel trick, he allowed me to swallow the whole cupful. Then, dripping and shaking, I went back into the house. There I was ordered to sit down, after which Deak tied my leg to a leg of the chair. At Milly's command, he draped an Army-issue woolen blanket over my shoulders and another over my lap. Those helped keep me somewhat warmer, though my feet, still encased in wet socks, were very cold.

I don't know how many hours passed. I became a little warmer, and, despite trying to stay awake, I nodded off now and then. Several times, one of my captors took a nap while the others more or less stood guard. Except when they were sleeping, they kept drinking. Once, Almond got up, but he drank another glassful of whiskey and then went back to sleep. Once, I came out of my doze to hear the woman and Deak mumbling about somebody called Harold.

"Yeah, he bit chunks outa his kids' arms, so they hauled him away, but not before he cut off Emmy's head and stuck it on a stake in the river." Hearing that, I slept uneasily again.

Suddenly, I was fully awake, aware that something had changed. Rain was drumming hard against the roof, and thunder and lightning were close by. The dark gray daylight had been replaced by the black velvet night. Sunset today was at 7:34, so it was probably a few minutes later than that. The kerosene lamplight was too feeble to exorcise the shadows in the corners, shadows looking like wolves, wombats, and weasels. Then my brain shifted its mental center of gravity, and the shadows became just shadows.

Standing a few feet before me, the lights behind them, swaying, their eyes blinking like fogged-over semaphore lights, were the woman and Deak. Almond was still snoring on the sleeping bag. The air seemed to condense into whiskey.

"Time for some answers, dick," the woman said. At least, that's what I thought she said, she slurred so badly.

I said, "I have to piss again."

"First, we wan' the whole story," Deak said, his speech even mushier than hers. "And don' lie, ashhole. We got work to do. Don' wanna waste time."

"I wouldn't want to inconvenience you," I croaked. My lips, mouth, and throat felt as if warm ashes had been sprinkled on them. "I'd like some water."

"No. We wanna get this over with," Milly Jane said.

"I can't stand it any longer," I said. "My bladder's going to explode."

"If you answer my questions quick," Milly Jane said, "you can go outside quick. If you don't, you can piss on the floor for all I care."

Deak turned around and staggered to the sofa and sat down

on it, seeming, like a black hole, to collapse in on himself. "Lesh queshun'm." And he passed out.

"Worthless as broccoli pie," she mumbled. She managed to get across the floor in a crooked path and to drag a chair behind her, her revolver in the other hand. When she sat down, a few feet from me, her buttocks sagged on each side of the seat. Like twin moons just above the horizon of the giant planet Jupiter. The six-shooter she pointed at me swung this way and that and went up and down as if afflicted with some metal palsy. She hadn't cocked it yet, so I wasn't worried about an accidental squeezing of the trigger.

"Know who you are," she said, "where you live, wha' you do. Wha' wanna know . . . how you got invwoved."

"Invwoved?" I said.

"Thash wha' shaid. Oh, shit. Can' even talk shtraighrt. Dumb, dumb, dumb! Gotta ge' coffee. Coffee."

I sat there, my arms and feet and buttocks getting more and more numb, while she made a big pot of coffee and heated it on the camp stove outside. I didn't know why she didn't bring the stove indoors. Maybe, she just wasn't up to it. She got two mugs, filled them, and poured half of one into my mouth. Though it burned my mouth and throat, it did warm me up somewhat. Then she dumped Deak off of the sofa and onto the floor, sat down, and drank three mugsful. After which, she rose unsteadily, lifted a bucket of water from the floor, and emptied it on Deak's head.

Sputtering, Deak came to. But he did not get up until she banged the bucket against the side of his head.

"Ain' no more time to queshion thish ashhole," she said. "Who caresh, anyway? Harly jush twied doublecrosh us, thash all. She hash a pay for tha'. But . . ."

Deak had managed to pour himself a mug of coffee without spilling all of it onto the floor. He stood by the table, drank some coffee, then said, "But . . . ?"

"Gotta get rid a thish guy. Now. 'Fore we all pash out, 'n he eshcapesh."

Deak drank some coffee, then said, "Up to me, shupposhe. Almond . . ." He hiccupped. ". . . gotta help me."

"One clown'sh 'nuff," she said. "Two . . . fuck up for sure. Come on, Deak, hep me untie him."

Neither one held a gun on me. But the woman had told Deak that I wouldn't be able to move for a while after the ropes were untied. She was still thinking more or less clearly in that soggy mist-shrouded brain. And she was right. Again, I was in agony as the blood started to flow. And my tortured bladder let loose.

Finally, the pain was gone, and I could get to my feet. The woman's revolver and flashlight were pointing at me. Deak had a rifle, a Garand M1. She said, "You go ahead. We right behind you."

Her slur was as heavy as before the coffee. But, since she was more than twice the men's mass combined, she should have been able to drink twice as much as they and still not be as intoxicated.

Blanketless, I stepped out into a hard cold rain, a hard cold wind, and loud thunder and frequent nearby lightning. The dog, drenched and looking miserable, got to its feet, but he didn't growl.

Neither of my captors had put on rain hats or coats. They were too loaded to think about them or they just didn't care. Maybe they wanted the cold rain to help sober them up. It might even be possible that they were in a hurry to get the foul deed done before their consciences stopped them.

I doubted that.

The flashlight shone half on me and half on the path ahead. Instructed by Milly Jane, I preceded them along a more or less straight path, my feet sinking into mud with every step, past oaks and cottonwoods and bushes. When we were about sixty feet away from the lakeshore, we came to another shanty. This was a trifle smaller than the other but leaned to one side.

The woman told me to stop. Deak went around me and opened the door. He stepped inside. Milly Jane said, "Go in."

Her flashlight illuminated the dirt floor of the only room. Part of it was occupied by open partitions of upright wooden beams holding shelves. Deak lit a kerosene lamp to give us a better look. I didn't have much time to inventory the stuff on the shelves, but I saw a dozen or so boxes with the imprint: DAIYANKI ELECTRONICS. Some held TV sets; others, VCRs.

There were enough steel traps of various sizes hung from pegs on the walls and enough fishing rods, hooks, weights, nets, and duck decoys on shelves to open a store for poachers. Coils of rope on wall hooks were above a pile of six rusty old lids for wood-burning stoves. In a corner stood a condom dispenser which these thieves had ripped off a restroom wall for some unknown reason. There were also three sledgehammers, an ancient Burma Shave roadside sign, and a damaged two-foot-long model of a Mississippi paddlewheeler. Blue overalls streaked with paint, mostly white, hung from a nail in a wall.

Milly Jane said, "You know wha' ta do, Deak."

He jerked a thumb at the pile of stove lids. "Ge' three a 'em."

"To weigh down my body," I said, my teeth chattering. I hoped my voice wouldn't quaver. It didn't, but that didn't make me proud of myself.

He laughed, and he said, "You go' ut."

Usually, I would have been able to hold a stack of three of the lids in my arms and walk steadily. But I was weak. After twice dropping them and jumping back so they wouldn't strike my feet, I said, "Two's all I can carry."

"No. Three," Deak said.

"Then shoot me now."

"Two'sh OK," Milly Jane said.

Deak pulled a long hunting knife from a sheath on his belt and cut three lengths of rope. He also stuffed a roll of electrician's tape into his back pocket and picked up an empty burlap bag from a pile of at least forty. That bag was to hold the stove lids and would be tied to my body. I staggered out of the shanty, the stove lids cradled in my arms. Their edges dug into my flesh. Fortunately, I only had thirty feet down the slope to the shore. Here a duck hunter's skiff rode the wind-pushed waves.

"Pu' 'em in boat," Deak said.

The water was warm compared to the rain and the wind. It only came to my calves as I waded out to the boat and slid the lids over the side onto the middle of the skiff. I wanted to drop them through the bottom. But, if I did, I'd be shot on the spot. As long as there was the smallest chance of my escaping, I wasn't going to do anything foolhardy. As it was, I was having more luck than I deserved. My captors were drunk, one passed out, the others neither thinking clearly nor reacting swiftly.

In other circumstances, I'd have been killed on the shore, my weighted body rowed out to the middle of the lake and dropped there. The snapping turtles and the fish would strip me to the bones in a short time. But Deak was just too lazy and too drunk to row the boat. Let me do it.

Deak took the flashlight from the woman and waded out to the bobbing skiff. "Ge' in. Do ut slow. No funny moves."

He seemed to be much more sober, and he was speaking more clearly. One thing was certain. He, too, was shivering and thoroughly miserable. And, maybe, he was beginning to realize that he might be in as much danger as I was. Though the wind did not have the tree-felling force of this evening, it was strong enough to kick up sizeable waves. The skiff, designed for much smoother waters, was rising and plunging. If the rain got heavier, he might have to start bailing before he got back. But he'd forgotten to bring a can or a dipper for that. And the lightning crashed just too often and too close for him. Not to mention for me.

I climbed into the boat and sat on the board, my back to the prow. I reached for the oars, which were already in the locks.

Deak spoke sharply. "Don't touch 'em till I tell you to!"

I hadn't intended to do so. Though he held the rifle in one hand and the flashlight in the other, he could shoot me before I could use an oar as a weapon. Besides, Milly Jane was still standing only a few feet away, the revolver in her hand. I sat there, my feet on the stove lids, my arms folded, while he rocked the boat dangerously when he got into it. He threw the coils of rope onto my feet, placed the flashlight on the seat by him so that it pointed at me, and drew out his knife. He drove its point straight down into the wooden seat beside the flashlight.

Hunched over, rain-soaked, he said, "Start rowing. Head for the middle."

My back was to the lake, but I was sure he'd correct any wandering off the course. His marks would be the lightning-illuminated wall of the dike about three-quarters of a mile due west. Besides, the old river rat knew this area so well, he could probably have rowed out here blindfolded.

I gripped the oar handles and put my back into the work. Behind me, to my left sixty or seventy feet from the shore, illuminated fitfully, was an islet, a ten-foot-high mound of wet mud from which a few willow trees grew. Erosion had exposed the roots of one; it wouldn't be long before it toppled into the lake. I remembered the islet from when I was a member of the nearby duck club. If I could somehow get behind that . . . forget it. It wasn't going to happen.

Deak was hunched down, staring at me, his face hanging

above the glow of the flashlight. While he talked, the tumor-tendrils around his mouth writhed like octopus tentacles probing an undersea cave. I slowed down my rowing, which hadn't been fast anyway. He didn't seem to notice.

"We get to the middle of the lake," he said, "I shoot you spang dab just between the eyes. Ain't nobody gonna hear it in this thunderstorm."

He paused. I suppose he wanted to see what effect his words had on me. I grinned, though I certainly did not feel like it.

"Then I tie the bag with the stove lids to you, tape you up, and into the water you go. Down to the bottom, where the carp and the snappers'll make short work of you. How ya like them apples?"

"I'm not crazy about it," I said. "I may die tonight, but you'll be along shortly thereafter. Those mouth growths are cancerous. They'll kill you in six months."

I didn't think it'd be that soon, but if he could scare me, I could scare him.

"Thus," I said, "it behooves you to repent of your sins and make your peace with God before you go down to the everlasting flames. I think you'll go there anyway."

I didn't believe there was a hell of sulphur and brimstone, but he might be uneasy about its possible existence.

"You some mealy-mouthed preacher?" he snarled.

I'd almost stopped rowing. The boat was rising and falling with the choppy waves, and the push of the wind had canceled the effect of my feeble strokes. Now was the time to act. Now! Now!

"You really think I'm goin' ta hell?" Deak said. "Le' me tell you, dick, you 'n me're in hell now."

At that moment, a bolt smashed into the lake not fifty feet away. Both of us started. But my foot, dug under the coil of rope he'd dropped near my feet, kicked upward. The coil flew at him. He flinched, then tried to rise.

I rolled over the side of the skiff, tipping it but, unfortunately, not turning it over. The rifle boomed. The bullet didn't hit me, probably went upward into the sky.

Just before the black water closed over me, I smelled its odor, a mixture of rotten fish, decaying vegetation, and ancient mud. Then I was moving along the shallow bottom, swimming toward the islet—I hoped.

10

Eyes shut, my fingertips touching the mud now and then, I swam. Before I'd gone very far, my right hand struck a hard mound. I passed over it, then turned around and groped. The object might be a rock. Or it might be what its sloping surface suggested.

I needed air. Right now. But, if the object was what I thought it was, it could be used, and I couldn't leave it to go to the surface. I might not be able to find it again. Desperate, I wasn't going to ignore anything that could be a weapon. This thing, if used properly, could be that, and I knew how it could be.

My hands slid along the hard dome. But when I pressed a little on it, I felt a leathery substance. The turtle—I was certain now that it was a turtle—started paddling away. I seized one side of the rough shell with my left hand and gingerly used the other to feel its shell. There was a smaller plastron under the big shell. That, plus my contact with a long tail with a crested ridge and its ten-inch-long shell made me certain that it was a snapping turtle. I was glad that the head of this antediluvian reptile had been facing away from my hands.

I imagined its hideous naked head, its profile that of an aged and malignant senator voting to repeal the Child Labor Act.

I couldn't hold my breath any longer. I was no longer the youngster who could hold his breath underwater for almost four minutes, and I was weakened by fatigue, lack of food and water, and the fear of dying. Yet, I couldn't release the snapper. It'd move on; I'd never find it again.

My hands along the sides of the shells, I raised myself and brought my knees up against my chest. My feet sank into the toothless sucking mouth of the mud. I pushed upward by straightening my legs. My feet sank up to my calves in the mud. Nevertheless, my shove loosed them, and my head broke the surface. I breathed out and in twice. Some of the stinking water got down my throat, and I had a hell of a time to keep from coughing. Then I sank back until my mouth was just above the surface, and treaded water.

Now I saw Deak standing up in the boat, the beam of his flashlight probing into the darkness. A second later, a bolt not eighty feet away behind the boat illumined him. It also enabled him to see my head even through the dazzle.

He shouted, dropped the flashlight, and brought his rifle up to his shoulder. If he fired it, I didn't hear it. I let myself sink down under the surface, my knees bent. The turtle was still moving its flippers, trying to swim away from my grasp. I estimated its length at twelve inches and its weight at approximately thirty pounds.

Again I came up, standing on the mud, though slowly sinking. By another flash, I saw Deak seated and rowing the skiff toward me. He was looking over his shoulder and might have seen me. I drew in a deep breath and sank back down. I walked underwater toward the boat. I was leaning forward, my feet sinking deep in the slime.

I could only estimate very roughly the distance between me and the boat. If I misjudged, I might come up beneath the boat and bump my head against the bottom.

I counted one thousand one, one thousand two, one thousand three, one thousand four. At one thousand five, I bent my legs, then straightened them as I thrust upward. Suddenly, the water was only to my midriff. The turtle became heavy. Another flash, this one behind me, smote my ears. It must have momentarily blinded Deak.

He was standing not a foot away from me, bending over, looking down, his rifle pointed at a spot a few feet from me.

He yelled. The rifle boomed. Out of the side of my left eye, I saw the muzzle flash. I tossed the reptile at him with a strength that only an adrenaline surge could have given me. The thrust drove me backward, and my feet were deep in the mud again, then I leaned backward, and my feet were free again.

As my head broke from the surface, another lightning streak, more distant than the previous one, showed Deak staggering backward. I could hear him screaming. My luck had held. I'd zeroed in on him. The ugly powerful beak was clamped around Deak's crotch. And he was falling over the side of the skiff. The boat rocked wildly but did not turn over. Another flash behind me, nearer this time, revealed an empty boat. The rifle, which he had dropped, had fallen upright, its butt on the bottom of the boat, its barrel leaning above the side.

Deak's screaming and thrashings came from beyond the other side of the boat.

I didn't have to climb back into the boat and chance completely turning it over. I was close enough to the shore that I could push it easily. Meanwhile, Deak's shrieks and his cries for help would have touched me deeply if the circumstances had been different and he was just another fellow human being who needed a Good Samaritan.

I looked again in his direction after I got the skiff moving. A flash showed that he was up to his waist in water. His face was twisted with agony, and the flapping tendrils around his lips made him look like some evil lake god who had tangled in mortal combat with an even more powerful lake monster.

"Help me!" he screamed. "Oh, God, help me!"

I ignored him for the moment. Before I came near the shore, I looked for Milly Jane. Another lightning flash. She wasn't there. I hadn't thought she'd stand in the cold rain and wind until Deak came back.

After I'd dragged the skiff almost completely out of the water, I got the rifle, the knife, and the flashlight. By the beam of the latter, I looked at the M1 Garand. Four shots left in the eight-round clip. The other clips would be in the pockets of Deak's jacket.

Since I had no belt or sheath, I put the blade of the knife between my teeth. I turned the flashlight off and jammed it under my left armpit. I advanced, the rifle held in both hands. When I got to the storage shed, I cautiously looked around the side of the open doorway. The kerosene lamp was still on. Nobody there, though. I didn't go in. I wanted to find out if Deak's screams could be heard at this point. Yes, but very faintly, during the brief lapses of the lightning and the thunder.

Then I saw Deak by the glare of a bolt. Somehow, he had waded ashore with that heavy reptile hanging from his crotch like a Scotsman's sporran. Now, he was now lying face-up on the shore mud, his feet in the water.

I couldn't have him behind me, though it seemed highly unlikely he'd be dangerous to me. I walked back to where he lay, his mouth working, his screams now sunk to moans, his eyes closed. I slammed the rifle butt against the side of his head. As an ex-LAPD officer, I knew the difference between a skull thumper and a skull breaker.

He quit groaning. The turtle still hung on. Folklore goes that it's impossible to break a snapper's grip. That isn't so. But it would take a surgeon to do the job.

I returned to the storage shack and carried out the big burlap bag containing the equipment Almond had taken from the trunk of my car. I put the flashlight, knife, and rifle on top of the bag. Then I went back inside and hurled the kerosene lamp against the wall. It shattered, and the flaming liquid spread over the wall and ran onto the floor. After putting the knife and the flashlight into the bag and then hoisting it over my shoulder, I left quickly. If Milly Jane saw the blaze, she'd be coming, and she wouldn't be unarmed.

When I got near to the shack, I heard the dog barking. The lamps shining through the window showed that the windowless door was shut. I stood partly behind a tree. Then the door seemed to explode wide open. Milly Jane, holding a double-barreled shotgun, charged through the doorway. I put a bullet into her left thigh. She fell heavily on her breasts. Her shotgun bellowed. I knew it had been accidentally fired because the pellets blew the dog apart.

I stepped out from behind the tree and shot at her head, but the bullet struck her shoulder. She grunted and rolled over. A moment later, she was screaming again.

I got quickly to her side and kicked the shotgun away. The butt of my rifle against her head silenced her. I picked up the shotgun with a finger through the trigger guard and threw it as far as I could. After which, I went to the side of the house and looked through its window. Almond was still lying on the floor, his mouth open, his eyes shut.

I didn't think he was playing possum, but I went into the shack ready to shoot if he did more than stir. Satisfied that he wasn't shamming, I knocked him deeper into unconsciousness and dragged him out into the rain alongside the woman.

It took a few minutes to tape over their mouths, to roll them over so I could tape their hands together behind them, and then tape their ankles together. It took longer to put my clothes and raincoat on my wet body, retrieve my keys, wallet, and other belongings from the table and stick them in my pockets, and scoop the money into the briefcase.

I took the briefcase and rifle outside before going back in and smashing both lamps against the wall. Then, I ran out before the flames reached the five-gallon kerosene containers I'd opened. Just as I did so, the kerosene containers in the storage shack exploded, and the fire billowed up above the tops of the trees.

I picked up the bag, briefcase, and rifle and headed for the end of the ridge. When I reached it, I heard the second explosion—Deak's shack. The night became day. However, the heavy rain would soon kill the flames.

My car was in a clearing off the road, the pickup close to it. I backed it over the weed-covered mud and drove down the dirt road. I hoped that I'd get out of Goofy Ridge before someone saw the fires. I didn't want the narrow passage blocked by people on foot or by cars.

I made it to the Mallard Club without seeing anybody, drove onto the paved road, then turned right. Instead of taking the same route back to Peoria, I'd decided to drive south on the county roads—very little traffic on them—until I got to Havana. Then I'd cross the bridge and go northward along the west side of the river. About two minutes later, I pulled off the road and turned off the motor. I was shaking like a dog passing worms. After a while, the reaction to the ordeal passed, and I resumed the journey homeward.

A little later, I passed close by a place where a tragical yet comical accident had happened. This was long ago, in 1866, during the latter part of a bright spring day. The sun was hanging above the top of the western bluffs when the *Minnehaha*, a sidewheeler steamboat, was tootling along northward in a stretch of river just wide enough for three boats abreast. Its flag whipping, smoke pouring from the tall black stack, steamwhistle shrieking and bells ringing, it would've gladdened any human being worthy of being called human.

Its owner and commander was Captain Augustus Minnie, a notorious drunkard, and it was carrying a cargo of pool balls and cue sticks from St. Louis to Peoria. Everything seemed fine. Then the boiler exploded with a roar that rang back from the hills and sped up and down the river. The boat was blown to pieces. There were no survivors.

Two duck hunters in a boat near the east bank of the river saw Captain Minnie soar from the wheelhouse high into the sky above the flames and the smoke. The westering sun silhouetted him, still upright, his plug hat on his head, a whiskey bottle tilted to his lips.

Before the hunters realized they were in danger from other than the flying fragments of the boat, the storm was upon them. One hunter was transfixed by a cue stick, fell into the river, and did not come back up alive. The other man, a shoulderbone smashed by a pool ball and an ear torn off by a cue stick, lived to tell his tale.

To this day, people sometimes find pool balls in the mixed sand and mud of the riverbanks along here. The wooden sticks, of course, decayed long ago.

My rising spirits nosedived when I suddenly thought about Glinna and the birthday party for which I was very late. When I got to Havana, I used a public phone booth to call home. No one except the message machine answered. I heard my own voice, the voice of that doomed creature, Thomas G. "Doghouse" Corbie, telling me to state name, telephone number, and time of the call, and he'd get back to me when able. I groaned. I'd thought I'd been in trouble. That was nothing to what I'd get at home.

But I had not expected her to throw me out of the apartment, which she did.

11

hree days passed before my true love phoned me at THE
TUM-TUM TREE MOTEL, Rooms by the Hour, Fresh Towels.

"Glinna!" I said. "Is all forgiven? Not that there's anything
to forgive. You want me to come out there and move my
stuff out right now? I really don't have any place as yet to
move it to."

"Bu-bu-bastard!" Her voice sounded thick. Phlegm? Fear?
Hatred? Love? Grief?

" 'Bastard' was your last word when you threw me out."

"I may have been wrong to do that. I don't mean calling you
a bad name. I mean telling you to get out."

"We all make mistakes. Or is it an error in this case? Never
could remember the difference. Are you apologizing and also
pleading for me to come home?"

"I'll admit I've been very miserable. But why did you take a
room at that fleabag house of assignation? Everybody knows
it's a hangout for whores."

"Sometimes, 'everybody' is right," I said. "Mostly, 'everybody' is wrong. In this case, however, a herd of harlots does graze here."

"You're evading my question."

"Though this place abounds in friendly women," I said cheerily, "I've remained faithful to you and will do so as long as we're married. I'm old-fashioned about fidelity, loyalty, chastity, that sort of thing. Besides, you know I wouldn't bed a whore no matter how desperate I was. It's all so mercenary and cold-hearted, and disease lurks in every humid crevice of the body for sale. Anyway, I gave you a whole week to get over your anger. Yet, here it is, only three days passed, and you're seeking a reconciliation."

"All right!" she said loudly. "I admit I was hasty! But it was my birthday, my *birthday!* All my friends waiting for hours for you to show up, looking at me like I was to be pitied. I got very angry, then I got worried. Then I got angry again when we got tired of waiting for you and went out to eat. I was so upset I could barely touch my food. Then I came home, worrying again, very distressed, and you're snoring away on the bed, reeking of whiskey, your face bruised and swollen, the kitchen in a mess, and you wouldn't say a word about what happened to you!"

"We went through this," I said. "I'd been on a strictly confidential case. I didn't even tell Mimi Rootwell what happened, and she got me the job. Anyway, I only had three ounces of Duggan's Dew of Kirkintilloch to soothe my inflamed nerves. Then I ate. Sorry about the dirty dishes and skillet. You know I always clean up my messes afterward. But I was just too exhausted."

I hadn't, of course, told Glinna about the $11,200 I'd brought home. If she knew that, she'd be sure I'd been doing something unlawful. Which, come to think of it, I had.

"Listen," I said. "This is twice you've cast me flaming with utter ruin and furious combustion down to bottomless perdition. Let's not have any more scenes. You've got to trust me. If I'm late coming home, it's because I've been on a case, not on a woman. You have to accept this. If you won't, much as I hate to say it, we're through. Sundered, riven apart, looking across an abyss at each other."

There was silence for a moment. Then she said in a much subdued voice, "OK."

"Be home in twenty minutes."

"I'll be waiting for you with bells on." She paused. Then, "Nothing else."

"Nothing is far more than something. I love you."

"I love you, too, though sometimes I wish I didn't."

She always had to have the last word, get the last lick in. Let her. It wasn't conceding too much.

Feeling as buoyant as a gas bubble in a baby, I quickly packed. Home again, home again!

On the way out of the room, I stuck yesterday's *Peoria Journal-Star* under my arm. An article therein reported the arrest of Deak, Almond, and Milly Jane (née Foushee) Mobard after they'd been attacked (they claimed) by unidentified men. All three had been taken to the Mason County District Hospital. The woman was in intensive care, her critical condition worsened by pneumonia. Deak was also still hospitalized, watched carefully because of his wound. His brother was in jail.

Most of the article was devoted to Deak's painful but comical tangle with the snapping turtle. It had not released its "death grip" until the surgeons had cut the beak off. How severely Deak had been injured, the article didn't say. But the reporter did state that Deak's lifestyle would be crimped from now on.

Meanwhile, the Society for the Prevention of Cruelty to Animals had asked the Mason County DA to charge Deak with mistreatment of the turtle and with removing it from its natural environment.

According to the reporter, two county deputies had been on one of their rare and nervous patrols through Goofy Ridge. They'd driven up the road leading to the Orion Gun Club and had seen the flames before the rain put them out. Investigating, they'd found the Mobards and then called in an ambulance. At the hospital, a detective recognized Deak and Almond and recalled that they had warrants against them for various burglaries.

The culprits had been questioned separately.

Deak Mobard described the assailant as a young, scar-faced black, seven feet tall, wearing a stocking cap, sweater, trousers, and "basketball" shoes, all black. Deak had valiantly fought him with a machete but had been forced to take refuge in the lake, where the turtle had grabbed him.

Almond said he didn't remember a thing because of a blow on his head.

Milly Jane stated that her attacker was a five-foot-tall Chink or Jap (her words) who weighed at least two hundred and fifty pounds, all muscle. His head was shaven, and he had a Fu Manchu mustache. Looked like a wrestler. After he had raped her repeatedly fore and aft, he'd had the gall to ask her to run away with him to California. She had refused, whereupon he had burned the soles of her feet, then asked her again. She had once more rejected the offer. The Asian had then shot her with Deak's rifle and had left her to die.

Yesterday, I'd phoned a Mason County sheriff's department detective from a Peoria public phone booth. Falsetto-voiced, I'd told him I was Nellie Bly, a new *Journal-Star* reporter who was writing a follow-up on the article. I was chiefly interested in the Mobards' family history. He replied that couldn't tell me a thing about that. However . . .

"Strictly off the record, OK? They'd have to look up

through a telescope to see a snake's belly. The Exalted Order of Idiots blackballed them because they're so dumb."

"That's not a politically correct statement," I'd said.

"I'm being very charitable. And, oh, oh! Wait just one moment! What shit is this? Who you trying to kid? Nellie Bly, my ass!"

"Tsk! Tsk! Shocking language to address to a member of the press. A woman who's having her period, at that. May I quote you on that?"

"If you're a reporter, I'm Lois Lane!" he had snarled. "I just remembered who Nellie Bly was! You think we're all ignorant hicks down here? It's a crime to make prank calls to officers of the law! Just who are you, clown?"

Using a very deep voice, I'd said, "My name's Clark Kent, and my mission is to destroy all evil. Thanks for the info, sir." And I'd hung up.

I did wonder how he knew who Nellie Bly was. Not many do nowadays though her name was once a synonym for "demon girl reporter." She became famous in 1889 when, working for the *New York Herald,* she dashed around the world attempting to beat the fictional record of Jules Verne's hero, Phileas Fogg, in *Around the World in Eighty Days.* Which she did. Her dispatches to the *Herald* were read by millions. Not so well known were her exposés on snake-pit lunatic asylums, tenement conditions, exploitation of women, and corruption in the New York state and city government.

I checked out of the motel in what was quaintly called a lobby. The owner and manager, Bella Watting, tall, gaunt, fifty-ish, was on a bar stool behind the registration counter. Her high-piled bright-orange hair was actually a wig. Underneath it was a thumbnail-bald head. The makeup covering the broken veins in her face was as thick and vividly colored as a pile of early autumn leaves.

In the best American tradition, a female Horatio Alger hero, she'd managed through hard work, strict discipline, and sheer pluck, to put aside enough (much of it hush money) to buy the motel. She was not an assembly-line stiff now; her piece work was behind her; she was the one on top.

Unfortunately, arthritis caused by long hours on her back rotating her pelvis at a high centrifugal speed or down on her knees like a prayer vigilante had crippled her. She now got around in a motorized wheelchair, even went to church in it. She was scheduled, however, for an operation to replace her diseased hips and knees.

Though I deplored her morals, I admired her undaunted spirit. She'd been beaten up often. Bananas, Coke bottles, six-packs of AAA batteries, and feather duster and fly swatter handles had been stuck up her vagina. Ice cream cones filled with peanut butter had been jammed into her anus just before a client rammed into it with his tallywhacker. (I love that out-moded word.) It was always creamy peanut butter except for the one man who insisted on superchunky. Many times, she'd been part of a trinity with johns and sheep. Once, Bella had ridden an ostrich while her client . . . I didn't want to think about it.

Through all this, meanwhile trying to cure her cases of syph, clap, yaws, herpes, chlamydia, and various imported venereal diseases, avoiding only AIDS and the blueballs, she had been a cheery optimist. She was not sullen or bitter; she did not whine.

If just surviving with a glad and ever-hopeful heart was ad-mirable, then she should get a medal. I truly admired her, though not because of her profession. That was grisly, grimy, dangerous, and about as glamorous as a pile of cold dog turds. The whores she'd started out with and many of two suc-ceeding generations had OD'd, been murdered, gone crazy, died slowly and painfully while their flesh rotted, or were homeless and prowling through garbage cans.

But Bella could say, like Ishmael after the great white whale sank the Pequod, "And I only am escaped alone to tell thee."

Because I'd gotten her out of a mess involving a high Peoria city official, a blackmailing woman, and her dog, I could room there free. However, I insisted on paying because I didn't want to owe her anything.

"Come back any time!" Bella said as I walked toward the exit. "But next time be more polite when you turn down Sherry. You hurt her feelings, you know!"

"Sorry about that," I said. "I lost my temper when she called me a queer. I've been having a rough time lately. I'll call her up, apologize personally."

"Oh, she knows you're not a fruit," Bella said. "She's getting old, can't take rejection like she used to. Got piles now, too. Ruined her specialty."

Bella was an excellent source of information about the scurvy antics of many of central Illinois' prominent citizens. For instance, a few years ago I'd been hired by the wife of Orson Bunhanger, a very powerful Peoria contractor and land developer, to investigate her husband. She suspected that he had a mistress. I'd found that he was supporting three women, not counting his wife. He also made weekly visits to the motel to enjoy Sherry, whose ass, painted like an archery target, its bull's-eye the anus, intrigued him. Though he always showed up at the motel wearing a false beard and dark glasses, he didn't fool any of the women. Bella, giggling, had told me that the contractor was so used to paying off politicians, union bosses, and city inspectors under the table that he insisted that Sherry take her money likewise.

While driving south on the road to Peoria, I thought about the Mobards. They'd be out of action for some time, so I didn't have to worry about retaliation from them just now. But they

knew my name and address—if their booze-soaked brains remembered them—and they could find me when they were
freed, though that might be a long time from now.

I doubted I'd ever hear from the Mysterious Stranger again.
She or the person who'd hired her would've read the news article about the Goofy Ridge incident. She or her client would
know I'd put the trio out of action. Probably, she was disappointed I'd not killed them. But she'd suppose that they
wouldn't trouble her anymore. In any event, she'd not be asking me to return the blackmail money, $10,000.

At 4:06 P.M., I turned off the car ignition in the parking lot
of the Rinky-dink Arms. Just after I slammed the door behind me, I saw Glinna waving at me from the French doors
by the balcony. Even from this distance, I could see that she
was wearing a necklace of tiny bells. Nothing else. Much
faster than was my habit, I went up the steps and into the
apartment. I was greeted by Glinna, who, besides the necklace, was wearing red high-heeled shoes. I was also greeted
by her perfume, which smelled like pumpkin pie and laven-
der. According to a scientific study, this combination is the
most sexually arousing for men. Next is a mixture of dough-
nuts and black licorice. Actually, I only needed Glinna herself.

We also didn't need the three copper pyramids and six cut-
crystal pyramids placed under the bed to focus cosmic sexual
energy on us. Nor did we need the cut-crystal Channeling
Chandelier above the bed. It was supposed to blow invisible
but blue orgone bubbles, a cosmic source of sexual energy,
down on us.

We literally leaped into bed, and it was good while it lasted.
I wanted to do it again. She said, "No. Once is for love. Twice
is for lust."

I'd been through this many times. Nevertheless, I protested.

"Look at This! Look at This! If This was a dirigible, This'd be the Hindenburg! It's inspiring angels to blow their trumpets, cherubs to sing, and whales to envy!"

"Maybe when we retire for the night. I'm hungry."

We showered, dressed, and walked down the road to O'Leary's Restaurant. I devoured a Denver omelette, and Glinna (diet be damned tonight) wolfed down chimichangas.

I said, "It seemed very quiet next door. What happened to Mutts and Wickling?"

She covered her mouth with her napkin before replying, thus subtly reminding me that I'd spoken with my mouth full.

"You know, the spell must've worked! I haven't heard a thing since I cast it on their stereo. Except for a lot of cursing."

"Really?" I said. "If you can do that, why not evoke an eviction notice for them?"

"You forget I don't put spells on people. Only evil wiccas do that."

I wondered how long it'd be before a technician or Mutts would discover that the power socket had no plugs. I found out when we returned home. The walls were shaking with "Your Rattlesnake Heart."

"I don't understand it," Glinna said. "It was a long-term spell."

"Maybe they hired an evil wizard," I said. "You better get your whole coven working on this."

She looked at me to see if I was kidding her, but I didn't smile until I walked away from her to go to the bathroom. That smile didn't last long. I just wasn't going to put up with my neighbors' barbarism a minute more than I had to. Early tomorrow, I'd act. Meanwhile, it would be earplugs and gritting my teeth and figuring out the best plan to get rid of the pests. Rat poison was out. So was arson.

At 9:00 A.M., tired after a fitful sleep, I was awakened by the phone.

Mimi Rootwell, sounding unusually cheerful, said, "Up and at 'em, sluggard! Get your heavy-metal ass over here! I got a job for you! Try to look respectable and stable, difficult though that may be. Wear a suit, tie, and white shirt."

12

Mimi Rootwell said, "Nothing big moves in this city without Simon Alliger's go-ahead. Yet, the Alligers are so publicity-shy that very few Peorians have even heard of him or his family."

She paused, then said, "A little history lesson. The first Alliger, twenty-year-old Johannes Frederick, came from Oberammergau, Germany, to Peoria in 1844. Most of its houses were log cabins, and the streets were mud. But it had the river for transportation, and it had very rich natural resources: grain, coal, and so on.

"Fritz Alliger got off the steamboat paddlewheeler with two dollars in his pocket and larceny in his heart. He made a fortune and so have most Alligers since. Some have been honest. A lot haven't.

"Now . . . Peoria was, from the 1840s on, for about a hundred and forty years, the supreme whiskey-making city in the world, except during Prohibition. During the Civil War, the tax district of Peoria paid for half of the money needed to run the federal government war effort.

"The Alligers were strong church-goers and members of the temperance unions. But they secretly invested deeply in the breweries and distilleries here. Then, in 1875, the federal government broke the Whiskey Trust. This was a ring of major distillers organized to monopolize the whiskey trade and cheat the government of its legal share of taxes. The Alligers narrowly escaped being indicted and publicly exposed as the hypocrites they were and are. But they kept the vast sums of money they'd made."

Mimi was forty years old, twenty of which she'd spent in a wheelchair. Her wasted body made her large head look even larger, reminding me of the movie scene where the Wizard of Oz's huge disembodied head is terrifying Dorothy and her buddies. Yet, she had a beautiful face, and she was admired and respected. She knew the secrets of every prominent family in this area, including the Alligers.

We were sitting in her office in the Andrew Bell Investigations and Security Services agency. Next door were Mimi's lawyers, the much-feared Sprenger, Kramer, Hammer, and Burnam. I'd done a lot of work for them.

"Simon Alliger will be seeing you in the office in his home," she said. "His downtown office is being redecorated, the first time in fifty years. He's tight, though not nearly as flint-fisted as his wife. She's paranoiac and so mean her anus could snap the ends off of steel rods.

"She puts bottles behind the curtains and drapes to check if the servants have been cleaning there. She checks the food in the fridges and the freezers and the booze in the pantries and cellars to make sure the servants aren't stealing them. She searches the servants' quarters when they're not home. She once fired a maid because she found an electrical vibrator in the woman's dresser. There's more I'll tell you about Alexandra Alliger, but not now.

"My Uncle Andrew had a lot of trouble getting his Alliger

bills paid, and so do I. You know how too many of the rich are. Anyway, I've told Simon he'll have to pay the whole bill on this case within a week after it's submitted. That he agreed without arguing means his problem is urgent. He was very cagey about its exact nature, said only it concerned an investigation of his daughter-in-law. He didn't want to reveal any more until he had a PI who'd handle the case. Said it'd be premature, whatever that means.

"I told him I had a good man to work for him, you. I just hope your bruised and bumpy face doesn't put him off!

"I'll tell you a story which, of course, you'll keep to yourself even though most of Peoria's upper crust know it. The first wife of Roger Alliger, Simon's only son—let's call her Antigone—suspected that Roger had a mistress. Antigone hired local PI, Autolycus, to handle the case. Two days later, he was shadowing the mistress—call her Medea. After a short time, he realized that Medea was following another woman, Electra."

Mimi laughed, then said, "What a farce! The PI is following Mistress Number One, who, it turns out, is following Mistress Number Two. But it soon became even funnier!

"Electra led the two shadowers to the Pimiteoui Yacht and Sculling Club, where Roger kept his two-master boat. Autolycus, the PI, parked his car in the lot. He waited until Medea had headed for the dock and Electra was hiding behind her car, then watched Electra from behind her car.

"To make the story short," Mimi said, "Medea went aboard Roger's yacht. A moment later, Electra followed her. When the detective got near the boat, he heard a tremendous shrieking and screaming. Medea had barged in on Roger and another woman, Jocasta, naked and in bed. She was the wife of a wealthy man, Roger's cousin, in fact. Very good-looking, the wife, that is, and very respectable. Medea tore into her. Then

Electra showed up and went at both women tooth and claw. Lots of hair pulling, slapping, and clothes ripping.

"What made it worse, really surprised the PI, was that Roger's wife, Antigone, suddenly joined the fray. She'd been following the PI! He was so intent on the other women, he hadn't noticed that he was also being shadowed."

Mimi laughed.

"It was a noisy bloody mess. Poor Roger, the unlucky son of a bitch, grabbed his pants and ran out. Not before his wife raked his genitals good with her nails, though. He probably still has the scars.

"The PI left the scene before a crowd gathered. The wife didn't even ask him for his report. Paid him off and took off for Reno the same day. There was nothing in the paper about the divorce. The Alliger lid was clamped shut."

"Four women," I said. "I'm envious. What a man that Roger must be!"

"An egotistic idiot," Mimi said. "And he has a reputation for being dishonest. What else? Oh, yes! Roger sniffs cocaine. And his father fired Roger's business agent when he found out the agent was robbing Roger blind."

Mimi told me something about every member of the immediate Alliger family and also about the servants. Then she handed me several pages of data to bolster my memory.

"Hustle on out to Simon's. Keep your smartass remarks to yourself. Don't antagonize him."

"I do have some intelligence," I said.

"It's not your brains I worry about. It's your attitude. Get going."

Twelve minutes later, my car turned off Grand View Drive onto the red-brick driveway leading to the Alliger residence. This curved for almost two hundred feet before I drove out of the dense growths of oak, fir, sycamore, and hickory nut trees lining it. I stopped the car for a moment. Ahead was a huge three-story house. Mimi had described it as a Colonial Revival style house with a porch and twelve Corinthian columns added. To me, it looked like an enormous white box which still was not large enough to contain all the troubles and woes of the owners.

Simon's grandfather had built it in 1910. This was the year that President Theodore Roosevelt visited the newly constructed drive and declared that it had the most beautiful view in the world. He may not have lied.

A TV monitor camera was mounted above the double front doors. It was part of the security system which Mimi's company had installed three years ago.

The twelve wooden pillars on the wide porch were three stories high. Like the house, they shone whitely in the eleven o'clock sun. The paint looked as if it had been put on a few weeks ago.

At a right angle to the left wing of the mansion and separated from it by fifty feet was a freshly painted, off-white building. Its lower story contained eight garages; the upper, the servants' quarters. Two monitor cameras on high white steel poles nearby pointed at the garage.

I drove up the semicircular driveway past the mansion and into an empty garage in the detached building. I supposed my client didn't want anybody to see a cheap automobile parked in front of his house. Only Lamborghinis, Porsches, Ferraris, and Rolls-Royces were allowed there. But you couldn't see the lower part of the mansion from the public road because of the trees.

A dark-skinned, short, and stocky man in brown sandals, green jeans, a white T-shirt, and an old gray Stetson hat had been working among the array of flowers planted along the house. I knew from Mimi that he was Juan Cabracan, a political refugee from Guatemala. He turned his head for a second, allowing me to see his profile. It was almost a perfect semicircle made up of a backward-slanting forehead, a large curving nose, and a slightly jutting chin. Just like those profiles carved on the stone walls and statues of ancient Mayan ruins.

Guatemalan secret police had tortured him because he was suspected of being a rebel. His right cheekbone was a bulging mess under the skin. Three deep parallel scars ran from his left cheek to the corner of his lips.

He was the gardener, but he also worked part-time as a house servant and chauffeur.

"And, no doubt," Mimi had said, "working his ass off for a minimum wage. Simon Alliger runs his financial empire, but his wife runs the house—most of it, anyway. Alexandra, as I've told you, is not noted for her generosity. By the way, there's a curious arrangement of ownership and power in that house. The grandmother, Faith Alliger, owns the house and lives in it. But she lets her son, Simon, and his wife, Alexandra, Sandy for short, run it, usually stays out of the way of her son and daughter-in-law. Faith is partial to Diana, Roger's wife, which displeases Simon and his wife."

I waited for Cabracan to come to me. The only sounds were the faint ones of his footsteps and, from behind the house, the territorial challenge of a male cardinal. Then I saw its bright red as it flashed like a falling star over the house and dived toward the woods in front.

Cabracan spoke a much distorted English in a deep voice. "Meester Corbie?"

"The same."

"Please follow me."

At least, that's what I thought he said.

He started to lead me around the corner of the left wing. Brakes screeching and tires squealing made me turn around. A red Ferrari convertible was still rocking from the sudden stop. The driver's door was open, and a young woman with bronze-red hair cut in a China chop was striding around the car.

She could jump-start a eunuch.

She was in her early thirties, stood about five feet nine inches, deducting the high-heeled shoes, and weighed maybe one hundred and twenty pounds, deducting the heaviness of her huge light-blue earrings. The tight crimson tank top, no bra beneath it, and the tight lemon-yellow jeans revealed her superb figure and long slim legs. Her face would've been beautiful if it hadn't been twisted by rage. Here was a woman gripped by hell's fury, though I couldn't imagine any man scorning her, even if her outfit was rather flashy for an upper-class woman, in Peoria, anyway.

She stormed into the house without ringing the bell or bothering to shut the door behind her.

"Diana Alliger," I murmured. "The second and current wife of Roger, Simon's and Alexandra's daughter-in-law. She lives in Millennia Oaks."

I followed Cabracan around the corner of the house to its south side. We passed two doors, above each of which was a monitor camera, but neither of which was operating at the moment. We stopped at the third door, which had a camera stationed outside it. This was, I assumed, the tradespeople's entrance. A lowly PI wasn't good enough for the front door, not that I blamed the owners for thinking that.

We stepped into a large hall. A code pad was on the wall just by the door. Its lights, two blue and one yellow, showed that it was off. To my right I could hear women chattering in Spanish and pots and pans clattering behind a half-closed door. In front of me was a narrow iron spiral staircase.

We went up it to the second-story landing and into a wide high-ceilinged hall. This was surprisingly cool though there were no air-conditioning vents or ceiling fans. The only light came through big open wire-screened windows at the ends of the hall. The carpeting was not as thick as it had once been nor were the walls as white as they should have been. Along the hall were a few elegantly framed French and Flemish masters on the wall. I couldn't tell if they were originals or not.

Cabracan pointed to the second door on the left. Or I should say doors, since you had to open a screen door to get to the second door. That was the first time I'd seen this arrangement indoors.

"Meester Alliger is in there," Cabracan said. "Knock."

He spun around and was gone quickly.

I opened the screen door and rapped once on the inner door. A man's high voice said, "Come in!"

Simon Alliger II was standing behind a huge ebony desk in a huge room furnished with huge dark leather chairs and sofas. Along the west wall behind him were many large, open, and screened windows. Their light erased the heavy darkness that would have been in this otherwise shadowy room.

The paintings on the dark-green and silver papered wall were mostly western or hunting scenes. The heads of African buffalo, rhinoceros, grizzly bear, jaguar, leopard, and a male lion looked down on me. They needed dusting. Against one wall was a glass-enclosed cabinet holding many firearms. So, this guy was a Nimrod, a mighty hunter before the Lord.

Shelves with many books lined two walls. I was close enough to the right wall to read the titles near me. I noted one by Rush Limbaugh and two by Ayn Rand. A few were biographies: Jim Fisk, John Jacob Astor, Richard Nixon, Ronald Reagan, Edward Teach, and Sir Henry Morgan. Most of the books were leather-bound sets of Dickens and other classical nineteenth-century writers. None of these, I'd have bet, had ever been opened.

On the desk to Alliger's left was a mounted photograph turned at an angle which allowed me to see its subject: Simon when he was a young and slim naval captain. To his right was another photograph displaying a young man and a young woman in hunting clothes and boots. Both held shotguns, and behind them was an open field with woods in the distance. I knew, from what Mimi had told me, that the couple were Simon's parents.

The rest of the furniture was what you expected in an office: telephones, modems, a fax machine, two computers, and so on.

"Corbie?" the man behind the desk shrilled.

I advanced. "The same."

He gestured at the big leather chair in front of the desk. "Sit down."

The Man was wearing a white shirt and white shorts, as if he intended to play tennis later. He didn't look as if he'd be much of a player, but he had won letters for swimming and tennis in high school and college.

Simon Alliger, sixty-six years old, was five feet seven inches tall, deeply tanned, paunchy, double-chinned, and apple-bald. Behind his round rimless spectacles were pale blue eyes. The areas under his eyes were as dark as if stained by sin, perhaps original sin. These also gave him a vaguely racoonish look. Or, considering his family history, a bandit's mask. His wide lips were very thin. His nose was long, thin, and hooked. Much like a red-tailed hawk's but without the nobility of that bird of prey.

Simon Alliger stared at my battered face but said nothing about it. Maybe he liked my looks. If his case was a tough one, I looked tough enough to handle it.

He drummed his fingers on the desk, coughed, then said, "Mr. Corbie, this is very difficult for me. Painful."

I looked sympathetic.

"Miss Rootwell assured me you were the soul of discretion. It's about my daughter-in-law."

Screeching voices came through the screens behind him. He sprang from the chair, saying, "What the . . . ?"

I followed him to the open but screened window. Below it was a sidewalk. Past that was a forty-foot stretch of grass ending in a large sunken garden bordered on three sides by honey locust and fir trees. A tennis court was on the right. To the left was a very large heart-shaped swimming pool.

The voices came from Diana Alliger and a woman I assumed was Simon's wife, Alexandra. She was dressed for gardening, a pale-brown wide-brimmed hat, ankle-length flowered-print dress, and white elbow-length gloves. A basket holding freshly cut roses hung from the crook of her right arm. A pair of large clippers was in her left hand.

"Christ!" Simon said. "They're at it again!"

"It" was one hell of a quarrel. What I could catch from the rapid gabble was that Diana resented her mother-in-law's interference with a guest list for a party Diana planned at her Millennia Oaks house. That Diana hadn't just called over the phone about it but had come over like a hurricane to confront Alexandra told me a lot about her character.

"Don't ever stick your big nose in my business again!" Diana shouted. "I've had it with you! You do it once more, and we're through! Your wimp son might back you, the ball-less bastard always does, but I'll put such pressure on him, he won't keep it up! You'll never see him again unless I say so! You got that in your devious busybody mind?"

Simon groaned softly.

Alexandra raised the clippers as if she meant to drive the points into Diana's breast.

Simon shrilled, "Sandy, for God's sake!"

"Try it!" Diana screamed. "Just try it! I'll take it away from you and stick it up your ass!"

This beauty certainly did not behave as ladies are supposed to. But then they seldom do.

Diana turned and strode across the garden, crushing flowers, ran up the steps out of the hollow, and disappeared into the house. The door banged behind her.

Macho pig that I am, I couldn't help wondering if she was as fiery in bed.

Simon put his hand on his forehead and groaned again. He certainly wasn't acting like a steel-nerved captain of industry, the secret king of the city, supreme master of the land roundabout. Men, however, seldom are of heroic stuff when they're dealing with their women.

Alexandra stood still for a moment while she looked vacantly toward the house. Though her body was fat, her face was long and narrow, like an arrogant camel's.

She threw the clippers down, hurled the basket of roses across the garden, tore her hat off, cast it on the ground, and stomped on it. After which, she raised her face to the sky and screamed.

Simon croaked, "My God! The servants, the servants!"

Suddenly, Alexandra quit screaming. But her mouth was still opened wide, and her face began to turn slightly bluish. Her hand went to her throat. I could hear the wheezing. It didn't entirely surprise me. Mimi had told me that Mrs. Alliger was asthmatic.

Simon shouted out of the window. "Where's your inhalant, Sandy?"

She obviously was in no condition to reply even if she heard him. She ran to the basket. By the side of the roses spilled out from it lay a large atomizer. She bent over, picked up the can, shook it, and sprayed a mist into her mouth. That didn't seem to help. She looked up despairingly at Simon, then began running toward the house.

"Don't run, Sandy!" Simon shouted. "You know that makes it worse!"

After she disappeared from my view, a door slammed.

I said, "Would you rather I'd see you another time?"

He turned. "What? Oh, no. She'll be all right as soon as she gets the other medications and lies down for a while in her room. She has asthma, high-blood pressure, and glaucoma, all of which require her to take medicines. She also takes diet pills and drinks wine, though our doctor has warned her not to because they work against her medications. But she'll be OK in a few minutes."

I had expected him to go to his wife's room to comfort or help her. But he said, "That bitch, Diana! She knows Sandy gets asthmatic when she's overexcited!" He pressed a button on the left wall. A section of the wall slid open to reveal a liquor cabinet in a recess. His hand shook as he poured himself several ounces of Wild Turkey. He downed all of the liquor before he recalled his manners.

"You want a drink?"

I was going to shake my head, but I said, "Why not? Scotch, if you please."

If I became his drinking buddy, I might get more out of him than if he were sober.

13

I'd expected Alliger to be in complete control of himself and others, like Captain Ahab before his leg was bitten off by the Great White Whale. What I got was a man who had to sail through the golden seas of alcohol, three sheets to the wind, before he had courage enough to spill out the family troubles. And he was as windy as Ishmael, the narrator of *Moby Dick*. He chattered on about everything except why he'd hired me. I waited, patient as a rock, on the outside, anyway, until he could no longer put it off. By then, we were halfway through our second three-ounce glass of whiskey.

His son, he said, had gone to Los Angeles a year ago on business and to visit friends. Eight days after arriving there, Roger phoned from Las Vegas, Nevada. He had just married a woman named Diana Rolanski.

"He wouldn't admit he'd done it on a drunken impulse. He said he loved her deeply, and we'd love her, too. I asked him about her background. Her father had been a plumber in Pasadena, a wage earner, not, mind you, a man who owned a business. And Polish, too! Don't get me wrong! I'm definitely not prejudiced! But some things . . ."

"No matter how low his or her status in society," I said, "everyone is unique. I firmly believe that, though I'll admit I can't prove it scientifically."

He stared at me for a moment, then said, "So everybody is unique. That doesn't make everybody equal to everybody else."

After a long swallow of Wild Turkey, he said, "Anyway, Mr. Rolanski died when Diana was thirteen, and she and her mother moved to Los Angeles. Shortly after Diana graduated from high school, the house burned down. Mrs. Rolanski died in the fire. Diana wasn't there when it happened.

"Roger didn't know how much insurance Diana'd gotten when her mother died. Actually said it wasn't important. Wasn't this America? Can you believe that?"

Roger had told Simon that Diana was an office receptionist for an oil company executive. But she was taking night classes at a business college.

"Things looked very bad," Simon said. "But I told my wife not to get hysterical. Roger would soon come to his senses, and I'd arrange a quiet out-of-state divorce, though it would be expensive. Then I'd lay down the law to Roger. No more disgraceful situations. This would be the last!"

Alexandra had then gotten angry at Simon because he'd told her not to get hysterical. After denying that she ever lost her control, she'd had a screaming fit and then an asthma attack.

I wasn't entirely surprised that he'd revealed that much about his wife. It was true that Mimi had described him as being very self-controlled, cold, and uptight. But people are often no more consistent than the weather. And he needed to tell someone about his long-time suffering. Apparently, and this was sad, he had no close friends to whom he could confide. He must have felt safe in telling his troubles to a man who was not a peer and would keep his mouth shut about them. Still, he had to uninhibit himself before he could do that.

Also, possibly, the old Corbie spell was working. There really was something about me which sometimes made people open themselves up like a flower to the sun. Or, as Mimi had said, make people unlock their word hoards.

Roger was right in one thing, Simon said. Diana was even more beautiful than his first wife, Nessy. But, like her, Diana was a dyed-in-the-wool bitch.

"Diana doesn't have Nessy's breeding. She's crude and tawdry, not at all restrained. But I do want to be fair. Diana's not really a, ah, bimbo, despite looking like one. Bimbos are supposed to be dumb, feather-brained, right? She's not. However, she's much more belligerent than Nessy. Dangerously so, I'd say."

I thought, But she wasn't the one who threatened with the clippers.

I said, "Not exactly the eye of the storm."

"You've got it. She's the storm itself. What's more, she's been trying to turn Roger against us. Despite what Diana told Sandy, Roger doesn't back his mother in all of their quarrels. That's a lie from the queen of liars. Lately, Roger's been caving in to Diana. I regret to say this about my own son, but he's ah, well, I won't say he's weak, but he's certainly not as strong as I'd like him to be. Takes after his mother. There's a weak streak in some of the Vongristers. Also, besides his unfortunate penchant for good-looking women, he, ah, I hate to say it, has been known to, ah, sometimes use something stronger than drink."

"It's the times," I said.

"That's no excuse. Not for an Alliger."

He didn't rise to refill our glasses as he had the first two times. "Be a good fellow, get the drinksh. I mean, drinks."

By now, his face and eyes were as red as a woodpecker's neck.

I went to the bar. Somehow, while my back was turned, he had hoisted himself up from the chair and walked to the window. The floor must have seemed to him like a plunging deck in a heavy sea.

"Come here," he said thickly.

I did so, and I handed him his glass.

He spoke very slowly to control his enunciation. He was losing his battle fast, though. "My only trouble isn't Roger. There's my wife, too. See there."

"Where?"

"Shtill . . . still in her room, I hope. Damn it, I'm not referring to her. I mean thoshe . . . those . . . beehivesh. Ah, hives."

Some of the hives were visible just beyond the line of pines on the west edge of the garden.

"There'sh . . . there is proof of how much she loveshe me!" he snarled. "The bitch knowzh I'm allergic to bee stingsh. I've already gone last year into anaphyl . . . anaphylactic shock from one. Shwell . . . swelled up fast . . . my arm, I mean. Would've died if I hadn't taken a shot of epinephrine the first time, Suphurin the next, and taken cortisone pills for five weeks. The next time, I may die."

He waved the hand holding the drink and slopped whiskey on the carpet. "Flowers. And . . . and honey locust trees. They attract the bees, you know, little black and yellow, fuzzy, striped bitches with stingzh . . . stings . . . that could kill me. Don' dare go into my own . . . garden."

"Why don't you get rid of them?"

"Flowers're the light of her life, one of the few thingsh she has left worth living for, she says. She won't hear of parting with them. Anyway, not going to admit in court I din't have the guts to stand up to her . . . Roger's pussywhipped . . . I'm not. How about torching those abominabobble inshectsh, insects? I can hear her screaming now."

When he spoke again, he did so even more slowly and with much less slurring.

"Mother's fond of Roger just because he's her grandson, though actually she doesn't dote on him. She knows he's a . . . well, I'll be brutally frank, pitiful case. Pathetic, pathetic. And she knows Rosemary, that's our daughter, is a worse case than Roger."

He drained the glass, turned, staggered to the chair behind the desk, and slumped down. A minute later, he was snoring, his head on the desk.

I'd messed up. I didn't even know what he wanted me to do, though I was sure it had to do with his daughter-in-law. Mimi would be very angry with me, not that I could blame her. Booze can be a useful tool for a PI if he handles it skillfully. But if the handler gets loaded, too, the screwer gets screwed.

What to do now? Probably, it'd be best if I wasn't there when he did come to. He'd feel ashamed and humiliated. I tore a page from the notepad on the desk, wrote a brief message, and left it in front of him.

Before leaving, I had to get rid of some of that whiskey. I opened a door midway along the south wall of the office. As I'd hoped, it was the bathroom entrance. The room was very large and furnished with lots of marble. Its faucets were gold-plated, and the purple toilet paper was monogrammed with big black A's which, I suppose, stood for Alliger. However, the wallpaper in a corner where wall and ceiling met was beginning to peel.

As I Niagara'd into the bowl, I glanced around. In a corner to my left were two small dark objects, the only dirt on an otherwise clean white tile floor. After I'd zipped up and washed my hands, I went to the corner. I'd told myself that keeping this bathroom clean was not my business. But here I was, hating myself for giving in to the compulsion.

My father says that I'm like my mother, I want to clean up the whole world. That's why I became a policeman and then a private detective. But I'll never be able to keep the world dirt-free, that is, crime-free.

Bending over, I saw two dead striped honeybees, *Apis mellifera*. Stingers, the kind that Simon Alliger feared so much.

How'd they get into the big room? It had screened windows and a screen door at the room entrance. And the bathroom door, I assumed, was open only when someone was going in or out.

I picked a bee up between my thumb and finger and looked at it closely. Its fuzzy half-inch-long body wasn't flattened out, though that didn't necessarily mean that it hadn't been swatted to death. I doubted that Simon had killed it. He would have gotten rid of them at once. If a servant had killed them, he would've flushed them down the toilet. I put both of them in one of the plasticine envelopes I always carry and placed it in my jacket pocket. I still had the Mysterious Stranger's plastic eyeball and shield in an envelope in that pocket.

After I'd downed a tall glass of water, I left the house the way I'd come in. I wasn't exactly sober, and I wasn't exactly drunk. Somewhere in between, but master of myself.

I'd been tempted to go into the kitchen and talk to the servants. Other than God, they know more than anybody else about the people upstairs. But there was so much noise there that I decided not to interrupt their work. When I got to the front of the house, I saw that Diana's red Ferrari was gone. I called Mimi on my cellular, and she heard me through without interrupting me.

She chuckled then and said, "Old Simon got loaded. Well, well. He's known to drink a little wine now and then, no more. Maybe your aura did it. You radiate something that makes people shoot off their mouth. Some kind of wild element."

She paused, then said, "Maybe it's not you. Glinna might be casting spells to help you."

One more surprise. I'd never said a word to her about Glinna being a wicca, claiming to be, anyway. I might've guessed, though, that Mimi knew.

"Come to the office for a powwow," she said.

As I backed the car out of the garage, I saw in my rearview mirror a white 1935 Cord, a wonderful antique, drive up to the front of the mansion. A hand reached out from the driver's seat and squeezed the bulb of the horn mounted by it. I paid it no attention until it had blared three times. I stopped my car.

The low-slung door opened. The woman who got out of it was dressed like a 1920s flapper. A sky-blue headband around her short dark hair, a glittering dark-red necklace, an azure-and-dark-red, expensive-looking, and knee-exposing dress, black stockings, and open-toed pale-blue shoes with medium-high heels. She was five feet five inches tall, and her arms and legs were thin. She had to be the ninety-two-year-old grandmother, Faith Alliger.

She waved at me. I backed the Ciera up until it was a few feet in front of the Cord, then got out and walked to her. Under her many wrinkles and folds was a delicate skull that told me she must have been quite good-looking at one time. But then I knew that from the photograph on her son's desk. The hair, of course, was dyed.

She got very close to me, looked up at me with faded blue eyes, breathed deeply, snorted, and backed away. Her voice was cracked but not feeble. "Young man, you've been drinking."

I bowed slightly. "Unless I'm mistaken, I'm addressing Mrs. Faith Alliger, the matriarch of this stately manor."

She smiled.

"Matriarch. I've never been called that, not to my face, anyway. Who are you?"

" 'Said the caterpillar to Alice.' My name is Thomas Gresham Corbie."

"Gresham? After the famous sixteenth-century financier, adviser of Good Queen Bess? Or is that a coincidence?"

"You hit it on the belly button," I said. " 'Bad money drives out good.' "

She cocked her head, looking like a bird trying to decide if I was a cat or some strange but harmless animal.

"I know who you are and why you're here," she said. "My son and his wife didn't mention you, but I have certain sources of information."

I thought, Another Mimi Rootwell.

After a slight pause, she said, "Speaking of PIs, which we weren't, I knew Raymond Chandler. Not in the Biblical sense. I also knew Georges Simenon, the creator of the Inspector Maigret series. He once tried to put the make on me. We were both past our prime, but it didn't seem to matter to him."

All I could say was, "Well!" Once more, I had to change my prejudgment of an Alliger. But I felt strongly that, despite the difference in our ages and class level, we were strongly attracted to each other. Glinna would have said we had been lovers in previous incarnations.

She put her hand on my arm and said, "You're probably wondering why I'm so candid with you. I really don't know. But there's something about you. Certainly, none of the people I associate with now that all my old friends are dead have it. What do you think?"

"I think you're having me on," I said. "However, I can truthfully say that I do like you very much. I don't know why. But I don't plan to leave my wife for you."

I grinned. She laughed.

"Simon and Alexandra want you to prove that their daughter-in-law has a sordid past."

"I can't tell you anything about that," I said.

"Young man, unless you have urgent business elsewhere, please come to my suite with me. I only want to talk to you for a while. Comfort an old lady, though you must have doubts about my being a 'lady.' You have no idea how bored and lonely I get. I'd like to find out more about you. You may leave at any time you wish. If you do, I won't be more than slightly hurt."

I smiled, and said, "I have an appointment with my boss. However, just now I'll go with you. Lead on."

After getting her purse from the seat of the Cord, she walked toward the house at a fast clip for her age. Her back was straight, not curved into a question mark like so many elderly women whose bones have softened. When she got to the door, she stopped to allow me to open it for her.

I arched my eyebrows as I did her the courtesy.

"All my life, I've thought that males make the best doormen," she said. "And I've never believed in the equality of the sexes. Women are the superior gender except for their stupidity in choosing mates. You agree?"

"I never argue about religion," I said as I closed the door.

So, now my social rank had been raised. I was suddenly entitled to enter through the front door. Ever upward, Raggedy Tom! Horatio Alger would be proud of me.

We went through a large foyer with a marble mosaic floor to the huge living room, though I didn't suppose the family lived in it much. The floor was polished hardwood. The furniture was Louis XIV or one of the Louies, I'm no authority. The ceiling was two and a half stories high, and a story-high gallery with an ornately carved railing jutted out from the west wall. Beneath it near the north wall was a mammoth fireplace of white marble. Above it was a large oil painting of a middle-aged and dark-haired man with a long flowing beard, hawk nose, and tight mouth. Below his eyes were the hereditary smudges.

"Old Fritz, the family founder," Faith said. "Died while counting his money. A fitting end."

I thought I heard a faint far-off wheezing. Was Alexandra still having the asthmatic attack?

We headed for a staircase that looked like the one up which Rhett Butler had carried Scarlett O'Hara for their only night of sexual passion. But we walked around it to an elevator shaft made of etched glass.

The elevator took us up to the top floor, the third. When we got out, she led me directly across the hall to a door, then gestured for me to open it.

14

*F*urniture, photographs, and paintings crowded the large room. My feet sank into an Oriental carpet as if it were quicksand. Overhead, several old-fashioned, big-bladed fans turned lazily. Though the room was warm, it wasn't the hothouse I'd have thought she'd need to keep her ancient blood coursing.

"You may take your jacket off," she said. She headed for a corner occupied by two overstuffed divans and an easy chair. She sat down in the chair. Before us was a large teakwood coffee table on which were black-and-white photographs in upright frames. I picked up the nearest one. I certainly hadn't expected to see the face of a young Ernest Hemingway, the author of *For Whom the Bell Tolls* and many other works of fiction.

Even more surprising was the handwritten dedication: "To Faith, a free spirit, with la grande passion, Ernie."

Another photograph showed two men standing on each side of a beautiful young woman, their arms around her shoulders.

"There you see me, the quintessential American flapper in the Paris of the late 1920s," she said. "Dutch bob, beaded headband, short skirt, rolled knee-high stockings, high-heeled shoes. The two men are Joan Miró and my lover, Avram Gessner. There's a Miró on that wall" — she pointed — "and one of Avram's over there."

Miró was one of the all-time greats of abstract art and surrealist fantasy. But Avram Gessner?

On the way to the opposite wall, I passed tables on which sat lamps with bead-fringed shades, a wind-up Victrola with a big horn, and a streamlined Art Deco chair made of jade and ivory. The Gessner painting, a rather large one, was hanging above an ornate Spanish chest.

This room was a jumble of different styles and periods, a temple to Faith's memories. Memories should brighten, not darken, and Faith had made sure of that. Each relic lit a lamp in her ninety-two-year-old mind.

Gessner's painting was surrealistic. A line slanting at a forty-five-degree angle across the canvas from left to right separated the sky from the surface and the deeps of an ocean. The sky was a much heavier blue than the depths below the line. A lone being with a fish's tail, a man's genitals, and a woman's breasts was swimming in the sky. Above him was a pair of human lungs. Floating in the sea was a human brain, nerves hanging from it as if they were a jellyfish's tentacles. A huge eye on the sea floor glared up at the swimmer. It seemed to belong to a monster buried in the mud but about to surge up toward the swimmer.

The viewer of cubist and surrealist art was supposed to look at the painting until he was drawn into it. In theory, it would be like stepping through the wall of our universe into another world. I did just that. Tried to, anyway. After a minute or so, I could feel the seawater — or was it the liquid air of the sky? — pressing down on me. I felt the tug of the countercurrent and heard the heavy sounds of the swimmer's arms moving in the water and the distant booming thunderish call of some great beast of the abyss. I could sense the desperation of the swimmer, lost, his breath gone, his intelligence only a glimmer, striving to get to his lungs and his brain, independent creatures floating away from him.

Not reluctantly, I stepped back into the world I best knew. I told Faith what I'd felt while I was "inside" Gessner's work. She looked pleased. "You must be very imaginative."

"I am, though some think I'm weird. For instance, when I was a child roaming the oak forest near my parents' house, I actually 'saw' Withihakaka, the trickster of Peoria Indian myths. He looked much like Bugs Bunny. I was awake then, though several times when I was young I spoke to him in dreams.

"Anyway, to tell the truth, I still prefer paintings like Ingres' *Oedipus and the Sphinx* or Winslow Homer's seascapes and Frederick Remington's Wild West art. Representational, realistic art. I just don't resonate deep down to Picasso and Miró. However, I'm not bewildered by modern art works, thanks to my father's art lectures when I was young. And I love surrealism and the absurd in literature, like Henry Miller's Dadaism in *Tropic of Capricorn*."

"Bless your fundamentally middle-class heart," she said. "At least, you're honest. There are so many phonies in the art world, you know. But enough of art chatter. Would you like some tea?"

"Tea'd be fine, thank you."

I expected her to call a servant to bring in the tea. Instead, she opened her small purse, sequined with tiny silver fish images, and pulled out a slim silvery flask. Directed by her, I went to a massive mahogany sideboard carved with leering or silently screaming gargoyles and demons. I brought back two beautifully cut rock-crystal goblets and set them on the table before her.

While she poured from the flask, she said, "I purchased these in Istanbul. The rascal who sold them claimed they were made for Harun al-Rashid. You know of him?"

What the hell was this? I wasn't bucking for a Ph.D. I felt as if I was being grilled by my father on some lecture he'd recently given his one-person audience — me. For a moment, I was back in my childhood, answering his questions on some book he'd made me read but desperate to be out playing with the other kids.

"Sure," I said. "He was the caliph of the Islamic Empire when it extended from Spain into India. Ruled in Baghdad, A.D. eighth century, I think. He also was a prominent character in the *Arabian Nights*."

She smiled and handed me a goblet holding two ounces of liquid. "Do I detect some anger?"

"I'm not the Encyclopaedia Britannica."

"You certainly don't look like it. Anyway, the merchant was undoubtedly lying about al-Rashid owning it."

She held up the goblet. It shook only a little in her hand. "Here's how! Salaam! And death to the infidel dogs."

I raised my goblet. "Death to those who prefer the letter to the spirit."

The "tea" was straight double-malt scotch. I sipped some and put the goblet down. "Great stuff. But I've had enough booze today to last me for months."

I was an interested audience, which she hadn't apparently had for a long time. She didn't want to let me go. That was fine with me. I learned that she'd been born and raised in Peoria, had graduated in 1924 from Vassar, and had then gone to Paris though her father, a wealthy banker, chairman of the board of this and that, didn't like her living unchaperoned in "that cesspool of iniquitous Frogs."

"I wrote them once a week, long letters in which I described the cultural sites and how fluent I was getting in French and how much I was learning about the culture and history and art. I wasn't lying. What I didn't tell them was that I was living in the La Ruche district near Montparnasse nor that my daily companions were writers and artists whom they would've considered degenerate beyond redemption. Nor did I tell my parents how quickly and smoothly I'd shed my midwest, small-city Lutheran rearing, like a snake sheds its skin. I seemed born to the bohemian life: sordid cockroach-ridden rooms, dirt, unwashed bodies and underwear, chamberpots, no plumbing. But the compensations were radical ideas, bold artistic experiments, and the soaring and fiery conversations in sidewalk cafés and cheap restaurants. Many of those men and women would some day be reckoned among the greats.

"My parents never came to visit me because they were very busy and my visits home during the summer and at Christmas time satisfied them."

She was silent for a while, her mind watching reruns of the vigorous, exciting, and sometimes dangerous days and nights of post-World War I Paris. I envied her.

She fell silent for a while, then said, "I had lovers. They ranged from a huge ugly brute of a mailman—but what a lover!—to some whose works hang today in the Louvre and museums and private collections from New York to Tokyo. I also caught gonorrhea twice, the crabs three times, and syphilis once. We didn't have antibiotics then, you know, so recovery was not so quick—in fact, you could die or go crazy or both from syphilis. That scared me. From then on, I became more discriminating in my choice of lovers. At least, I tried to."

She paused, then said, "Do I shock or embarrass you?"

I shook my head.

"I didn't think so. To continue. Then I met Avram, a Russian Jew who spoke French with a Yiddish accent. After the Communist revolution, he learned quickly enough that anti-Semitism was far from dead in Russia nor was censorship in literature and art passé there.

"I fell deeply in love with him, and I was faithful to him, no easy thing to do then. I think he would have become famous if he'd lived longer. We had three years of great happiness—after I got him to quit eating so much garlic. And then . . . then he died of typhoid fever.

"I became very depressed then. I drank a lot of absinthe and smoked hashish, much more than I'd been doing. I lost all interest in sex. Eventually, I decided to go home. I'd marry a local boy, one of the country club and yachting set, of course, make my parents happy, make protective mimicry my way of life. The prospect even seemed attractive. That tells you how low my spirits were, how lonely and homesick I was."

"I don't think you made a good chameleon," I said.

"Oh, no. You're wrong. I actually convinced myself I was happy, very much a member of the booboisie, as Mencken called them. And, of course, I didn't talk as frankly as I do now. I'm a very old and very rich woman now. I don't have to pretend to be what I'm not. However, my relatively mild and innocuous behavior embarrasses my family. All Alligers were born with a ramrod frozen to absolute zero stuck up their anuses and deep into their brains. So they keep me in the background as well as they can."

She chuckled.

I said, "What happened after you came back from Paris?"

"I dated a lot, in my own set, of course, because that was expected. I played bridge, tennis, and golf. I became an expert at skeet shooting and duck hunting. I did a lot of charity work, headed fund drives, was very active among the civic-minded. Peoria, you know, has always had a great community spirit. Per capita, we have more civic-minded people than, I dare say, New York or Chicago. No lack of them.

"Then I started to date Simon Alliger, and he taught me to fly. That was fun. He was a dashing and handsome young man, a sportsman, an athlete, a Harvard graduate with an M.A. in business administration. All that stuff that so impressed his elders and his contemporaries. He didn't know beans about art, literature, science, or history, but that made no difference in his circles. He could be witty when he was tanked up on bootleg whiskey — for about half an hour."

"But you married him anyway?"

"Not right away. Though everybody regarded him as the catch of the year, as if he were some sort of record size fish, I couldn't bring myself to say yes to his proposals of marriage. And then . . . then . . ."

I waited. She frowned. Evidently, she didn't like the particular rerun in her mind.

"First, my mother died of cancer. She was buried October 22nd, 1929, a week before Black Tuesday, the day the stock market crashed, the beginning of the Great Depression. Banks closed, factories shut down, the soup kitchen lines formed on the right."

Her father's bank was wiped out, and his own fortune was gone. He'd been unable to face disgrace, poverty, and a possible jail sentence for illegal use of the bank's funds. He must have thought there was only one escape from all that. What happened then was reconstructed by the police. He had taken an elevator to the tenth floor of the Peoria Life Building, at that time the highest structure in the city. Apparently, he had intended to jump from a window or blow his brains out with a pistol.

"He was leaning out of a window, the cocked gun in his hand, still unable to make up his mind. And then his heart decided for him. It stopped. The gun fell ten stories to the sidewalk from his dead hand, and the impact caused it to fire. The bullet drove at an upward angle through the brain of a stockbroker, a close friend of Father's."

She was silent for a few seconds, then laughed.

"The stockbroker was on his way to jump from a window in the Peoria Life Building. A note left in his office said he was ruined and would be indicted for misusing his clients' investments even though he had not intended to defraud them. Like so many, he'd been buying stocks on margin, and the crash had wiped him and his investors out.

"According to witnesses, just before the gun fell onto the sidewalk, he'd stopped before the entrance of the building, stood still for a moment, then turned around and started walking away. He must have changed his mind about killing himself and was returning to his office to get the suicide note before anybody found it. But it was too late for him. Fate had already cast his lot."

"So much for free will," I said. "The universe doesn't play fair. Destiny is not always determined by character."

She said, "I'd been rich, then suddenly I was very poor. But the canny Alligers had gotten out of the stock market before things started going bad. Though their many businesses suffered, they rode out the storm. So, I married Simon, and Simon Junior came along a few years later. I realized later that I wasn't much better than a whore in doing this, but I was a rich and respectable whore. Though I never loved Simon, I was fond of him, and I had my books and music, and I painted, though my talent for that was limited. Out of all the people I knew, my cousin, Bobbie Gerichter, was the only really kindred soul. She was always wonderful fun."

She paused, then said, her voice breaking, "Bobbie died three years ago. Since then, I've been very lonely."

"I'm sorry," I said. "I mean it."

"I have no right to complain."

I said, "I saw the photograph of you and your husband in duck-hunting clothes. I'm curious about you two. A friend of mine" (I referred to Mimi) "mentioned you and your husband had to shoot your way out of an ambush, an attempted abduction. It was on the road near the Duck Inn after you two had been hunting. Made quite a splash in the papers, I understand."

She shrugged, and said, "I'm not proud of that, and I don't like to think of it. But it had to be done. A man and a woman, poor people, poor because of the Depression, thought they'd kidnap me and ask Simon for ransom. They were desperate amateurs, which we didn't know until after the shooting, though that wouldn't have made any difference in what we had to do. They were armed with rifles and revolvers. We had shotguns, of course, but also pistols which Simon insisted we keep in the car for protection."

She grimaced. "Their car forced ours off the road, and they came at us on foot with rifles. We fired first. It took a second for me to kill my man instead of a lifetime, if you get what I mean. And it took Simon the same time to kill his woman instead of taking a lifetime."

"That's one way of putting it," I said. "Thank you. I used to hunt, but I, well, I got to feeling sorry for the birds and animals, and I quit."

"I understand quite well," she said. "I quit hunting after that . . . incident, though I kept up my skeet shooting until ten years ago."

For the first time, I looked at my wristwatch. I said, "This has been extraordinarily pleasant and instructive. But I have to be going. However, I'd like to see you again."

She smiled. "Call me soon. I'm sure we can get together and have another tête-à-tête. Now, I'm going to take a little nap. You'll pardon me if I don't call a servant to show you out."

"Sure," I said. "I'm a PI. I can make my way through any maze."

She got up and walked unsteadily across the room—the two ounces of straight scotch had hit her hard—and disappeared through a doorway. Before the door closed, I saw part of a large canopied bed and a huge entertainment center cabinet. So, she didn't disdain modern technology; she wasn't as stuck in the old days as she had seemed.

When I stepped onto the front porch, the heat hit me. It got worse when I stepped into the sunshine. Before I could get to the garage, however, I heard my name called. I turned and looked upward.

Simon Alliger was leaning out of a second-story window. He bellowed, "Corbie! Get back up here!"

15

I started toward the side door. Simon shouted for me to wait until Juan came to escort me. A moment later, the Mayan trotted out from the front door. As he went by me, he motioned for me to follow him. I walked slowly to the side door, forcing him to wait for me.

"I'm not a dog," I said. "I don't run when the master calls."

He grinned, showing large, blocklike teeth. I followed him into the house and up the steps to the second-story hall. He opened the screen door and knocked on the office door. The master shouted, "Come in!" I sauntered in and placed myself in the chair in front of the desk. I wasn't going to wait for Simon to invite me to sit down.

A large pot of coffee and a half-filled cup of coffee were on the desk. Like so many, he mistakenly thought that a lot of caffeine would sober him up faster. The afternoon sun was shining through the window behind him, outlining him and half-blinding me. I moved the chair to one side to escape the glare. He looked at me sternly from red eyes.

"I've been told that you were talking to my mother."

"It was her wish."

He scowled. I didn't tremble.

"Listen, Corbie. You must understand that my mother is old and just a little, ah, senile, though she's always been, ah, eccentric. She likes to shock people to . . . ah . . ."

"Épater le bourgeois," I said.

"What?"

"Beat the Philistines. Shock the middle class," I said.

"Oh, yes. Anyway, you can discount anything she may have said to you. She tells the most outlandish things to people, anybody who'll listen, even strangers, just to embarrass us. I don't know why she does that. We've always treated her as if she were a queen. I suppose she tried to find out why you're here. I hope . . ."

"She does know I'm a PI you hired, but she doesn't know why you did it. Nor will anybody know unless you tell me it's OK to tell them."

He leaned back. "Good!

Evidently, he wasn't going to offer me any coffee.

"Let's get down to business," he said loudly.

Whatever had opened him up during my first visit had vanished. He was now the boss, and I was just a working stiff in a business suit.

"Did Mother say anything about Diana?"

"Nothing for us to worry about."

A smile skimmed batlike across his mouth.

"You witnessed that scene between my wife and Diana. And I believe I said something about their relationship."

"Not much. Why don't we start all over again?"

He leaned forward, his lower arms on the desk, and he church-steepled his hands. While he talked, he glared at me, though I think he would rather have looked anywhere but at me. His fixed stare was the threatening look which the leader of a baboon pack gives an inferior in the pecking order. If I looked away, I acknowledged that he was the purple-assed king.

So what? I wasn't going to be pulled into his game. Keeping my eyes on his would be painful, especially since I'd have to look into the bright light. Again, I moved my chair to my right. This forced him to swivel the chair toward me. Of course, the sunlight through the next window was full on my face. I shaded my eyes with my hand.

Muttering something forceful, he got up and drew down the blind behind him.

I said, "Thanks." And I moved my chair back to its original place. After that, I mostly stared up at the ceiling or down at the desk. Now and then, just to show him I could do it, I'd look into his eyes. The dark skin below them seemed to get darker every time I did this. More and more, his face resembled a raccoon's.

"Very well," he began. "I dislike very much bringing strangers into the family affairs. But the situation is such . . . anyway, you are to find out all you can about Diana's past. What happened . . . my wife and I were shocked when Roger phoned from Las Vegas and said he'd just gotten married. But I told you that, didn't I?"

"Something about it," I said. "Not enough."

I wondered if he really didn't remember or if he was probing me to find out if I'd drunk so much I didn't remember either.

"OK," I said. "You wouldn't be unhappy if I uncovered dirt you could use to get your son to divorce her. Am I being too frank for you?"

He drew in air, held it, then breathed it out slowly.

"No. You're not too frank. But I want to make this perfectly clear. I desire the truth and only the truth."

"That's all you'd get from me, anyway," I said.

"Roger knows nothing about this investigation. We haven't told him because he's too infatuated with her, blind to what she is, a low-class . . . uh, I won't call her a tramp, not yet. I have to be fair. Anyway, for the present, this will have to do. After you read it, you can proceed on your own."

He opened the middle desk drawer, pulled out a large manila envelope, and held it out to me.

"Here. AAA Abendale Investigations' report on Diana."

Though surprised by this unexpected item, I didn't say anything. I pulled out the folder inside the envelope and then its contents. It was a case file prepared by Lorna Mordoy, an operative of the Chicago outfit. Date: exactly three months after Diana had married Roger Alliger. Simon hadn't dillydallied much before loosing the hounds.

I took my time reading the entire file. In essence, it confirmed everything that Diana had revealed to the Alligers about her past, though that wasn't much. She had been born on May 24, 1956, in Pasadena, California. The long-form birth certificate was enclosed with the report.

I noted automatically—Glinna's influence—that Diana was a Gemini, the astrological sign of the Twins.

Her father was William R. Rolanski; her mother, Myrna Groat Rolanski. He was born in 1936 in or near Monkeys Eyebrow, Ballard County, Kentucky. Birth certificate enclosed. Died in 1970 in Pasadena, California, of a heart attack. Death certificate enclosed.

I'd once tracked an embezzler to Needmore, a hamlet near the abandoned hamlet of Monkeys Eyebrow. That's the only reason I would ever have heard of this place. The most plausible story accounting for its name is that the hamlet was on a ridge topped with bushes and this looked to some traveling salesman like a monkey's eyebrow. The sparsely populated Ballard County is in western Kentucky and across the Ohio

River from Metropolis, Illinois. This Metropolis is not the city where Clark Kent worked as a reporter. But the newspaper is called the *Daily Planet,* and there is a huge statue of Superman there.

Myrna had no birth certificate. The enclosed Ballard County marriage license, dated April 1, 1956, gave her age as about eighteen. The Reverends Heber and Angela Boomall of the Descent-of-Doves Pentecostal Church had conducted the ceremony. What the Rolanskis did from 1956 to 1960, Mordoy did not know. In 1960, the Rolanskis arrived in Pasadena and rented a small house. In 1970, a month after Mr. Rolanski died, Myrna Rolanski purchased a small house on West 17th Street, a lower-class neighborhood in Los Angeles. The money came from Mr. Rolanski's insurance policy.

Myrna Rolanski's death certificate stated that she had died of smoke asphyxiation when her house on West 17th burned down on August 20, 1975. There was much other enclosed data re the parents, such as real estate records, employment and state agency records, et cetera. Also enclosed were the reports of the fire department and insurance investigators. They agreed that the blaze had been caused by a short circuit in the forty-year-old electrical wiring.

Diana was nineteen when her mother died. From her mother's savings and life and fire insurance, Diana got $52,000 minus taxes. After buying a used 1970 BMW convertible for $10,000 and taking a small apartment in Westwood, she entered UCLA in September. School records for her first two years were enclosed along with the automobile sale, DMV, rental, and scholastic records. Her grades were good, mostly B's, but C's in her science courses.

In addition to the car, she had purchased expensive clothes and jewelry. An itemized list of the sale at a Wilshire Boulevard store was enclosed.

When I saw that, I looked up and said, "A $10,000 BMW, $12,000 for lingerie and dresses, and $25,000 for diamond and emerald necklaces, gold brooches, and bracelets!"

He grimaced.

"That woman has no concept of the value of money."

"Went ape," I said. "But I suppose she'd never had much money until then."

"That's no excuse. Her wastefulness and extravagance have really upset Sandy and me. They also drive Roger up the wall, but" — his lip curled — "he's too gutless to raise hell with her. The only complaints he makes about her reckless squandering are to us. Never directly to her."

I murmured, "As you said, pussywhipped."

"What?"

"I was just exclaiming."

I paused, then said, "Of course, gold and jewelry are good investments."

His face got red, and he snarled, "Not if you're stupid enough not to insure them!"

"Ah?"

"The brainless bitch! So, what happens then? Just what you'd expect! While she was absent from the apartment, the jewelry was stolen! It wasn't insured, either! It was a break-in, probably by some sleazebag radical student or some black!"

He slammed his fist on the desk.

"And then," he said, "she wrecked her BMW, which she had no business buying even if it was used! Read on!"

To sum it up, the insurance company refused to pay for a new car, and she was arrested for drunk driving. By the time a lawyer got her off, she was broke.

I said, "Well, she was going to college. And she wasn't on drugs. At least, the police report indicates she wasn't."

"She never finished college."

The record of her movements was a blank from August 10, 1977, until the evening of September 9, 1995. Mordoy could find no records of any sort during that time.

On that evening, Diana met Roger Alliger at the Hollywood Hills home of a movie producer. The producer, Cosmo Evershiv, had made only B movies, mostly beach, campus, and jungle films featuring bikini-clad women, muscle men, space aliens, and clichés. His biggest moneymaker was *Snake Women of Atlantis versus Pectoral Man*.

The Chicago operative, Lorna Mordoy, had interviewed Evershiv once for twenty minutes. He stated that a friend of his, couldn't remember his name, had brought Roger Alliger with him to the party. Evershiv hadn't known Alliger before the party and didn't remember much about him.

He had a better memory of Diana though he didn't recall her surname. Evershiv did say that someone had told him Diana had played bit parts in some movies. Mordoy had phoned Simon from Los Angeles and asked him to find out the name of the friend who'd taken Roger to the party and who, apparently, had introduced Diana to Roger. Simon had casually asked his son about it. Roger claimed that he had met the man in a bar. He remembered only that the man's name was Rupert Something-or-other.

Lorna Mordoy had interviewed the minister who'd married Roger and Diana at 4:35 A.M. in Las Vegas. The Reverend George Boocherneff and his wife, encouraged by a hundred-dollar bill, had admitted that the couple had liquor on their breath and that the speech of the bride and groom was somewhat slurred. Except for the summary, that was the end of Mordoy's report.

I said, "What's Diana's explanation for the unaccounted-for period of time?"

Simon frowned, and he said, "I didn't ask her about it, of

course. Surely you're intelligent enough to know that. If I had, she'd have been tipped off I was investigating her."

"I can't take anything for granted," I said. I wasn't nettled by his comment about my brain power. I'd had ruder clients.

"Surely," I said, "your son must've asked her about her past?"

"I once tried to question him about it. I did it very casually so he wouldn't get suspicious and tell Diana. But he said that all he knew was she'd told him she'd worked at various odd jobs and moved around a lot. She met Roger at a party given by a movie producer. Doesn't that indicate that she might've been a call girl? Or maybe a street walker this Rupert knew?"

"If she was a street whore," I said, "she'd have a police record. Mordoy checked those. She wouldn't be allowed direct access to them, but I suppose she bribed some cop to look them up for her. As for your assumption that Diana was a whore . . . well, you don't have any evidence that she was."

He grunted, and he said, "What you say is true. Objectively, there's no real evidence. But if she wasn't a whore, how did she support herself after she dropped out of sight?"

"She could've been in some other state for a while. If you want to extend the investigation . . ."

"That'd be very expensive! No, we'll confine this to California. To the LA area, I mean."

When I was in the LAPD, I'd played poker with cheaters. This guy had aces up his sleeve. He knew something he hadn't told me yet. When I saw him smile smugly, I knew I was right. He opened the middle desk drawer again and pulled out two sheets of 8 1/2-by-11-inch Xerox paper. He slid them across the desk and said, triumph in his voice, "Read that!"

One sheet bore a copy of the face of a 3 5/8-by-6 1/2 envelope. It was postmarked fourteen days before the present date. Hollywood Station, California. No return address.

The other sheet was a copy of a handwritten letter, its words small and its lines pressing against each other. While Simon Alliger kept on smiling knowingly, I read it.

16

There was no date or return address on the letter.

Dear Diana,

Or shud I call you Minnie Dix or Clio Brooks?
Depends on if your in a blue mood ha! ha! right?
Those were the days! I never had so much fun in
my life as when we was in Cast Your Broad Upon
The Waters and The Last of The Merkins, they was
riots, I never laft so much in my life! Anyway, I got
lucky, lucky! This guy Sid is rich and he aint a bad
guy. He dont beat me when hes drunk or pist off
except with his big rammer and I aint complaining
about that ha! ha! His wifeys a real bitch, wont
blow him or let him eat her pussey or cornhole
her so him and me, we go to it. You know me I
love it tho when you get down to it and I do Id really rather just fuck. And Sids good for a hell of a lot
more loot than those cheapskate titeass sleezeball
producers ever gave me. I aint doing bad for a

country girl from East Gnawbone Indianna. From haystack to Hollywood pad you might say and I do.

Ran into our old agent Irving Dingenzick who cud forget that name, right? Hes getting old and shaky tho not too old not to try to get me into his bed again even tho his hart's bad. He asst about you I said I didnt know where you was.

Thanks for riting me tho as you said you shudnt have cause it was too chancey for you. Thanks also for asking me how the opration came out. Guess you can tell Im doing alright now. Shudnt have no more trouble. Your letter shows your AOK, a real pal. You got a big hart behind that tough bitch style of yours. I wont rite no more less I get another letter from you. Your well fixt now and dont want nobody to find out about your passt. Dont blame you Id do the same.

Lots of Love
Weena

I looked up at him. He was still grinning smugly.

"Might I ask where you got this?" I said.

He sat back and frowned. "No. You may not."

"I need to know. How else can I determine if it's genuine? Also, it might give me a lead . . ."

His face got red, and he leaned forward. "What do you mean genuine? Are you suggesting . . . ?"

"Suggesting nothing personal, sir!" I said sharply. "But how am I going to use this if I don't know where or from whom you got it? I need leads, and I can't ignore any just because they might reflect unfavorably on someone."

I sat back with the air of one who speaks with the authority of experience and won't take nonsense from anyone.

"Reflect unfavorably?" he said. He chewed his lower lip for a minute. Then he surprised me by smiling.

"You're shrewd, Corbie. Very well. But what we did was quite justified, considering the circumstances. Last week, my wife and I went to my son's house when they were not there. We let ourselves in with a key, Roger gave it to us sometime ago, and we had his permission to enter the house at any time."

"Pardon me, sir," I said. "Did Diana know that Roger had done that?"

"No. Why?"

"Does she now know?"

"No. Neither does Roger."

"Legally, it wasn't breaking and entering," I said. "But if Diana found out about it, she could file suit for invasion of privacy and theft of property and who knows what else."

He winced. He was envisioning the publicity and the scandal. "Well, there's no reason why that should happen."

He continued his story. He and his wife has gone through the desk and files in Diana's office. They found nothing incriminating there, though they did find some bills for very expensive clothes.

"She has no sense of values," he said. "She's wasting his money."

I didn't reply to that though I did think about Roger's yacht.

"Then we went into her bedroom. They don't sleep together because she's too restless and easily disturbed if somebody else is in the bed. Anyway, we found this letter inside a pair of, ah, panties at the bottom of a stack of underwear in a dresser drawer. We made a copy on Roger's copier in his office and put the original back where we found it."

Neither of us spoke for a minute. He was leaning back in his swivel chair, his fingers church-steepled again, his eyes fixed on the ceiling. Perhaps he was projecting an interior

film on it, Diana in disgrace and exiled from Peoria, his son
Roger restored to the bosom of his family and free from cocaine, adultery, and fiery-tempered bimbos.

Suddenly, he leaned forward. "What do you make of this letter, Corbie? Surely, it contains the leads you need?"

"It suggests that the writer, Weena, last name unknown,
was an actress, possibly in blue movies, possibly hardcore
porn. But she could've been in sleazy T & A movies with no
genuine nudity . . ."

"T & A? What're those?"

"Tits and Ass. The women dress in bikinis or the minimum
of underwear. You see flashes of bare breasts and long views
of bare buttocks."

His upper lip curled, and he said, "I wouldn't know. That letter also proves that Diana was in that kind of movie and what
kind of slut she was and is. Just like her close friend, Weena,
I'd say. Roger puts up with a lot from her, but if she was like
this Weena . . ."

"Apparently, Diana had at least two stage names," I said.
"Clio Brooks is OK. But Minnie Dix! Come on!"

He looked puzzled. Then the pun became clear. He said,
"For God's sake! However, Corbie, there is something I don't
understand. This movie, *The Last of the Merkins*. What's a
merkin?"

"It's a pubic hair piece, a wig for the female pubes. Comes
in brunette, redhead, and blond varieties. Used sometimes by
whores and amateurs. The titles of the movies sound as if
they were outright porno films. But titles aren't proof. You're
going to need a lot more than this letter to use as an effective
weapon against your daughter-in-law."

"I know that, Corbie! But is this enough for you to trace her
career as a Hollywood porn actress?"

"Probably," I said. "You made a lucky strike with that letter.
The name of the agent and the movie titles should be enough.

I might not even have to go to Los Angeles. I can use a private detective who lives there. He's not cheap, but you'd save money if I didn't have to fly out there, live in motels, and drive a rental car."

"By all means! When can you get started?"

"Within the hour. But I'll need your written authorization for the investigation. And a check for my estimated expenses. And an advance based on the estimate of the agency's total services. As you know, my boss, Mrs. Rootwell, requires that."

He didn't look happy, but he said, "That'll be taken care of as she wishes. However, I'll expect daily and direct reports from you. First, though, just what did you mean by that remark about the genuineness of the letter?"

I shrugged, and I stood up.

"A paranoiac is someone who doesn't believe in coincidences. He believes that everything is connected, is one cosmic spiderweb. PIs are not paranoiacs, but we have to think as if we are."

"I don't like it that you might have considered for one moment that Sandy and I faked that letter and envelope. That is what you were considering, wasn't it?"

"For two seconds," I said, grinning. "But neither of you would know enough to successfully fake that letter, pardon the split infinitive." Then, I said, "Why didn't you use AAA Abendale to follow up the case when you found the letter?"

"I suppose it really wasn't this Mordoy woman's fault that she didn't uncover Diana's actress career," he said. "But those who work for me don't fail. If they do, they're out!"

He handed me the copy of the file. I said, "Thanks," and I walked toward the door. I looked back when I opened the inner door. He was standing at the window, his back to me, probably contemplating . . . what? Who knew what anybody was really thinking about?

I looked at my wristwatch. 3:11. Glinna wouldn't be home

from her part-time job until six or so. While driving home, I'd report to Mimi Rootwell on the phone, explain why I'd not called her back at once, and then report to her. I was sure she'd agree that we should get Garry Deb, the Pasadena operative, to investigate in the LA area.

By the time I'd thought about this, I had passed the south side of the mansion and was heading for my car on the driveway. Faith Alliger's Cord had been moved. Just before I was about to get into the car, I heard a motor throbbing and then brakes squealing. I turned. There was Diana Alliger getting out of her rose-red, brand-new Ferrari convertible. Its top was down, but her hair didn't look wind-blown.

She was now wearing high-heeled open black shoes, black stockings, and a very short black sheath with a deep scoop neckline. Very fetching, I thought. I doubted that Simon and Alexandra would approve of it, but they wouldn't approve of anything about her.

Evidently, Diana had not gotten over her mad. Or she was off on a new one. She stormed up onto the porch as if she meant to walk through the closed door. But the Mayan, Juan Cabracan, stepped out from it. He held out a hand, a stop signal, and said something.

She said loudly, "Out of my way, Juan, unless you want to get knocked over!"

He smiled and made an imploring gesture. I still couldn't hear his words. Instead of getting into the car and driving away, minding my own business, I walked to the porch near the steps and watched them from an angle. Actually, this scene, anything about this family, was my business. Private detectives have a divine right to know everything.

I could now hear Cabracan's low pleading voice.

"Pleess, Missess Allikeh, Meesteh Allikeh, he say no. Meesses Allikeh . . . still seeck. You can' not enter. You . . . shut out, stay away till Meester Allikeh say iss OK. He say you mek his wife sick."

"Are you telling me I'm barred from this house?" Diana screamed.

Cabracan nodded, stepped back inside, and closed the door. Its lock clicked.

She whirled around and saw me. "Who the hell are you and what the hell you doing here? Eavesdropping?"

"I could be downtown and still could hear you," I said.

She started to look even more furious, then, suddenly, she was laughing. "I am a hellcat sometimes," she said. "When I have good reason, though. Sorry I jumped on you like that. But . . ."

I wanted to talk to her, draw her out, and find out much more about her, possibly things which the undoubtedly biased Simon Alliger would never have told me. But to do that, I'd have to tell her my name. That might lead to her finding out just who I was and why I was here.

So I said, "I'll just go. I came over to see if I could aid a lady in distress and all that, but I think the distress was suffered by that man."

I started to walk away from her.

"I don't know," she said. "Things're falling apart."

I halted and turned. She wasn't looking at me, and her lips were moving silently. She hadn't been talking to me.

Once more, I started toward the car but again stopped and turned. A beat-up, blue, and somewhat rusty 1983 Dodge van came out of the woods and around the curve of the road. It stopped behind Diana's car, while from it blared the latest rock hit, "Busted Blue Orgone Bubbles." Music by the Rimmer Cockroaches, I believe. The two occupants of the van stared at Diana and me, then got out of it.

Mimi Rootwell had described Rosemary Alliger, Roger's nineteen-year-old sister. This very short and very skinny woman had to be she. Her face would've been pretty if it'd been more than skin tightly drawn over the skull. Her pale blue eyes bulged above dark half-moons. Her tangled chestnut hair, bound by a red headband, fell to her buttocks. She wore a long-sleeved, brown-and-white checked granny dress. The sleeves would be covering needle marks. Brown sandals enclosed her skeleton feet.

This woman, I thought, was going to die by evening unless she got a milk shake and hamburger under her belt.

The man, who'd gotten out of the driver's side, leaned against the closed door. A black headband bound his long dirty-blond hair. He wore a black long-sleeved shirt, an old leather belt, almost-white blue jeans fashionably torn at the knees, and scuffed rawhide cowboy boots. A burning cigarette dangled from a corner of his thin lips.

He, too, was very skinny but stood several inches over six feet. His eyes were a muddy brown, and a hammer-shaped ring hung from his large right ear. His narrow shoulders were bowed; his chest, sunken. His skin was as rough and as red as if it'd been sandpapered. A very thin mustache ran along the edge of his upper lip, which was curled into a sneer.

This was Burt Kordik, a native of Jefferson Park, a Chicago area. Many fine people have been born there, but Kordik was not one of them.

17

Diana Alliger was now facing the newcomers. Rosemary Alliger walked halfway up the steps, then stopped, looking up at her sister-in-law.

She spoke in a piping little-girl's voice. "Hello, Diana."

Diana smiled tightly. "You're just in time to see me get locked out, too, Rosemary. We're in the same boat, and it's sinking fast. Too late to start bailing."

"What is it now?" Rosemary said. "You and Mother . . . ?"

"Your father, too," Diana said. "I told Alexandra she has to quit interfering with Roger and me and quit nosing into our private business. Now . . ."

"And I suppose she had an asthma attack?"

"Doesn't she always? Your father accuses me of causing her attacks, but who causes most of them? He does! He doesn't really give a damn about her, he hates her, and she hates him! Otherwise, why would she cultivate those bees when they're such a danger to your father?"

Diana looked beyond her at the van. Kordik waved at her. She didn't wave back.

"I suppose you've come to ask for money again?" she said to Rosemary. "Forget it! They told me you're not welcome in this house until you get rid of that snotbag!"

She pointed at Kordik. "And maybe not then. You'll have to get therapy, and . . ."

Rosemary's voice was very cold. "I don't like the way you talk about Burt. Just because he's not rich . . ."

"Look at him, look at how he treats you," Diana said. "He's a creepy crawly slimy slug, and he got you on drugs and is keeping you on them. He's only interested in your money, your parents' money, I should say. I've met blowhole larvae like him before. Far too many."

"Shut up!" Rosemary screamed. "I love him, and he loves me! Anyway, who are you to talk? You're only interested in Roger because of his money! Mother and Father said so, and they . . ."

She stopped. The lack of logic in her thinking must have struck her.

Diana smiled and said, "That creep made passes at me, and he even tried to put the make on Cabracan's wife. He'd fuck a snake if you held its head."

I hadn't heard that old folk phrase for a long time. Where had she picked that up?

"I won't let you insult him!" Rosemary cried. She stepped up onto the porch, her face and hands clenched, and stood very close to Diana. She had to bend her neck far back and look upward.

The door and then the screen door opened. Simon Alliger stood within the entrance while he held the screen door open with one hand. His face was red, and he was quivering.

He shrilled, "For God's sake! You're making public spectacles of yourselves! You're dishonoring this house! Get off my property, all of you! I don't want to see any of you here again until I say you can come!"

He paused, then yelled, "Do you understand that!" And he slammed the door.

Rosemary cried out, "Father!"

Kordik called out in a high thin voice, "Come on, Rosie! It's hopeless! Your old man has really got the red ass for us!"

Rosemary swung toward me. She said, "Do you have business here? If you don't, why the hell don't you get out of here?"

I turned and walked away. But, once more, I stopped and reversed direction. I'd heard another car coming up the driveway. This was a low-slung white convertible Lamborghini. It stopped just behind the van. A medium-tall, stocky, and blond man wearing a white shirt, solid dull-red tie, and gray business suit got out of the car. I estimated he was in his early thirties. He had a handsome though bland face. The long sharp nose and dark crescents under his eyes made Roger Alliger look as raccoonish as his father.

Old home week at the ancestral mansion. Everybody here. The joint is jumping. Prime-time soap opera!

Roger swaggered around the van toward the porch. Frowning, he spoke loudly, deeply, and authoritatively.

"What's going on here, Diana? Why'd you call me here?"

"Your father has forbidden me to enter the house. He says I'm a disturbing influence, I've upset your mother too many times, made her have asthma attacks. You know that's a crock. Everybody stimulates her asthma. I just wanted the old biddy to keep her nose out of our private business. If you're a real man, you'll tell her to do just that."

Roger suddenly looked as if his flesh had turned to wood. He spoke in a much more subdued voice. "What do I have to straighten out now?"

"No, Roger," she said scornfully. "When you try to straighten things out, you always get them even more crooked. Forget that. I just wanted you to be here and at least appear to back me up. But now your father won't even let me in the house."

She gestured at Rosemary.

"He won't let her into the house either."

Kordik said, "So what's new about that that? Come on, Rosie. Let's blow. Your parents got it in for us. Nothing more we can do about that. Forget about them."

Rosemary turned to face him. "We can't! We need money! What're we going to do?"

"We don't need 'em," he said. "Come on!"

I swatted at a bee buzzing around my face. Simon had better stay inside the house, I thought. A second later, the doors opened again. Simon's scowling face appeared.

"All of you go home!" he roared. "I mean it! Meanwhile, I'll be thinking about changing my will! Get out, get out!"

"Sure, or you'll call the police!" Kordik said. "That'll be the day! All that publicity!"

He sneered, blew cigarette smoke out, and sneered again. But he did climb into the van.

"Father!" Rosemary said, her hands held out to him. "We need money!"

"Have you no shame?" Simon said. "Begging before all these people. Here!"

He took his wallet out, removed a bill, crumpled it, and threw it at Rosemary. She picked it up from the porch floor and ran to the van.

"Buy some more drugs!" Simon shouted. "Shoot it up! Get high! My God, Rosemary!"

His voice broke. Rosemary turned, her face twisted. "I can't help it!" she shrilled. "You won't help! Nobody'll help!"

She got into the van. The motor started, the van backed up until its rear bumper was touching the front one of Roger's car, went forward until its bumper touched Diana's car, went back, went forward, Kordik wresting the wheel right and left, then the van sped away with its tires screeching.

I walked away feeling ashamed of them and of myself for staying there to witness the hatred and the humiliation.

I heard Diana yelling. "Well, Roger, you coming with me or you going to stay here and kiss your father's ass?"

"He's not coming in today!" Simon shouted. "And you, Diana, Diana *Rolanski*, you'll apologize and promise not to make trouble anymore or you'll find this door closed forever to you!"

I'd had enough of this. I drove off without looking in the rearview mirror to see what Roger was going to do.

Back onto Grand View Drive, I drove northward. The road climbed as it curved along the top of the western bluffs along the river. Before I'd gone far, the cellular phone rang. Simon Alliger's voice was loud in my ear.

"Corbie! You witnessed that scene on the porch! I'm sorry about that, very sorry! It was degrading! But even in the best of families . . . anyway, you *will* keep all this to yourself! I couldn't tolerate anybody talking about this!"

I said, "I'm a professional, so don't worry."

"I know. But . . ."

He seemed close to weeping.

"Where's all the tenderness and love and caring? Where's the respect? What happened to my wife, my children? Things change, they change, and things fall apart!"

I hadn't hired out to be a psychological counselor. Anyway, he was as much responsible for the situation as anybody else involved. But he wouldn't take kindly to my saying so.

"Flux is the essence of time," I said.

"What the hell does that mean?"

Good. He was angry again. I preferred him to be. If he'd started sobbing, I might've felt sorry for him.

"It means . . ." I said. I stopped. Then, "I'm glad you called. You remind me of something I meant to ask you. Did you just get back from a business or vacation trip?"

"Why?"

I told him about finding the dead bees in his bathroom. He didn't say anything. Maybe shock had gripped him.

"That's why I asked you if you'd just come back from a trip," I said. "I think the bees starved to death. It's the only reasonable assumption."

His voice was as thin as a ghost's. "I got back yesterday from a business trip to New York. Seven days there. But I haven't used the bathroom since I got back. Not until today, that is."

"It's possible that they somehow got into the bathroom on their own."

"Nobody was even supposed to be in my office," he said. "Not even Juan. He cleaned the office and bathroom just before I left town. I saw him do it. He did it while I was working there."

His voice became stronger.

"My God, Corbie! This means . . . ?"

"Maybe," I said.

"But why . . . who?"

"Never mind that," I said. "Not just now, anyway. Do you keep your office locked when you're not using it?"

"What? Oh, yes, I do. Except that, well, quite often, if I leave the room but don't leave the house and I intend to return soon, I don't lock it."

"Besides you, who has keys to the room?"

"No one. Not even my wife."

"Do you always carry yours with you?"

"Always," he said.

"When you go to bed, where do you put the key?"

I turned the car off the main road and onto a lane formed by a concrete-bordered island of grass. I stopped it beside a wooden plaque on posts, a historical marker, and turned the motor off. I'd seen Diana's Ferrari, tailed by Roger's white car, coming up the road behind me. Apparently, they'd not left the house at once. But they were going fast now, exceeding the speed limits for this road.

"I put the key in the drawer of my bedside table."

"You said you always carry the key with you? But do you really? I mean, if you go to a social gathering or, when you take a trip, do you have it then?"

There was a pause. Then he said, "Well, sometimes I leave it. Not on purpose, though. A few times, well, I've forgotten to take it with me. But this trip, no, I didn't forget. I took it with me."

I didn't remind him that it's easy to take a key, make an impression, and make a key from the impression. He'd probably already thought of that.

The two cars sped by the island. I doubted that either Diana or Roger had seen me. They looked angry and intent, and their eyes were fixed on the road.

Alliger said, "I just can't believe that anybody's trying to kill me. But . . ."

"Just be careful," I said. "Don't accuse anyone. That'd be a mistake, and it'd put the guilty person—if there is one—on guard. It's also possible that there's an explanation for the bees being there. We just haven't thought of one."

"Listen, Corbie," he said. His voice was low and angry now. "First thing I'm going to do, I'm going to write a report of this. I'll give it to my lawyer, Jack Crotal, to keep in confidence. If anything should happen to me, he'll give it unopened to Mimi Rootwell. She can conduct a discreet investigation, and . . ."

"Sir, she'll have to give it to the police," I said. "She can't proceed otherwise. I know you want to avoid scandal and all that, but some situations . . ."

He barked, "That's the way I want it, and that's the way it'll be!"

I shrugged. No matter what he wanted, it was going to happen as I said. If his lawyer were informed of the paper's contents, he'd tell him the same.

"I want you to go ahead on the investigation," Alliger said. "I think Diana is the one who put the bees there. She's got a lot riding at stake, and if I'm out of the way . . ."

He paused. Apparently, he couldn't think of just how removing him from the living would benefit her. I was sure, though, that he'd eventually come up with rationalizations to satisfy him.

Of course, he could be right.

"Just sit tight, sir," I said. "If you accuse her, anybody for that matter, you might have a lawsuit on your hands. No way could the newspapers repress that. You need proof. Look, sir, with all due respect, you're in a messy situation. You're going to be plastered with publicity. You can't avoid it."

"Oh, yes, I can!" he said harshly. "What if the person planning the murder was to die, but it looked like an accident!"

He hung up, leaving me puzzled about just what he meant. Maybe he was just blasting hot air. I waited, expecting him to call back at once. He'd tell me to forget what I'd just heard because he'd spoken in anger. He'd then tell me to go ahead as if things were normal. He himself would only do what I'd suggested. He'd be cool.

But he didn't call.

18

On Grand View Drive near its north end is a wooden marker. It gives some dates and the various names for Peoria from 1673 on. It's on the edge of a bluff which at this point is 328 feet above the Illinois River and its valley. I parked the car here to enjoy the view, which is indeed grand. On a clear day, you can see northward for twenty-five miles past the broad expanse of river the Peoria Indians called Pimiteoui. Land of the Fat Beasts.

"Peoria" is a Native American word the most valid interpretation of which seems to be "turkey." There are many in this area who think that that is very appropriate, but cynics are everywhere. They also insist that there's a good reason why one of the French settlers' names for Peoria was "Pissville."

And these cynics love the Peoria Indian myth about With-iha, the Great White Hare, the prototype for Bugs Bunny. The myth goes that, in the early days after the creation of the world, the long-eared trickster spirit invented corn. After he'd eaten the first batch, some undigested kernels in his droppings took root and became the first human beings.

There's another Peoria Indian legend which supposedly really took place on the edge of the very prominence on which I stood. It has some of the basic and conventional elements other similar legends have. But it also differs in some important aspects. My father says that the differences are because of the "Peorianess" which floats in the local air. Whatever that means, here's how it goes.

A maiden named Mishiwapo was pining away because her lover, Kwasim, had failed to return from a raid on the far-away Iroquois. She waited a long long time, and then she got word that he'd been killed. So, after making a suitable farewell speech to the Great Spirit, she leaped off the bluff a few feet from where I stood.

But, instead of hurtling to her death, she was caught in the branches of a tree growing almost vertically from a crevice in the rock about fifty feet below the edge of the bluff. The branches broke, but those of another tree eased her fall somewhat.

Undaunted by this mishap, the bruised and bloody maiden crawled back up the cliff. After resting a while, she again jumped off, though from a different place. This time, she bounced off a spur of rock she'd not seen from above and cartwheeled through the air onto a bush, which broke off. Then she fell fifty more feet before ending up in the branches of a small tree.

Though bleeding and hurting in body and dignity, she climbed to the top again. In a few minutes, having found a spot which promised an unimpeded descent, she cast herself into space once more.

This time, a big male black bear happened to be ambling along on the narrow trail a hundred feet below. The maiden, instead of bouncing off the hard rock of the projecting trail and on down to her death, landed on the relatively soft back of the very fat bear. It died. But she suffered only a temporary loss of breath, a permanent loss of some teeth, several broken ribs, a shattered nose, and battered flesh in many places. Not one to give up easily, she again climbed to the top of bluff.

There, groaning and moaning while hauling herself over the edge, she looked up into the face of her presumed dead lover. He was on his way to the village to announce his escape and to introduce the Iroquois woman who was deeply in love with him and had abandoned her own tribe to flee with him.

The legend does not record what Mishiwapo said when Kwasim told her this. But it does record that she hurled Kwasim and the woman from the edge of the cliff to their deaths and then went home to marry the local flint-chipper, One-Eye.

I first heard this story from my father when I was nine years old. Even then, he told me that the legend was different from all other similar native American legends. "There's something unique about Peorians. I can't as yet put my mental finger on it."

When I came back from LA to Peoria, he brought up his belief again. And he said, "You're a detective, a human bloodhound. Why don't you sniff out the essence of this difference? Give your poor old father some answers to his questions?"

I'd tried to satisfy him, but, so far, I'd failed.

In any event, as of today, the largest employer in this area is Caterpillar Tractor, the Yellow Giant, the world's largest manufacturer of earth-moving equipment. St. Francis Medical Center is the second largest employer. Drug-dealing youth gangs, murderous and mindless, are the third largest.

Many thousands of the citizens of this metropolitan area of 250,000 believe that magic and witchcraft really exist. At least thirty-five percent believe that there was once an Atlantis, that the Earth was once or still is flat, that the stars are little lights hung from a solid sky, that snakes talk, that the sun and the moon ceased to circle the Earth so that Joshua and his Is-raelites could win a battle, and that UFO beings will be our saviors. Hardly anybody here or anywhere, however, believes that most politicians are honest.

But Peoria also has much to be proud of, and it has a civic spirit unexcelled by any other city. I'm far from being embarrassed when I tell people I'm a native.

And then there's that well-known question, "Will it play in Peoria?"

President Nixon often wondered that aloud while he and his gang were conspiring to screw the American people. The city was an icon of conservatism, a representative of Everyperson. Thus, if what Nixon did or said was approved by most Peorians, most of the country would also approve.

However, "Will it play in Peoria?" was a famous phrase as far back as the middle of the nineteenth century. Even then, show people said that Peorians made a tough audience. If you could make it there, you could make it anywhere.

In any event, Peorians were and are pretty much like other people everywhere. That's too bad or that's very good, depending upon if you're a pessimist or an optimist.

■

As I drove homeward, I thought about the Alligers.

We're taught in geometry class and common sense tells us that parallel lines never meet. But there's a system of geometry, invented by a German mathematician named Riemann, in which parallel lines do eventually meet. The Alliger family members were on this kind of tracks, laid down by the self-will of each, and there was going to be a hell of a wreck when the locomotives, going full speed, whistles blowing, bells clanging, crashed into each other at the Riemann Express Junction.

Just now, though, I must consider the present, not the future. The letter to Diana from the woman named Weena was a lucky find for Simon, an unlucky one for Diana. Meanwhile, I had to think about the dead bees in Simon's office bathroom. Anybody who had access to it could have put live bees in it the day Simon was expected to return from his business trip. But he'd stayed away so long that the bees had died.

On the other hand (why is there always another hand?), someone may have placed dead bees in his bathroom just to scare him. There wasn't much point to doing that, but I've seen even less pointless deeds.

Just after I'd turned northward onto Prospect Road, I called Mimi Rootwell and told her what happened at the mansion. She heard me through to the end without commenting.

Then she said, "Soon as you can, fax the letter and a written report to Garry Deb at his Pasadena address. He can start his investigation at once. You can go to LA yourself if he doesn't turn up anything we can use."

"I'll stop at the agency and report directly to you," I said.

"I'm downtown. Stop at the agency anyway, make the report, fax it and the letter to Deb, call him, fill him in, leave me copies. Good-bye."

A half-hour later, I parked the car in the apartment building lot. Usually, at this time, Glinna would have been home. But she was going after work to a dinner at the house of a sister wicca and then to a coven meeting. She wouldn't be home until after midnight.

I phoned the answering machine in my office in the Antique Center building downtown. No calls from would-be clients. I was lucky that Mimi was using me now. Otherwise, I'd have been unemployed, not that I mind that if I've got plenty of money in the bank. I didn't, but I did have that $11,000 cached in the hollowed-out book in my bedroom. I hadn't reported that yet to Uncle Sam and the State of Illinois, and I wasn't sure that I would. However, my conscience, that necessary evil or not always desirable good, depending on how you look at it, was biting me. Or, if not biting, was at least nipping at me.

I was standing by a French door in my apartment and looking down at the parking lot. I saw Sheridan Mutts drive his pickup truck in, park, get out, and stride toward the entrance. Swinging at the end of his gorilla-sized fist was a twelve-pack of beer. I swigged on my ice tea and waited for the verbal explosion. A minute later, I heard his heavy footsteps, the click of the key being inserted. The knob on his door rattled. He said, "What the hell?"

Followed more tuggings at the door. He could feel the key turn all the way, so he knew that it was unlocking the door. More tuggings and swearing. A crash as he dropped the twelve-pack and pulled with both hands. More oaths.

Then, shouting, he beat on the door with his fists. When that did not solve his problem, he went down the steps. I pressed my forehead against the French door and looked down. I could see part of his yellow safety helmet and his outer shoulder as he went toward the other door on the ground level. As I had supposed he would, he came back with the manager, Selinda Tuneball. As usual, the poor woman was drunk. To keep her from falling, he was gripping her left elbow. Even so, she stumbled often. I could hear him swearing at her as they passed below me and then, a minute later, as they came up the staircase.

Mutt's loud voice and Tuneball's slurred mumbles came to me. Finally, he bellowed, "You're useless as tits on a boar, you pinhead lush!"

But that was nothing to what he roared a moment later. Evidently, she had passed out. Then I heard the snap of a can opening, a splashing as he poured out cold beer on her to waken her. That seemed to have failed. I heard his loud gulping as he drank the rest of his beer and the clang of the can when he hurled it against the wall.

For a minute, there was no sound except for his heavy breathing. But I jumped when he began beating on my apartment door.

"Goddammit, Corbie, you yellow-bellied dickhead! Come out and face me like a man! I know you're in there! I seen your car in the lot! I don't know what you did to my door, but you fixed it so it won't work! Just like I know you fucked up my stereo! Come on out, take your beating like a man, you lily-livered skunk!"

I said nothing. He slammed his fists on the door again, shouted some more clichéd challenges. Finally, he became silent, then I heard his bootsteps on the staircase. I looked through the French door. He was by then in the parking lot and opening a long tool case in the back of his pickup. He took out a short-handled ax, slammed down the lid of the case, and strode toward the building.

He looked up and saw me before I could step back. He shook the ax at me and shouted something I couldn't hear because of the traffic noise. I phoned 911, quickly gave my name and address, and described the situation. "Hurry! This Mutts is threatening to kill me! He's armed with a big ax!" Then Mutts was bellowing outside my door.

"Last chance, you scumbag! Come out and confess what you done, you ball-less wimp! If you don't, I'm going to chop your door down! And then I'm going to carve your head so you'll be even uglier'n you are now!"

I said loudly, "I got a shotgun'll blow your head off if you come in!"

That wasn't a bad idea, but I wasn't going to do it unless I really had to.

"Show your hand, Corbie, 'cause I'm coming in!"

He'd seen too many John Wayne movies.

The first blow of the ax came a few seconds later. It wouldn't take long for him to destroy the very cheap and thin door our tightwad landlord had provided for us. I walked to the French doors, opened them, and stepped out on the little balcony. The hot air streamed over me. But I was already sweating. I wasn't as calm and as cool as I'd thought I'd be.

I closed the French doors, went over the iron grille railing, let myself down, hung there for a second with my hands, and then dropped to the sidewalk. I did it without injury by bending my knees when my feet struck the cement, by falling bent over to the ground, and rolling. Then I got up.

At that moment, the glass in both the French doors above me shattered. Shiny sharp fragments flew over me. Mutts appeared on the balcony. He shook the axe at me.

"There you are, you fucking pansy coward! I'll be down in a minute and chop you up like kindling! First, though, I'm going to wreck your place! You comin' up 'n try to stop me?"

His face was as red and as swollen as the hind end of a female baboon in heat.

It wasn't until then that it occurred to me that things had backfired on me. What if he destroyed my books in the living room? My God! My special edition of Henry Miller's *Tropic of Capricorn* illustrated by Grandma Moses? *The Mysterious Stranger,* first edition? Amanda Ros' signed first edition of *Irene Iddlesleigh?* And then there were the very expensive computers and all those floppy discs with their files of data and the printers! And the hollowed-out book with the $11,000 in it! And . . . and . . .

I looked along Willow Knolls Road again. No flashing lights speeding on it from the east or the west. No sirens.

And then I heard a thud as of some hard object hitting flesh, followed by a loud grunt. I looked up just before two hundred and sixty pounds of fat, muscle, and bone flattened me out beneath it. In that microsecond before I blacked out, I recorded Selinda Tuneball's face looking down at me, the silvery cylinder of Glinna's tachyon emitter in her hands, and the clang against concrete of the axe Mutts had dropped when Selinda had slammed the cylinder against the back of his neck. I also remember, or think I remember, the faint far-off wail of a siren.

Events for a long time the rest of that day were fuzzy and seemingly far off. I half-awoke briefly in the hospital emergency room. I saw a niche in a wall in which was a statuette of Matthew, the patron saint of accountants.

Fadeout. Then someone, Glinna, I think, saying, "Where is the doctor?" Fadeout. Then the face of the doctor—I think he was one—looming over me, wiping mayonnaise from his thick black moustache and breathing garlic on me.

That face merged—when, I don't know—with another face and then became the bearded Neanderthal visage of Sheridan Mutts. It dissolved, and it re-formed into the demonic features of the driver who'd almost rammed his van into my car outside the Duck Inn during the storm.

Next, I was lying in a hospital bed. Glinna was by me and chanting a healing spell under her breath. My father and his companion, Sheba Peece, looked gravely down at me. Later, Mimi's big pumpkin head was turning away from me as she rotated her wheelchair. Then, someone was holding my hand.

At one time, I became aware that I was being X-rayed, though that didn't last long. But, suddenly, someone said, "He'll be OK," and I was. Partly OK, anyway, and in my full mind, whatever that really was.

Then came the cops and the questions about what had happened at the apartment building. I found out more than I would have if I'd just been an ordinary civilian. My police contacts told me that Mutts had been arrested and charged with various felonies, including resisting arrest and assaulting officers of the law, but he was out on bail. Later, he would bring suit against me for malicious damage to his apartment and for provoking him to attack me. Mutts would also sue Tuneball, charging her with unprovoked and murderous assault on him.

Mimi's much-dreaded law firm, Sprenger, Kramer, Hammer and Burnam, was bringing suit against Mutts and the landlord, Katzenwinter. His law firm, it turned out, was the greatly feared Crotal, Redast, Upasian, Snooker, and Hempen. Using them, Katzenwinter would countersue me and Mutts for vandalizing the building and would ask for $250,000 for the cost of repairs and as much for the emotional damage and nervous tension and psychological upset we'd inflicted on him. Tuneball wouldn't sue anybody because she'd had a completely paralyzing stroke immediately after I was taken away in the ambulance. However, her nephew from Chicago (this was the first I knew he even existed, and I'd find out he was under indictment for embezzlement) would bring suit for her against Katzenwinter, Mutts, and me.

This would happen a few days after I was released from the hospital. Meanwhile, I was suffering from a concussion of the brain. My skull wasn't fractured, though. Somehow, my ribs and my spine were not cracked or broken.

In any event, the hospital had discovered that my insurance would pay for at least three days' stay, and the doctors had found out that the insurance would cover all their bills. So, everybody was happy except me and those who cared about me.

The second day I was in the hospital, Mimi Rootwell called me. After asking how I was feeling, she said, "I know you used to hunt ducks around Goofy Ridge. You might be interested

NOTHING BURNS IN HELL ■ 179

in an article that appeared in today's *Pekin Times*. The *Journal-Star* hasn't picked it up yet. You remember reading in the paper about the big fire in Goofy Ridge and the arrests of the Mobard brothers and a woman named Milly Jane who was living with them and their ridiculous and contradictory stories about being assaulted? You remember reading about that poor bastard with the snapping turtle hanging from his dong? It happened the same day you took on the case of the mysterious client even though I advised you not to."

"Of course I haven't forgotten that article," I said. I wondered if the call was just a coincidence. I suspected that Mimi had connected me in her mind with the events in Goofy Ridge that night.

"Yeah. OK The two men were in the Mason County jail and the woman was in the hospital with pneumonia. Well . . . the woman died last night of pneumonia and complications. A Pekin Times reporter happened to be in the hospital when she died, and he talked to the attending physician. The doctor told the reporter her last words, and he was so struck by them that he recorded them."

Oh, no! I thought. Had Milly Jane made a dying confession and named me and described what I'd done? I was in a hell of a mess if she had.

"OK," I said. "What were her words?"

" 'I saw the light in the swamp. She smiled. And all the bull-frogs sang green hosannas.'

"I don't know what they mean, yet they seem to make some sort of sense."

I saw more sense in them than Mimi could. Once upon a time, hard though it was to believe, the tremendously obese and morally degenerate Milly Jane had been a little girl. She may even have been pretty, slender, happy, and innocent. Maybe, just maybe, when she was a little girl, she'd been wandering in the swamps along the river. And, just for a moment, she'd had a mystic experience, a vision. Our Lady of the Swamp had appeared in glorious light and smiled at Milly Jane. And the frogs had indeed sung like a choir of angels.

These images made my skin cold and made the blood rush to my head.

And maybe I was too imaginative.

But I liked to think that my scenario had actually happened.

It was sad, though. The vision, the light, the smile, the divine singing of frogs had not led the child Milly Jane to a high plane of spirituality. Others seized with such images and sounds became saints. Milly Jane . . . what you might have been . . . what you did become . . . I mourn for you.

"You there?" Mimi's voice said.

"What? Oh, yes. Sorry. I was thinking."

"There's more, Tom. The night she died, Almond and Deak Mobard escaped the jail. Apparently, someone slipped them a .45 automatic, just who, just how, nobody yet knows. The brothers stole a car and disappeared into the area around Goofy Ridge. Two hours later, the Mason County sheriff's deputies found Almond."

She paused, then said, "He'd been shot in the back of the head. Deak hasn't been found. No wonder you've always been so interested in that place, Tom. There's always something unusual and outré going on in it."

Far more than you'd suspect, Mimi. Or, maybe, you do suspect.

19

*T*oday was When-Do-I-Get-Time-to-Use-the-Bathroom? Day.
Garry Deb's express mail package from Pasadena arrived at my apartment at 9:00 A.M. It contained the four video tapes Deb had promised me on the phone yesterday morning.

After calling Mimi Rootwell to tell her they'd arrived, I ran them off on the VCR. First, *Cast Your Broad Upon the Waters.* Second, *The Last of the Merkins*. Third, *Surf Studs Versus the Amazon Werewolves.* I ran many sections of these at fast forward because I was only interested in the parts where Diana Rolanski, a.k.a. Clio Brooks, was present. But I ran the fourth, *The Trojan Harlots,* at normal speed. Diana, starring as Minnie Dix, was in almost every scene.

I had no doubt that Dix and Brooks were one and the same. The many closeups of the face on the screen — far fewer than those of her body — proved that. The first three films were soft-core porn — that is, there were no actual shots of genitals though there were many scenes of simulated three-input sex.

However, *The Trojan Harlots* went all out. Yet, it was a high-class production for a hard-core film.

During my phone calls to the Los Angeles area, I learned from Garry Deb that, now and then, some schlock porno producer would hire a writer with some education and creativity and actually follow his or her script. More or less, anyway.

"This Woods Yeckman, who provided me with the copies, he's world-wide famous for his porn collection, told me the people who made this movie had the brains to steal from an ancient Greek writer named Lucian of Samosata. You know him?"

"Yes. My father had an illustrated copy in his library. Lucian lived about A.D. 120–180. Actually, he was a Syrian who wrote in Greek."

"Always the pedant," Deb said.

The Trojan Harlots began just after the ancient city of Troy had fallen to the Greeks at the end of the ten-year-long war. King Agamemnon, the Greek leader, burned down the temple to Aphrodite, the goddess of love, and so caused her to hate him even more than she had before the impious deed. When Agamemnon decreed that the temple priestesses were to become slaves to the Greek leaders, he made the goddess doubly furious.

But the chief priestess, Clitorpatra (played by Diana) talked Agamemnon into a contest. If the women could outscrew the Greek leaders, they'd be given their freedom and a ship to sail to wherever they wished to go. The women won, of course. But the villainous Agamemnon broke his oath to free the priestesses. Lying on his back, panting, drained after his heroic efforts, he ordered his men to slay the women. They, however, were too exhausted to rise from the floor.

Unopposed, the temple prostitutes sailed away in a galley. Many adventures, mostly sexual, followed. The big one was when an evil wizard on an island turned the women into trees which had the women's faces, breasts, and vaginas. When a crew of sex-starved shipwrecked sailors copulated with the half-trees, they found that they couldn't get loose even after their penises shrank. The priestesses' vaginal sphincter muscles were too tight.

I learned one thing. Diana's dark red-bronze hair was not dyed. I also relearned what other hard-core porno movies had taught me. For the first ten minutes, those well-built naked females and the sex excited me. After that, I got bored and then disgusted.

I felt sad for Diana. Maybe she'd been broke and desperate and so had taken the only way to support herself. But it seemed to me that she could have found another kind of employment. However, I was judging her without knowing the circumstances that had led her into that awful profession, if you could call it a profession.

And how about Glinna, my only beloved? She'd put herself through college by providing urine to be drunk by men whose compulsion the psychologists still can't explain. And then she had gotten religion and become, as she said, born again and clean of body and soul.

However, for all anybody knew, Diana had also renounced her old way of life, her sins, and was now on what some call the straight and the narrow.

Also, I wasn't in a position to judge others. Look at me. What kind of profession was I in? Some would say it was slimy, and, at the moment, I agreed with them. If I sent the tapes to her father-in-law, which I was going to do, I'd wreck her, expose her to shame and humiliation and who knew what else? Doing this made me feel dirty. On the other hand, she had chosen her path, and she'd have to endure the results of her choice. She had free will; she wasn't a robot.

I shrugged. On to the next steps. Actually, I had my own troubles to worry about. For one thing, Simon Alliger was upset by the publicity caused when Mutts and I tangled. It had been reported in the *Journal-Star* and on the local news channels. Furious about this, even though the reporters didn't know about my connection to the Alligers, Simon had phoned Mimi and raised hell about me. Not one to take unearned reproaches from anyone, Mimi had defended me and told him to cool down. But he had threatened to remove the agency from the case and hire somebody else.

Mimi had told him that was his right. Then, she'd bade him good-bye and hung up. So far, Simon hadn't fired the agency. However, Mimi said she might have to use another operative for Simon.

I didn't like that at all. I needed the money, and I was deeply interested in the case. I wanted to follow it through to the end, to be, in fact, the man who brought about the end. I also itched fiercely to know the principals in this case far better than I did. Although some of my comments might make it seem that I don't like people, they give a false impression. I like most people—the poor wretches—very much, and I'm very interested in those I loathe. In far too many of my cases, I've had no chance to know the people in them well. I've also been on too many cases where I was just getting below the surface of events and those concerned when the case abruptly ended.

So far, I knew Simon fairly well, though not deeply. The others were still enigmas because my contacts with them had been, though intense, brief. I wanted to know everything I could possibly know about them even though that still wouldn't show me all about them. The human soul is the deepest well in this world.

After I rewound the last tape, I started to reread the reports Deb had faxed me last night. The phone rang; I picked up the receiver.

"Tom," Mimi said. "How you doing on the case?"

"I just finished the last video. I'll bring them over in fifteen minutes. Our client will be very happy with them."

"I kind of expected that," she said. "I've just read the reports Deb faxed me last night. This detective Mordoy has some explaining to do. Either she's very negligent or there's something funny going on or . . ."

"I plan to call her today," I said.

"Not necessary. We'll point out to the client what Mordoy should have done. If he wants to, he can chew her out. Not our business. By the way, Tom, Selinda Tuneball died last night. She never came out of her coma."

That was a minor shock. I didn't feel any grief, only a general sadness that most people feel when somebody they've been involved with but don't feel deeply about dies. It was tinged with a grayish and shallow sorrow—how else describe it?—that she'd never had a good life and had been driven to deep drinking. I'd thought, until very recently, that she was an ignorant uneducated cowardly lush. So much for my perception. That she'd come to my aid by slamming Mutts with the tachyon emitter, even though she feared him, revealed her basic courage. And all those malapropisms, esophagus for soffits, arthurized for authorized, and such expressions, well, they were just her way of being humorous.

I'd found that out several days before the Mutts incident. She and I talked a few moments. Somehow, we got onto the subject of the American judicial system, which we agreed was a disgrace. But I kept backing away from her because the fumes of imported Albanian wine, Old Red Star, made my eyes water.

Then she said, "The courts are as slow as the procession of the equal knockers."

"What?" I said. "You mean . . . ?"

She smiled slightly, and a twinkle shone through the redness of her eyes. "I wasn't referring to a parade of well-matched beauty queens. You must know what I meant."

"The precession of the equinoxes is an astronomical phenomenon, a cycle, which takes 26,000 years to complete."

"Right," she said. "The verbal equinox occurs about March 21st. The ottoman equinox occurs about September 22nd."

It wasn't until then I realized she'd been putting me on all these years with her malapropisms. I grinned, though I felt very foolish, and I said, "Right. The verbal and the ottoman, which some people call the vernal and the autumnal."

"I've not always been what I am now," she had said. "Once . . . well, it doesn't matter now. Don't worry. I'm not going to tell you my life story."

Now, I wished she had told me.

Two seconds after Mimi hung up, the phone rang again. I picked up the receiver. Mutt's rumbling voice said, "Hey, Corbie! My lawyer told me not to talk to you, but what do those shysters know? Look! We can settle this out of court like real men. I'll meet you at The Last Stand, and we'll slug it out, winner take all? How about—?"

"Are you nuts?" I said. "You're going to prison for this! Don't call me again, or I'll get a restraining order on you."

I hung up. Again, I started to read Deb's report, but the phone rang. Mimi said, "Sorry, Tom. But I got a call from Simon Alliger. His daughter-in-law had phoned him and chewed him out up and down, forward and backward, sideways, all ways. His voice was trembling. I could feel the heat of his anger over the phone. And I didn't need him to tell me his wife was having an asthmatic attack. I could hear the rasping and the wheezing in the background. I don't think she was in the same room with him, though."

"Come on, Mimi," I said. "Why did Diana attack them?"

"She'd found out about their copying the letter from

Weena. She said she was going to take them to court. She was going to accuse them of illegally entering her house, invading her privacy by going through her possessions and making a copy of a personal letter, her property, without her knowledge or permission. She said their sneakiness and vindictiveness would be exposed to the public. And so on. I think she was just blowing off steam or trying to get them to call off the investigation. And . . ."

"How did she ever find out about the letter?" I said.

Mimi chuckled, then said, "Rage and hate have made more people do stupid things than anything else I can think of. Listen to this, Tom. You won't believe it, but it happened."

"All right. I admit it. You're the master of suspense. Now, what in hell did happen?"

"Alexandra herself told Diana about the letter!"

For a few seconds, I said nothing. Then I rallied. I said, "Why?"

"I suppose because she just couldn't resist crowing about it. She just had to tell Diana that she was doomed, that the Alligers would soon be rid of her, that Roger was going to find out what a slut he was married to. She wasn't thinking, of course, but then thinking was never Alexandra's chief achievement. Probably not even a minor one."

" 'Nothing burns in hell, except self-will,' " I said.

"Right. From the *Germanica Theologica*, a medieval German work."

I've never been able to quote anything the source of which she couldn't name. Sees all, hears all, knows all. That's Mimi Rootwell.

"Simon was furious, of course. He went to his wife's bedroom and verbally flayed her, I'm sure. I'm sure he caused her asthmatic attack. Then he called me and asked me what we could do about damage control. I told him Diana has probably confessed everything to Roger. What'll happen now is anybody's guess. But Simon says that the tapes will do the job, turn Roger against Diana. He wants to see them as quickly as possible. So, you'd better rush them over to him now. Take a copy of Deb's report, too."

"I haven't had time to make file copies of the tapes."

"Deb has copies he can send us. Now, get going."

It took me half an hour to get to the mansion. I had to shave quickly with an electric razor, dress (no time for a shower), and then run off copies of the report. At 3:11 P.M., I rounded the curve of the Alliger driveway and saw the house. I also saw three police cars, the coroner's car, an ambulance, and Roger's and Diana's cars. The cop who approached me before I could get out of my car was Cassius Belli. I was lucky. Cassius was one of Mimi's informants, a well-paid one. Even so, I had to explain what I was doing there before he'd tell me what was going on.

"Mrs. Alliger died about twenty minutes ago," he said. "I would've told your boss if I'd known she was involved."

"Which Mrs. Alliger died?"

"Mrs. Simon Alliger. Alexandra."

20

Mrs. Alliger, aged sixty-five, was forty pounds overweight and very nervous. She suffered from migraines, acid stomach, diarrhea, asthma, insomnia, frequent head and chest colds, glaucoma, high blood pressure, and a failing heart. It was a wonder she hadn't died some time ago.

"Especially," Mimi said, "when you consider her family physician."

She and I were in her office, three days after Alexandra Alliger died, discussing the case.

The family physician was Winley Cubitt, M.D., sixty-seven years old, a man with a wonderful bedside manner and who, marvelous to tell, made house calls—if the patient was rich. Dr. Cubitt had just settled two malpractice suits and was deep into a third. Though his insurances rates must have been enormous, he refused to retire.

This was the man who had directed Alexandra to take, all at the same time, diet pills, sleeping pills, tranquilizers, digitalis for her heart (it lowers blood pressure), propanolol for high blood pressure and angina, epinephrine for asthma, and a monoamine oxidase inhibitor for tachycardia (heartbeat rate irregular or too fast or both). Alexandra was also taking Contac for a heavy cold, another drug which a competent doctor would have forbidden her to take with the other medications.

Her opthalmologist, definitely not a quack, had prescribed eyedrops containing a beta-blocker for her glaucoma. Nothing wrong with that if it were taken by itself. But Alexandra, when asked to list her other medications, had not told her eye doctor about her pills.

Alexandra shouldn't have drunk any wine that morning, especially when she hadn't eaten her breakfast. Some of her medicines were time-release capsules, and alcohol could, and in her case did, dissolve the outer coatings and let loose the contents all at once.

She was found by Maria Cabracan, who had entered the room to take the breakfast tray away. It was untouched, and Alexandra was stretched out face down, her right arm reaching out toward the door.

The coroner discovered that the alcohol content of her blood was .14 percent. (The legal intoxication level in Illinois is .08 percent.) Moreover, there were very heavy traces in her blood of Inderal, epinephrine, Dristan-AF, and Nardil, twice what there should have been.

Whoever was to blame, Cubitt was lucky. Simon Alliger wasn't going to sue him.

"Don't you think that's strange?" Mimi said. "Simon is not the man to pass up making money, and he's got a sure winner here. Old Whiskey Jack" (she was referring to John Crotal, head of the law firm of Crotal, Redast, Upasian, Snooker, and Hempen, sometimes referred to as the Five Horsemen) "has advised Simon to ask for twenty-five million and settle for one. But Simon won't bring action."

"Very strange," I said. "Of course, he may be reluctant because of his distaste for publicity."

"Maybe, maybe not," she said. "Listen to this; think about it. Even stranger. The bottle of wine she'd been drinking from—no glass, she'd drunk straight from the bottle—was in the wastepaper basket. Empty. With it was its screw-on cap. No cork for that bottle. Alexandra was drinking a very cheap wine, which, knowing what a flint-fisted tightwad she was, doesn't surprise me.

"Now, Maria Cabracan, the maid, is a near-illiterate Mayan peasant, but she's no dummy. She told the police that that was the first time Mrs. Alliger had ever put anything in the basket. Always before, she'd left bottles, caps, any trash, dirty Kleenexes, dirty clothes, newspapers, crumpled letters, hairpins, and other things on the table or the floor.

"Detective-Sergeant Stubecannon, you know him, sent the empty bottle to the lab. It was analyzed, and it contained almost nothing but tap water. Someone had washed it very very thoroughly on the inside, had taken his or her time and removed almost all traces of drugs. There were, of course, very slight traces of the drugs I've mentioned, but these could have come from sputum when Mrs. Alliger drank the wine.

"If anyone dumped pills into the wine, they'd been smart enough to wear latex gloves and smart enough not to wipe off the fingerprints on the bottle. All were Mrs. Alliger's. Which suggests that somebody dumped pills into the wine and then removed the evidence. However, Alexandra usually took counteracting medicines anyway, and she drank wine, though she knew she wasn't supposed to."

"And the cops suspect Simon?"

I said that only because the suspect is usually the spouse if the killer is unknown. But what would Simon's motives be? And I'd hate to be the cop handling the case if Simon became

the chief suspect. He has such wealth, power, and high reputation that the evidence against him would have to be over-
whelming before the DA would order his arrest.

"Of course they suspect him," Mimi said. "But he wasn't
the only one who had motive and opportunity to dump the
contents of time-release capsules into the wine. Several people who could be suspects were in the house that morning.
Diana Alliger, for one. Rosemary, Roger's sister, for another.
And who knows how many other potential suspects might be
uncovered if the police start a full-scale investigation. Which
I doubt they'll do, though you never know."

"Diana? Rosemary?" I said. "But Simon had forbidden them
to enter the house."

"You forget it's owned by his mother. She's the highest authority, and she permitted them to come into the house. That
must've teed Simon off, but he could do nothing about it.
Diana, with Roger, was in the house from seven until ten of
the evening before Mrs. Alliger died. Diana was in the house
the next morning from eight until nine-thirty. Both times, she
was ostensibly there to visit Faith.

"Diana could have been in the house for some time before
she went up to Faith's apartment. Faith, Diana, and Roger said
that what they talked about was none of the cops' business,
and Faith and Diana repeated that when asked about the subject of conversation during the evening.

"Rosemary also visited Faith the previous evening and the
morning of the next day, the day Alexandra died. Subject of
their conversation was unstated. She, like Diana, may have
come earlier or left later than she told the police. The security
system, including the monitor cameras, was off the previous
evening. The alarm system wasn't turned on until ten. Then
Juan Cabracan, acting under Simon's orders, activated it. That
time's verified by the agency monitor."

"OK," I said. "Either Diana or Rosemary could have slipped into Alexandra's suite that evening and emptied the contents of cold and diet time-release capsules and other no-nos into Alexandra's bottle of wine. They had the opportunity. Simon, of course, would have much more opportunity. He hates— hated—his wife, has done so for years. Why then would he suddenly decide to kill her?"

"That's for the cops to find out," I said. "But you and I know that a man or woman can be on the edge of committing murder but not do anything about it for years or maybe never. Then, something happens, one thing too many, and they leap out of the circle they've drawn around themselves."

"And who has very good reasons, from their viewpoints, to off Alexandra?"

"Diana," I said. "And let's not forget Rosemary."

"Do you think those two women could be partners? What one couldn't accomplish, the other might."

"In cahoots?" I said. "It's possible. But consider Diana first. By now, Simon must've shown the tapes to Roger, unless he's waiting until the funeral is over and before Alexandra's will is read. But if Simon did show the films to Roger, what happened then? You don't know, I don't know. All's quiet on the Alliger front, from the outside, anyway.

"As for Rosemary being the murderer, she certainly could have a strong motive. She's going to be cut out of the will entirely if she doesn't drop her sleazebag lover, Burt Kordik. But if her parents died before the will could be changed—although it may already be changed—she could inherit a fortune. I'm sure that those dead bees in Simon's bathroom are the evidence of a failed attempt at murder. No way I can prove it. Not yet, anyway. So, now, Alexandra is dead. The police may not think she was murdered. I do."

"I, too," Mimi said.

"I'd say Rosemary wouldn't do anything on her own. I doubt she'd have the will to take a bath or eat a meal unless Kordik told her to. But with him pushing her, she might be capable of anything.

"Diana might have tried to murder Simon and may try again. Meanwhile, she sees her chance to knock off Alexandra and make it look like an accident, just as Simon's murder, if it had been successful, would've looked like an accident. But, if Simon hasn't shown the tapes to Roger, if he's waiting until the funeral's over, then Diana might try to kill Simon quickly. Rosemary would have the same reason for haste in murdering her father. The will."

"Agreed," Mimi said. "But the police don't have all the facts. They don't know about the dead bees or our investigation into Diana because . . . well, you know."

I nodded. Despite Mimi's urging Simon to tell the police chief about these things, Simon had refused. He insisted that he'd settle this family affair himself and thus avoid any publicity. Mimi had honored her client's wishes—so far, anyway.

That was the situation as of the time I drove away from the agency. When I got home, I sat down at my desk in the study and listened to Mozart CDs while I reviewed Deb's report for the third time. I hoped that this time I'd find the pearl of revelation in the oyster. Actually, I wasn't sure I'd even found the oyster.

One thing I *was* sure of. Lorna Mordoy had lied in her report to Simon Alliger. Mostly, she'd lied by omission, but, nevertheless, she'd lied. Take the dog license. One of the ways to find the location of a person is to check on the county or city licenses for pets and the record of the animal's vaccinations. If the subject had gotten a license or taken the pet to a veterinarian, his address and time of license purchase could be determined. Mordoy had stated in her report that she'd checked out pet licenses. But Garry Deb, following my orders, had found that Diana Rolanski was in the official files as the owner of a female Shetland sheepdog during the three years just before she'd met Roger Alliger.

Several months before this, she'd taken the dog to a Pacific Palisades veterinarian to be put to sleep. That is, killed. The animal was old and suffering from strokes and mental confusion.

Deb had gotten several addresses from the licenses, the last one being the residence of a Joe Galazzo. Inquiry at the first two revealed little about Diana except that the landlords considered her to be a quiet tenant who paid her rent on time. When Deb phoned Galazzo to get permission to visit him for an interview, he was told that Galazzo was dead. But the informant, Orbert Wimville, Galazzo's nephew and only inheritor, was eager to talk about Diana. It was obvious that he hated her. He said that the slut was going to marry his uncle, an old man, for his money, several millions or so. But—here the nephew laughed like a hyena for almost a minute—his uncle died two days before the wedding. He had a heart attack while on top of the gold-digging bitch.

But, before she'd left the house, she'd opened the old man's safe and removed his cash, stocks and bonds, and jewelry. Wimville couldn't prove this, though he knew that the fortune, worth about $300,000, was gone. Unfortunately, Wimville couldn't notify the police of the robbery. Wimville wouldn't say why he couldn't, but Deb got the impression that the police would have been interested in certain items taken from the safe.

"Probably," Deb had said to me over the phone, "it was something Wimville didn't mention. Like accounting books with information implicating Galazzo and Wimville in illegal activities. Diana must have taken them with her as insurance. Anyway, Wimville said he didn't know where Diana had gone.

He hoped she'd die of AIDS, the whore. But all that's in the report."

"I like to get it directly, too," I'd said. "The real kicker, to me, anyway, was that Mordoy had interviewed Wimville. Not a word about that in her report."

"Yeah," Deb had said. "How about that? She going to lose her license because of that?"

"The client doesn't want anything done about that yet."

"Yeah? Anyway, I got a kick out of what this Mordoy woman done to Wimville after he made a pass at her. He said she would've made a *Playboy* centerfold easy. But she knocked him down and then kicked him in the balls. He hated her as much as he did the Alliger woman. That Mordoy, though, she must be a tough one."

"A crooked one, for sure," I said. "What was in it for her to lie?"

"Blackmail," Deb had said. "Who was she blackmailing? This Diana, of course."

"It's possible," I said.

There were several other items that Mordoy had not reported correctly. Her report stated that she'd looked for people who remembered the Rolanskis. She'd investigated both neighborhoods in Los Angeles and Pasadena where Diana and her parents had lived. She'd found no one who remembered the Rolanskis. All the former neighbors had died or moved away, addresses unknown. Or so Mordoy had claimed.

But Deb, following her tracks, had uncovered one old woman in Pasadena who had been the Rolanski's next-door neighbor. (One more item Mordoy had failed to report.) She remembered the parents and the daughter, though not vividly.

"Her memory's failing," Deb had said. "Actually, I was lucky to get to her when I did. She was scheduled to go to a nursing home in a week."

The neighbor had told Deb that she did remember that the girl had given her parents some trouble. Something to do with drugs, nothing unusual then or now in California. And she'd run away for a while. Rumor had it that she'd gone East with a black man her age. The old woman didn't remember his name. The police had not found her, but, one night, Diana had shown up without the man. The neighbors didn't know where she'd been. While she was gone, Mr. Rolanski had died, and his wife had had a nervous breakdown. That hadn't lasted long. At least, Mrs. Rolanski had come home after a stay at a hospital and she was there when Diana reappeared. Shortly after that, Mrs. Rolanski had sold the house and moved with Diana to Los Angeles. It was also rumored that Diana had been pregnant but had gotten an abortion in Los Angeles.

"The last thing the neighbor remembers about the Rolanskis," Deb said, "is that someone came around some years later and inquired about the daughter. Only, this is funny, the woman, said she came from Kentucky, asked about Angela. Not Diana. Angela."

"Ah!" I said. I was suddenly excited, though I wasn't sure why. "What was the name of the woman?"

"Her name was Angela, too. She said Angela was her daughter, and she'd only recently found out that her daughter had been living with the Rolanskis. That doesn't make sense to me. Does it to you?"

"Not yet," I said. "What was the woman's last name?"

"My informant said it was Boomer or something like that. She wasn't sure. Then, while we were talking about something else, it came to her. It was Boomall."

Ah! I thought. Boomall! The Rolanskis' marriage certificate! Myrna Groat married William R. Rolanski. Groat? I got to check something! Soon as I get through talking to Deb.

Deb continued his report. Irving Dingenzich, the old producer mentioned in Weena's letter to Diana, had died five days before Deb had begun his investigation. He seemed to have left no relatives. Deb tried to get information from the Screen Actors' Guild about Weena and Diana, but they told him that such information was confidential. He should go to Diana's agent, if he knew who the agent was. Deb didn't.

However, Deb didn't need SAG or the agent. Having learned from a policeman friend about the multimillionaire, Woods Yeckman, who had the largest collection of pornography in the world outside of the Vatican, Deb went to him. Deb had no trouble getting the copies of the tapes I'd seen. Weena was listed in the credits of two of them as Godwina Hott. This, it turned out, was her natal name. But Weena seemed to have disappeared. Though Deb tried hard to locate her, he failed.

After I'd gone over the report twice more, I thought about it for at least an hour. Then, I did what I knew I shouldn't do. But Aries men are impulsive. At least, that's what the astrologers say, though I couldn't use that as an excuse since I thought astrology was nonsense.

First, I attached to the phone my voice-changer machine (I got through a catalog available to the public), then set its controls so that I would speak with a tenor voice and a slight Irish lilt. I got Mordoy's agency office phone number from her report to Simon and punched it in. Of course, I used the caller ID block to keep her from seeing the number on her caller ID display, if her phone had one. She'd be able later on to find my number and name. I didn't care about that. I just wanted to scratch this mind itch I'd had for the last hour. Then, let hellfire burn what it would.

The switchboard operator at AAA Abendale Investigations in Chicago asked for my name and the reason I was calling. What I told her was not the truth.

Within ten seconds, a voice said, "Lorna Mordoy speaking."

For a second, I was in the vacuum of outer space, no light, no air, no pressure to keep my body from exploding. Jackpot!

I should have hung up then, but I needed a few more words to make the ID absolutely certain. "I'm calling from Los Angeles," I said, "on behalf of Vandeleur, Stapleton, and Mortimer Investigations, Incorporated, Number 3 Turpey Street. I'm John Clayton, an operative in their employ. Ms. Mordoy, we have reason to believe . . ."

Her voice had been sexy and sultry. Now, it became shrill and harsh, a hawk's scream.

"Yeah, pissant, and I'm the Hound of the Baskervilles! Are you calling from Grimpen Mire? Just who are you, dickhead, and what're you trying to pull? Vandeleur, Stapleton, and Mortimer, my ass!"

I hung up. Once again — how did I do it? — I'd been caught. The smartass, me, wasn't so smart, or he was having very bad luck. Who would've thought that Mordoy would be so knowledgeable about A. Conan Doyle's Sherlock Holmes story, *The Hound of the Baskervilles?* How many people know that John Clayton was the cab driver in the story and that he lived at No. 3, Turpey Street, London? Or that Vandeleur and Stapleton were aliases of Rodger Baskerville's villainous son, Jack? Or that Mortimer, a skull-collector, was also a character in the story?

My chagrin quickly passed away. I was too happy to be downcast, too exultant about my discovery. The last time I'd heard that voice had been in Lakeside Cemetery in Pekin during a violent storm. Her last words then had been, "I'll call you tomorrow, find out what happened."

She had not called, and I hadn't expected her to do so.

It was then that I remembered what I was going to do

when I quit talking to Garry Deb. I did so at once. Thanks to the computer age, I got a reply to my question a half-hour later. But I was disappointed. The marriage certificate for Deak Mobard stated that his bride (his first wife, I assumed) was Mary Eldins. It was not at all what I'd hoped for.

21

Why did I call Lorna Mordoy?

There had been many knots tied in the line leading from Diana Alliger to Lorna Mordoy. I hadn't been aware of them. I hadn't even known that there was a line. Suddenly, up from my brain's dark center rose a thing which had handed me the line and said, "Here you are, stupid." And it left it up to me to untie the knots.

The first knot in the line, I'd say, was the fresh white paint job on the Alliger mansion. Something about it had been tunneling toward light in my coal-mine brain for a long time. But I hadn't known what it was.

The second knot was Mimi Rootwell's remark that Alexandra Alliger was a flint-fisted tightwad. This led to the thought—finally—that she would have hired nonunion painters because they'd be cheaper than union workers.

The third knot was the memory of the Mobards' storage shed and the pair of overalls streaked with dried paint which had hung in it. Moreover, Almond Mobard's cap had been spotted with dried white paint. Obviously, he worked at least part-time as a nonunion painter.

Another knot was a big one and central to the unraveling. That was finding out that Mordoy had failed to report certain very significant facts about Diana Rolanski.

Here's the way I figured it. Mordoy had blackmailed Diana about something Diana had done in LA. Mordoy had discovered this while investigating Diana for Simon Alliger.

And then Almond Mobard, hired by a scab contractor, had come to the Alliger mansion to help paint it. He'd seen somebody he had not expected to see. Diana Rolanski. Probably, Diana had not seen him. Almond had told his brother, Deak, and their shared wife, Milly Jane Foushee, about her. The Mobards had threatened to expose Diana to her husband and in-laws. They would have had to find out about her marital status and whatever they needed to know before proceeding with the blackmail. They'd probably made a phone call to her. Diana had reacted to their demands, though not as the Mobards had expected. She'd gone to the woman who was already blackmailing her, Lorna Mordoy, and asked for help.

"You have to protect me. And your own interests."

And Mordoy had done just that.

I was sure now that Mordoy had planned to kill the Mobard brothers in the Pekin cemetery. She'd hired me to back her up and had hoped I'd help her kill Almond and Deak when they attacked her. (She was sure that they would because she planned to provoke them if they didn't act on their own.) Then she'd kill me and arrange it so that it'd look as if I'd killed the two but had been fatally wounded while doing so.

But how could Diana be connected with the Mobards? She'd been born and raised in the Los Angeles metropolitan area. She'd never been to Illinois until she got married.

The Mobards, as far as I knew, had never been out of the midwest.

And getting a copy of Deak Mobard's marriage license hadn't helped a bit.

That mystery would have to stay in the holding pattern for a while.

When Mordoy read about the Mobards in the Peoria paper (no doubt Diana sent her the articles), she knew the true story at once. Mordoy figured out that I had to keep my mouth shut about the affair, and, anyway, I didn't know who she was. However, one of the Mobards might reveal everything if offered immunity or a lighter sentence by testifying against the others. Moreover, unless the Mobards were killed, they'd start blackmailing Diana again. Mordoy had acted swiftly and had somehow smuggled in that gun to the Mobard men. They'd broken out of jail. Mordoy had followed them, killed Almond, and tried to kill Deak. But he'd escaped.

After pondering a while on what to do next, I decided to phone Mert Plateburn, a Chicago operative my agency had used several times. I'd explain as much about Mordoy as I thought he should know, and I'd have him investigate and, perhaps, shadow Mordoy. But that would take money, and I couldn't expect to get it from Simon until after the funeral was over. Maybe not then. I lined up the facts as if they were on dress parade and reviewed them.

Diana's father, William Rolanski, was born near Monkeys Eyebrow, Ballard County, Kentucky, and he'd married Myrna Groat there. Though there was no birth certificate for Myrna Groat, or there didn't seem to be, it could be that she'd been born there or near there.

The north and west borders of Ballard County were on the Ohio River. Across the river was Illinois. The thinly populated county was the site of several wildlife preservation areas. Monkeys Eyebrow was now a ghost town, and the nearest centers of population to it were the hamlets of Needmore and Bandanna.

The Ohio River half-surrounded Ballard County. Where any big river flows by lightly populated but heavily forested land, there are houseboats and riverside shacks in which poachers live. These people often move around a lot up and down a particular river and sometimes go to other rivers for a while. The Mobards were poachers and river rats.

Could William Rolanski and Myrna Groat also have been river rats? Had they decided to give up that life and try for another one far away from their native land and river? Had they, while still quite young, shaken the river mud off their feet and traveled to the golden state of California?

Who might be able to tell me about their parents and family and their childhood? The Reverends Heber and Angela Boomall had conducted their marriage ceremony. But would they still be alive? Could I locate them if they were?

There was only one way to find out. I'd have to go to the area around now-deserted Monkeys Eyebrow and make my inquiries. However, everybody who'd known the Rolanskis could be dead. And anybody still alive who had known them might not want to talk to me, an outlander and probably a cop. The Ballard County citizens might be as clannish and tight-mouthed as the Goofy Ridge denizens.

I'd decided to call Andy Murchmassey of Louisville, Kentucky, and set him to sniffing on the Boomall trail around Ballard County. If he found the Boomalls, I'd go myself to question them. But that would be expensive, and I certainly wasn't going to spend my own money. So, I'd wait until Simon could be approached about it. Meantime, I considered calling Faith Alliger and, as they say, extending my sympathies. But it seemed to me that I'd better wait until after the will was read, though I doubted Faith was grief-stricken. I'd just send her a card.

I reached for the phone to call Mimi. Just as I touched it, it rang. I jumped, then picked it up.

"Hello."

A land mine, Mimi's voice, exploded in my ear. "Tom! Bad news!"

The agency's gone broke?"

"Always the joker! No, Tom, not yet, but since Simon can't pay our bill, we may go broke."

"What do you mean, can't pay the bill? Can't?"

"He's dead, Tom. Apparently, a bee was chasing him, and he fell down the steps from the second-floor hall and broke his neck."

22

A cold front had moved in last night. At ten this morning, the sky was clear, and the west wind was pleasantly cool. However, by three this afternoon, the spoilsport sun would remind us that summer's end was not yet here.

I was in my car, which was parked just off a hilltop in Springdale Cemetery. Founded in 1854, this was Illinois' second largest and its oldest continually operating boneyard. The area I was in was rundown and weedy, looking like a set for a spooky movie. Yet, its once-richest citizens were entombed here.

A few feet behind my car was the grave of my four-times great-grandmother. She was the daughter of Isaac Dripps, one of my few ancestors with a claim to fame, however slight. In 1833, Isaac Dripps invented the cowcatcher for the steam locomotive.

I was in the front seat of my car and looking through binoculars at the top of a hill to my right. It was approximately seven hundred feet distant. My powerful Bausch & Lomb glasses enabled me to see in detail the Alliger burial party.

Two cemetery workers, two limousine chauffeurs, two undertakers, the minister, the family lawyer, and four mourners. And, of course, the coffins of the two recently deceased.

Just beyond them was the Alliger tomb, a gray granite box a story and a half tall. Over its entrance, now bricked up because of vandals and grave robbers, were the incised letters of the family name, flanked by two crux ansata, the ancient Egyptian crosses with looped tops. Juvenile dimwits had painted graffiti in large letters on the side of the tomb. The cemetery workers had tried to clean off the black paint but had failed. Beneath the gang codes were lines spraypainted by a slightly higher order of cretin.

NEVER BLOWS SO RED/THE ROSE AS WHERE SOME BURIED GEEZER BLED. Underneath this: LET THE GOOD TIMES ROLL.

The very tall weeds that had surrounded the Alliger tomb had been mowed yesterday. It was now easy to see the upright granite stone of Simon's father. He'd been buried outside the tomb because it was full. Near his grave, on the hoists above open graves, were the medium-priced coffins of Alexandra Alliger and her husband, Simon.

A bee or bees had killed Simon, though not directly.

The police had reconstructed the events leading up to Simon's death. But they were, of course, only speculating.

It had happened at nine in the evening two days after Alexandra's death. Simon had just finished working in his office on the second floor. He had used the intercom to tell Juan Cabracan to start his bath. Simon would be down to his rooms in a minute. But, after he'd locked the door of his office behind him, he had encountered a bee or bees. Probably, it or they had been between him and the locked door.

He must have run as swiftly as a fat, out-of-shape, short-legged man in his middle sixties could. His panic may have spurted enough adrenaline into his blood to give him the power to leap out for three or four feet over the stairwell at the end of the hall. If he'd grabbed for the railing when he came down, he missed it. He then shot out over the steps, half-turned around and partway over in midair, and struck the side of his neck against the edge of the step just above the first floor. The impact sheared one of his neckbones and severed the nerves therein.

The police had found two live honeybees in the hallway of the second floor and four in the hallway at the foot of the steps. They had established who was in the house that day and where they said they'd been during this time. Mimi's informant had told her that Diana and Rosemary Alliger had been out in the garden cutting flowers for Alexandra's funeral. But they'd been there at different times and were alone.

Mimi had told me that each one could have collected bees to release later in the hallway. There were two handy little vacuum-sucking bee catchers in the house with which Cabracan, following Simon's orders, quite often skimmed bees off flowers and drowned them.

My binoculars were zeroed in on Diana's face. Her black veil didn't conceal her sad expression. Either she was a good actor or I'd misjudged her and she did have some feeling for her parents-in-law. Whatever, she was beautiful. I didn't altogether approve of her tight, very low cut, and bright yellow blouse or her black miniskirt. Not during a funeral. Bad taste, I thought, though I did admire her legs.

Rosemary's expression was her usual—haggard and sullen. She wore a microskirt. Very bad taste. Not only showed a lack of respect for the dead but a grave lack of aesthetic sense. Her legs were skinny and straight up-and-down, broomstick-shaped, and her knees were very knobby.

Faith Alliger looked more thoughtful than mournful. Roger was sitting by his grandmother. His face was as empty of expression as a trash can lid. Perhaps, I thought, he's in shock. Not just from the unexpected deaths of his parents, though that could be part of it. He may also have read my report and seen the video tape. If that was it, he hadn't told Diana about it. I'd bet on that. She didn't look as if she were deeply worried about anything.

The red face of "Whiskey" Jack Crotal, faithful family lawyer, shone in the sun. He stood behind Faith's chair, his hand resting lightly on her shoulder.

I had just put the binoculars down when I saw a flash on the high side of the hill to the north. I trained my glasses toward where the light had been and moved them up and down and back and forth. When I saw the flash again, I steadied the glasses and adjusted the focus.

I reognized at once the man who was crouched between two bushes and looking through binoculars at the funeral. The motto on his cap and the tendrils of flesh around his mouth were plain to see.

The watcher was Deak Mobard.

23

Why was Deak Mobard spying on Diana? Was he just checking up on her before he tried to resume blackmailing her? Or was he going to do something violent to her? I forgot my speculations when I saw near Deak a huge form partly hidden by an old fallen cypress. I adjusted the focus. The form became a man wearing a beat-up blue porkpie hat from beneath which brown and greasy-looking hair spread out over massive shoulders. He had a thick black Fu Manchu mustache and a wisp of beard on his out-thrust chin. His eyebrows were very thick and met over his small eyes. Just below the left eye was a ragged scar. His cheekbones bulged. Something, nature, accident, or a fist, had smeared his nose. Another ragged scar made a crater at the right end of his thick lips.

I couldn't see the lower part of his body. But I didn't doubt that he was armed.

By now, the coffins were being lowered into the graves. In a minute or so, the mourners would be going home. I started my motor and moved the car slowly, hoping that Deak and his

Frankenstein's monster would be concentrating on the ceremony and so not see me. In any event, I was going to get much closer to them, though not too close, and then see what happened after that.

Up ahead the road forked, turning southeastward for about eighty feet. Then it headed straight south and forked again close to the Alliger tomb. But I was going to stop at the point where I could go southward. I'd wait. If Deak followed Diana, he'd have me on his tail, though not too close. If I saw him drive north toward me, I'd drive the car out of sight on the eastward road.

When I came to the fork, I saw a beat-up and dirty Dodge pickup truck pulling away from the grass onto the road. It was headed south. Deak's buddy was driving. I couldn't see Deak. Then his cap lifted from the bed of the truck. He was lying down on it.

Looking straight down the road, I could see the chauffeur helping Faith Alliger into the limousine. The other limousine was just in front of it, and the chauffeur was shutting the right rear door.

Suddenly, I stiffened. I said, "What the hell?"

The truck had picked up speed. It was going so fast that it would slide if its driver tried to turn it onto the west road. Even if he slammed on the brakes, he'd probably skid off the road.

I didn't know what Deak and his King Kongish pal were up to, but I had to follow them. I backed the car up a little and then drove forward and turned south.

The truck did swing onto the westward road, its brakes squealing, its cab swaying. Almost, it left the road and soared up the incline of earth. If that had happened, it would have crashed into the Alliger tomb. But the driver managed to keep it on the road. By then, all of the funeral party were staring at the oncoming truck. I glanced at the rear limousine and saw a white face in a window, its mouth forming a big black O.

More shrieking of brakes. Deak got up onto his knees, one hand gripping the side of the bed, the other holding a revolver. My heart, which had been racing, now felt as if it was wrapping itself around itself. I thought sure he was going to shoot at Diana. But, though he was so close to his target, he was going too fast and bouncing too hard to have much chance to hit her.

However, he pointed the gun skyward, and fired two rounds. After that, accelerating, the truck turned east and then north. Deak was warning Diana. I was sure of that, though just what message he was sending, I didn't know. What I did know was that Deak must be desperate to threaten her in the view of so many witnesses. Of course, Diana and I were the only ones who knew whom he was threatening.

Deak was as reckless and as stupid as ever. For all he knew, the chauffeurs would be carphoning the police. If the cops were quick, they could shut off the two entrances to the park.

I drove past the limos, which had stopped, without looking at them. The pickup had sped northward and had passed the giant dead oak by which I had parked. I let the car fall back until I could glimpse the truck only now and then. However, the only exit for the public was the entrance on Prospect Drive. When I had the chance, I drove off on another road, and I got to the exit before Deak did. My car was well back and parked along the road when the truck sped into sight. I followed it up to War Memorial, which was also State Route 150. A short distance eastward down the hill, the McClugage Bridge crossed the Illinois River. I didn't know which direction the truck would take at the other side, but I felt confident that it'd be southward.

Using my hand tape recorder, I described the truck. I couldn't see the numbers on the license plate because it was smeared with dried mud.

As I'd expected, the pickup went through East Peoria and then Pekin and then, just as when I'd tailed Deak the first time, it went south on the Manito Road. The truck had to be heading for Goofy Ridge.

I stayed far behind. Since I had nothing to do except shadow the truck, I phoned home. I left a message to Glinna that I might be late for dinner. If I didn't show by six, she should go ahead and eat.

Then I called my office phone for messages. There was only one, and it was from Andy Murchmassey, the Kentucky PI I'd hired to inquire about the Rolanskis and the Boomalls in Ballard County, Kentucky. He'd had less trouble getting people there to talk than he'd anticipated. However, few remembered the Rolanskis, and those that did had only vague memories. No one remembered the Rolanskis returning to the county for a visit after they'd left for California. That meant that they didn't even know that the couple had had a child.

He had, however, determined that the Boomalls had retired to Florida. I'd told him to continue investigating to the point where he located the Boomalls. Then, he should call me. Now, he had apparently succeeded. Feeling hopeful, I phoned him. He picked up his phone at once.

He said, "Tom, you're in luck. I found out there's a national directory of retired ministers of the particular Pentecostal organization Boomall belonged to. He died ten years ago. But, since Angela is also a minister, she was listed. She resides in a retirement community near Deerfield Beach, Florida. It's called Glory Gardens, if you can believe that. I talked to the manager on the phone, had to tell him my business before he'd tell me anything about Mrs. Boomall, and that was very little. Talking to her on the phone is out. Seems she regards the phone as an instrument of the devil, and anyone who wants to speak to her has to do so directly."

He paused, then said, "The manager hinted Angela Boomall

isn't always all there. I mean . . . he said her mind might wander now and then. So, do you want me to go there and talk to her or do you prefer to go there yourself?"

"I'll handle it myself," I said. "Just give me all the information I'll need before I go there."

"OK. But the manager also said that if I wanted to talk to her, I'd better hurry. He put it delicately, but I clearly understood that her mind is going fast."

I got the data I needed, thanked him, told him to send the bill to ABISS, and said good-bye.

I was a mile behind the pickup when it turned onto the highway leading to Goofy Ridge. The truck didn't turn in at the road to the wooded section of the hamlet. After fifteen minutes on the back-country county roads, the truck slowed down by a field planted with clover. I coasted onto the shoulder of the road, no brakes, thus, no lights from my car to get their attention. But I was at least three-quarters of a mile behind them, easily keeping them in sight because the land was so flat. When the car came near the top of a slight rise, I tapped the brakes. My quarry wouldn't see the flash of their lights.

The top of the car was above the rise far enough for me to observe the truck. It had stopped by the fence around the field. Deak was out of the vehicle and lifting a crossbar. A moment later, the truck drove through the opening in the fence. It stopped. Deak replaced the crossbar and got back onto the truck. It rolled over a muddy path along the side of the fence running toward the river. Then it turned at an angle to the left and was swallowed up by the woods.

The field, the fence, the crossbar, and the woods looked somewhat familiar. It took me a minute to recognize the place. I'd gone by it many times while hunting. The last time was at night when I was driving to Mason City after escaping from the Mobards. On the other side of the woods was the river. It was there in 1866 that the boiler of the sidewheeler, the *Minnehaha*, exploded. And its cargo of pool balls and cue sticks soared into the sky along with the captain. It was near the eastern riverbank that the sole surviving witness was badly injured by a pool ball.

I waited for five minutes. Not a car passed along the road. Then I drove slowly to the fence, stopped, got out of the car, and put the crossbar on the ground. A minute later, I was driving the car in the muddy tracks made by the pickup. When I got near the woods, I turned my car to face the road. I might have to leave this place fast, and I wanted to be headed in the right direction when I did. I lowered the window, turned off the motor, and listened while looking in the rearview mirror.

I heard the harsh cry of a bluejay, the skreek of a red-tailed hawk circling above the field, and a faint call, a sharp descending kyoooo, made by a green heron along the river's edge. The only things I saw were the hawk and a distant flight of crows, no doubt bent on doing something wicked some place.

Five more minutes passed. Then I got out, opened the trunk with my key, and took out the Smith & Wesson six-shot .44 Magnum revolver. I attached an eight-inch-long barrel to it to extend its range. I put it in my right jacket pocket. A box of cartridges went into the other pocket. I dropped the car keys into my shirt pocket and my tie into my rear left pants pocket. The tie might be useful. I didn't lock the car.

The path over which the truck had been driven was just wide enough for it. I followed it, getting my shoes and trouser cuffs muddy. Many pin oak, sycamore, walnut, willow, and hickory nut trees pressed around me. Where the field had been bright with sunshine, the woods were dark enough to be gloomy. They were also strangely silent. Not even a squirrel barked.

Outside the woods, the temperature had been seventy-eight

F. Inside, it felt as if it were ten degrees cooler. There was little wind at my level, but the leaves near the treetops rustled.

Then, I felt wind, the air got warmer, the light became brighter. When I got near the end of the path, I moved to the left into the bushes. I crouched behind a tree and looked at the river, not sixty feet away. To my right, the land curved westward to make a sort of bay. Here, where the current was slower, marsh grasses and reeds grew thickly. To my left, but still part of the bay, was a beach made of sand and earth. Near it, a two-roomed shack with a corrugated-iron roof stood on a gentle slope. To its right was a small wooden wharf. Tied to it was an old abandoned houseboat about twenty feet long. This looked like the Ark would have looked if it had been built while Noah was on a long drinking binge. But I supposed it had once been serviceable enough.

The truck was parked by the wharf. No humans were in sight. A sleeping dog, a big scruffy mongrel, was chained to a wooden post near the shack. I was glad that the breeze came from the west. However, I certainly had to be careful about making noise here.

This was a good place for Deak to hide out. The woods and the field belonged to a farmer who'd never, as far as I knew, taken any interest in this section of land. He probably didn't know about the shack and the houseboat. It didn't matter. Deak was here. He could answer many of my questions. First, though, I'd have to catch him. And to do that, I was sure, I'd have to deal with Deak's pal, the hairy brute.

Deak suddenly stepped out from the cabin of the boat onto the deck. His belt held on one side a sheath with a big hunting knife and, on the other side, a holster containing a large revolver. He tipped a bottle containing a fluid which I doubted was water to his lips and drank deeply.

I took the gun from my jacket pocket and looked around the tree trunk for the big man.

He—someone, anyway—fired at me. The bullet ricocheted off the side of the tree and wheeed past my ear. And I saw fire spurt from the muzzle of the gun pointed at me from the window of the shack.

I fell to my left side against the wet earth and rolled until I came up against a bush, then got up on all fours and scuttled into the woods. Deak and the big man were shouting, and the dog was barking. Two more shots sounded.

By then, I was dashing through the woods, skirting bushes, and leaping over fallen logs. My revolver was still in my hand. Behind me came more shouts and a baying as deep as that of the Hound of the Baskervilles. Then I got to the path, and I ran faster. A glance backward showed me that the three were also on the path, the huge dog bounding far ahead, Deak behind him, and the big man close behind him. Deak had his revolver. The other man was carrying a rifle in one hand. Though he'd shot at me with a revolver, he'd grabbed his rifle to hunt me. Good thinking. For him.

I stopped, spun, dropped to one knee, and aimed at the dog. My shot got him, I think, in the throat. Wherever it struck, it dropped him. Deak hurled himself from the path into the woods. The big man threw himself face down and then lifted the rifle to his shoulder, his elbows on the ground, to fire at me.

I snapshot at him and rolled from the path.

Deak fired twice. His bullets didn't come near me—as far as I could tell.

I got up and ran, crouching, deeper into the woods. When I looked from behind a tree, I could see the upper part of the big man's body. He was still lying face down, and he wasn't holding the rifle.

Deak's voice was shrill, loud, and quavery. "Teal! Teal! You OK?"

Teal could be playing possum. To find out, I shot at his ribs. I didn't expect to hit him, but his body shook at the impact.

"You asshole!" Deak howled. "I'm gonna kill you! You kilt Almond, now you kilt Teal! I'm gonna blow your fuckin' brains out!"

He didn't know who'd murdered his brother. I saw no reason to enlighten him.

The explosions and the shouting had stilled the wild life. I left the neighborhood as noiselessly as I could. But I angled southwestward toward the river. I was sure that Deak would go the edge of the woods near the road. He'd expect me to try to escape in that direction. And he'd undoubtedly do something to keep my car from operating. Unless, that is, he didn't want to leave the protection of the trees. In any event, finding I wasn't there, he'd figure I'd gone to the shack or the houseboat to ambush him.

I decided to wait awhile. If Deak came back to get the rifle . . . I tensed. There he was. But he was wary. He looked from behind a tree on the other side of the path, then disappeared. Maybe he was thinking that I might be expecting him to retrieve Teal's rifle. And he'd gone to the shack or the houseboat to get his own rifle.

I didn't know where he was. But I didn't care to wait here for more than two minutes. These passed slowly. After which, I snake-bellied away from the path past two trees. I cautiously got up and ran bent over for several yards before stopping behind a great oak. From there, I went slowly to the edge of the woods near the river again. But now I was south of the shack about eighty feet.

I waited, and I watched. The birds were again singing; a nearby squirrel was chattering angrily at some animal or bird. Or, I hoped not, at Deak Mobard.

After fifteen minutes, a tug pushing ten barges slowly went

downstream past my hiding place. These were loaded with coal and made a train a quarter of a mile long. After a while, it was gone. It was then that I saw Deak run from the woods and leap up from the wharf onto the houseboat and jump through the cabin doorway. I wished then that I could have been inside the cabin waiting for him. But, for all I'd known, he might have been there if I'd gone straight from the woods to it.

Keeping my eyes on the boat, I made my way quickly through the brush and trees. I didn't see Deak. There wasn't any porthole in the rear of the cabin. If he wanted to find out if anybody was sneaking up on him from aft of the boat, he'd have to stick his head out of the porthole or window on the starboard or right side of the cabin. I took off my shoes and socks, stuck them behind a bush, and rolled up the bottoms of my trousers. Then I ran to the river until the water was up to my knees. I began wading toward the boat on its blind side. I was glad that its builder had been too lazy to put a window in the rear of the cabin.

I thought, if I had to kill Deak to keep him from killing me, I would. But I was hoping just to subdue him and then ask him The Question. That is, what was the connection between him and Diana?

After I'd got that out of him, I didn't know what I'd do. I couldn't hand him over to the police without ending up in jail myself. But I also couldn't let him loose again. Especially since he'd kill me as soon as possible.

Logically, there was only one thing to do then. But I didn't believe I could execute anybody.

Don't get ahead of yourself, I thought. But it was too late. I was ahead, and, as I would find out, I couldn't step back.

I was now crouching at the rear of the vessel, my butt and legs wet with riverwater. I put the revolver in my jacket pocket, reached up, and grabbed the top of the low wooden railing with both hands. I was still half-crouched, my knees bent, my bare feet digging into the soft muck of the riverbottom. My eyes were just below the level of the deck. One heave, and I'd be boarding this craft like a pirate of the Spanish Main.

Up I went like a rocket.

And Deak's face was two inches from mine.

I had a fleeting glimpse of his upraised hand holding his revolver by the barrel. Then, yelling, he slammed the end of the barrel down on my left wrist. He may have aimed for my hand, but, if so, he missed.

At the same time, my right arm went around his neck. It was a reflex action, no thought in it.

I went backward, my arm pulling Deak with me. His revolver fell to the deck as I pulled him over the railing. I hit the water on my back. He was on top of me, his face now pressed against mine. Those long fleshy tumorous tendrils ground against my mouth. But I was so occupied with the shock of encountering him, the numbness of my left arm from the wrist up to the shoulder, and the suddenness of what had happened I didn't feel the repulsion I'd have had under other circumstances.

Deak bore me down under the water until my back sank into the bottom mud. I released him then because I couldn't do anything with my left arm and holding him close to me would only allow him to get his knife into me. As it was, when I rose to the surface, I saw his knife blade just in time to move my head.

It was not far enough. The blade edge seared my right cheek.

I fell back and kicked with my right leg through the water. My heel must have struck his crotch. He yelled in pain, but he was not paralyzed. He came at me, his knife held just above the surface. I turned and waded toward shore with a desperate burst of energy. As the water fell away, I went faster. Just as I got to the shore, I felt another burning pain. This one was in my lower back.

But the knife hadn't gone deep—as far as I could tell. The wound didn't stop me from running as fast as I could along the shore or keep me from reaching into my jacket pocket for the Smith & Wesson. When it was in my hand, I stopped and then whirled around. Deak was fast and strong for an elderly man. Head down, he rammed into my belly and knocked me flat on my back. Then he dived and grabbed the revolver and twisted my hand.

I was trying to suck in my breath. But I did kick out and bring up my legs, which were half-under Deak, and so rolled him partway over. He had my revolver by then, but I had his knife, which he'd dropped when he went for my gun. It was in my right hand—I still don't know how I managed to get it—and I brought the knife edge down on his wrist. He yelped and dropped the gun. But he got to his feet and kicked the gun away and then leaned down and grabbed my wrist and twisted once again.

I dropped the knife. Before he could do anything, I leaped to my feet, my wind recovered, though my left arm hung uselessly and hurt so much I wanted to scream. No time for that. Not if I wanted to live.

Deak had gone after the revolver. I ran at him and stiff-armed him with my good arm. He staggered into the river and then fell down. I looked around for the pistol. Where had it gone?

Deak thought it was in the water. He was bent over feeling along the bottom. It probably was in the river. I certainly couldn't see it. But I could see the knife. I ran toward it. Deak must have abandoned his search then. If I had the knife, I'd have him, or so he must have thought.

Again, he was too fast. He shoved me hard from behind. I staggered forward, tried to keep going on two legs, couldn't, and sprawled forward. I turned over at once and started to get up. But I hesitated. When I'd fallen, my right hand felt something round. It was almost completely buried, but enough was just above the top of the wet sand-earth mixture for me to feel its shape.

I was almost certain I knew what it was. I dug in with the fingers of my right hand and then had the object entirely in my hand.

Though it was still covered with shore dirt, it was undoubtedly hard and round.

By then, I'd turned and was up on my feet.

Deak had the knife, and he was grinning.

He said, "Now I'm gonna cut you up into little pieces, asshole."

He was about twelve feet from me. He'd not tried to close with me. He was sure I would be an easy prey for him, and he was in no hurry. Besides, like me, he was breathing very hard. He'd get his wind back, then get close enough to me to carve me up with great deliberation and great pleasure.

I wound up as I'd done many times while pitching for my high school and college teams.

My dead and painful arm handicapped me. And my grip on the ball was not the best. I had no time to try to clean it off. Nevertheless, the object left with much velocity and a true aim.

Deak's eyes opened wide. His mouth spread wide open.

He tried to duck, but he failed.

The pool ball caught him in the center of his forehead. He dropped, and did not thereafter move.

That ball had been waiting for me since 1866, ever since

the explosion of the *Minnehaha* had hurled that particular ball onto the shore. It had been buried many times. The rains had eroded it somewhat and partly washed off the earth many times to expose it to the air and rain. But the ivory ball had been buried again and again.

It had been waiting to save my life for close to one hundred and thirty years.

24

Deak Mobard lay on his back, eyes open, tendril-ringed mouth open, blood from his nose covering his mouth and chin. His pulse had gone with his soul, if he had had a soul.

The ivory pool ball I'd hurled at him was rotting. Its surface was pitted; large chunks had broken off at the impact. And my throw certainly wasn't near my best, nothing like what I delivered when I pitched for Richwoods High and UCLA. The world record for the speed of a ball thrown by a human being was 104 miles per hour, made by Bob Feller of the Cleveland Indians in the 1940s. My ball had been hurtling at least between eighty to ninety miles per hour when it struck the bridge of Deak's nose. It must have broken many blood vessels in his brain and perhaps driven bits of nose bone into his brain.

I put the Smith & Wesson into my jacket pocket and stood by his body until I'd gotten my breath back. Meanwhile, using my good arm, I felt the slash on my cheek and the wound in my back. Blood flowed fast from them. I left the riverbank and walked through the woods toward my car. The dog and Deak's pal, Teal, looked dead. The flies were buzzing around and on them, and more were coming. Bad news for some is good news for others.

When I got to the car, I opened the trunk and took out my first aid kit. Despite the pain of my injured wrist and my inability to use my left arm, I managed to get a bandage on my cheek. Then, after getting my coat off and shirt and undershirt open and rolled up, I got a bandage on the wound in my back. Not easy to do, and I lost more blood.

I got a cloth and splints from the kit. Though I hurt badly and was clumsy, I made a sling for my left arm and put it on. For the pain, I swallowed three aspirins and washed them down with a soft drink from the ice chest on the back floor of my car.

With several more tools from the kit in my coat pocket, I went back to Teal's corpse and the dog's carcass. It wasn't easy to dig out the bullets in them because I could use only one hand. After ten or more minutes, using a long pair of tweezers and an ice pick, I had both bullets out. I wrapped up the bullets in a bandage and stuck it in my pocket. There was no use my looking for the bullet that had bounced off the top of Teal's skull and into the woods.

I returned to Deak's body. By now, the flies were crawling in and out of his mouth. Though I hated to throw the ivory ball, a historical souvenir, into the river, I did it. Deak's knife also went into the water. As for my footprints in the mud and the woods, there were too many for me to try to erase them. I'd get rid of my shoes later and hope rain would erase the bare-feet prints.

There was also nothing to do about covering over my car tracks in the field. It seemed very improbable that the police would ever connect the tire tracks to my car. Nevertheless, I'd have to get rid of the tires and get new ones or retreads, never mind the expense.

After I was on the road to Peoria, driving with one hand, wishing I could have a shot of Demerol in the wrist, I had time for regrets. I'd hoped I'd get some answers to some very puzzling questions from Deak. And I'd hoped that these would enable me to get some kind of hold on Mordoy so she'd quit blackmailing Diana and also quit trying to kill me. The only ones who had answers for me now were Mordoy and Diana Alliger, and I doubted they'd talk. There was, of course, a chance that Mrs. Angela Boomall, now living in Glory Gardens, Florida, might enlighten me.

First, though, I needed medical help. I didn't want to go to a hospital for treatment. The interns would report my obvious knife wounds to the police. There was but one doctor I knew who, for a certain sum of money, would take care of me and keep his mouth shut. That was old Doc Schiessel, the resident physician at the Tum-Tum Tree Motel. He was a drunk who'd long ago lost his license to practice medicine, his reputation, his wife, his dog, his house, and most of his money. But when he was sober, he was a competent sawbones. He treated the motel whores, and, if rumor was correct, wounded criminals hiding from the law.

So, I went to the Tum-Tum. I was lucky. Old Doc was only half-loaded. He stitched up my cheek and back wounds, not hurting me any more than I had a right to expect, and put on new bandages. He also adjusted the sling and splints. But he advised me to have the wrist X-rayed. It had turned black and swelled up and might be broken.

I paid him and drove away, though carefully and slowly because Doc's pain pill was clouding my brain. At the hospital, I told them I'd fallen and sprained or broken my wrist and had put the splints and sling on myself. Of course, I had to lie about the "accident," and I didn't mention my wounds, though the intern and nurse must have wondered about the bandage on my cheek. The X-ray showed that the wrist bones were not broken. The only damage was to the muscles and blood vessels.

Once home, I fell into bed. I couldn't keep my wounds from Glinna, of course. She was so distressed that she broke The Rule by asking me what had happened. I told her, as I had before, that she was better off not knowing.

Though Glinna nursed me, she talked to me as little as possible and was as cold as anyone can get without turning into real ice. There were times when I thought I'd rather be in prison.

Days passed, and nothing appeared in the news media about Deak and Teal. Unless the Mason County police had a lid on the news—and why should they?—the bodies hadn't been found. Glinna had started to warm up to me, and Mimi Rootwell called to tell me about the wills of the elder Alligers. She'd found out about their details though they were not yet of public record.

"To be brief," she said, "Alexandra's will gives half her estate to Simon, and the rest to Roger, if he divorces Diana. Rosemary gets one dollar. Simon's will gives one dollar to Rosemary and the rest to Roger, if he divorces Diana, except for certain amounts to certain charities, gun clubs, and universities."

She paused, then said, "Both parents suggested that he give her a substantial sum to keep her quiet. If, however, Roger refuses to abide by this, he's to lose all the inheritance, except for one dollar. If Roger doesn't kick Diana out of his bed and home, the money goes to charities."

"Is that legal?"

"It is unless a judge finds it isn't."

"What's Roger going to do about it?"

"The ancient Romans brought out the lions. Today, we bring out the lawyers. Diana isn't waiting for her husband to contest the will. She's hired legal ninjas, the firm of Grendelson and Owlmonger, to fight for her. And Rosemary is also contesting the will. Her lawyer is John "Flank Attack" Orcus, a real demon. The Alligers have ducked publicity for over a century and a half, but they can't get away from the fireworks now."

On the fourth day, I felt recovered enough to sally forth, though gingerly, on business. But I had no business. And I was somewhat nervous and jumpy. I knew that Mordoy would be doing something I wouldn't like at all. The only question was when and where she'd strike at me.

At 9 A.M. that day, Faith Alliger phoned.

Her voice sounded reasonably strong for a ninety-two-year-old woman whose son and daughter-in-law had recently died. After we'd inquired about each other's health, she got down to the reason she'd called.

"I called Rootwell and told her I want her agency to continue the investigation of Diana. But I want you to spearhead it. She said that was fine with her. So I told her I'd speak to you about it. Are you able to meet me at twelve at Stephanie's for lunch? We'll discuss this then."

Stephanie's was a high-class place with basically French cuisine. Nothing snooty about the decor or the waiters, and it served very good food. I was in my best suit and tie when I showed up. Faith Alliger was in an ankle-length print dress, light and flowery. A lot of lace around the neckline hid her bony chest. In front of her was a long-stemmed glass of wine. She looked at the cheek, now Band-Aided, and the sling, but she did not comment.

"A hard fall," I said. I sat down, refused her offer of a drink, and ordered coffee.

After the waitress had left, I said, "Do you mind telling me why you're continuing the investigation? I . . ."

"Thomas, I've read your reports and Mordoy's reports on Diana, and I know what's on those tapes, though I see no reason to view them. I want the investigation pursued until Diana's life is laid bare, no more surprises about her. Besides, I have a feeling, I don't know what causes it, there's something momentous, maybe really criminal, in her past. I must know for sure.

"Simon and Sandy hated Diana. But I liked her from the start. I especially liked the way she stood up to them."

"I tended to sympathize with Diana," I said. "I try to be objective while I'm working a case, but I don't always make it. However, now . . ."

"Now?"

"I won't say anything pro or con," I said. "The facts are a long way from all being in. But let me get this straight. You're hiring me to go along the same lines that Simon hired me for?"

"Not exactly," she said. "I don't care what she might have been before she met him—unless she was a child abuser or murderess. Or, say, a bigamist. But I do want to know for my own personal knowledge. And for Roger's."

"What's he think of the will?"

She raised her eyebrows. "You know the terms?"

"Those that count. And the latest developments, Diana's and Rosemary's lawsuits."

"Mimi Rootwell," Faith said. "That woman knows what's happening in this city before it happens."

She opened her purse, removed a dollar bill, and handed it to me.

"Give me a receipt. That'll make it official, right?"

"Right. You're my client. Anything you tell me from now on is confidential. But what does Roger think about the will?"

"He and I've talked about it," Faith said. "He's still in love with Diana. But the boy . . . I don't like to say this . . . he doesn't have enough backbone. He loves money and hates turmoil and trouble, and I've heard—never mind from whom—that he uses hard drugs. But he's read the reports and seen the tapes. He still hasn't made up his mind about her."

I said, "I've also talked to her. She knows I'm simpatico. I even asked her straight out to reveal all of her past to me and to Roger. Doing that, I told her, would save a lot of time and money and emotional pain. But she insisted she had no more to hide. Roger, she says, now knows all about her. She's given him three days to make up his mind. If, by then, he still can't accept her for what she is now, she'll leave him forever."

"Well, we now know who's going to make a lot of money," I said. "The lawyers. But if you want me to investigate Diana further with the idea that she'll come up smelling like a rose and Roger won't then have any doubts about her, that may or may not happen."

"You do what you have to. Now then . . ."

She paused so long that I said, "Well?"

"Oh, I don't know."

Then she straightened up. "Yes, I do! I might be overly suspicious. But something happened two nights ago . . . it may be nothing. However . . ."

"Just tell me what it was."

"Early this morning, I awoke. That's not unusual for me since I often awake during the night. But this was with a start. My heart hammered. I felt that someone had been in the room. The bedside clock indicated it was 1:17 A.M. Then I heard a noise, a slight one, something like a door closing in the next room. You know, the room where you and I talked. But I should have seen a momentary light from the hallway through the doorway if the door had been opened.

"I waited for perhaps a minute before I got up and looked

around. All the firearms are in Simon's office, so I took the poker from the fireplace in my bedroom. Just what I thought a feeble old woman could do with it, I don't know. But it made me feel better. Then I turned on the bedroom light. Everything looked normal. I went into the living room and turned its lights on. It seemed to be just as it was when I'd gone to sleep. The door to the hall was locked. I opened it.

"Then I knew something was wrong. The hall lights were out. I went down the hallway, feeling along the wall until I came to the main switch. I thought it was possible that all the bulbs had burned out, though it didn't seem likely. There are six overhead lights, you know. The switch was off.

"Somebody has a key to my suite, I thought, and he let himself in, looked around, then left. But it could all be my imagination. Or the noise that awoke me could have been from outside the house."

I said, "Who else has a key?"

"Simon and Sandy each had one. I don't know where their keys are now."

"Anyone who wanted to get a copy of your key could have done it. Who was in the house that night?"

She thought a moment, then said, "The servants, the Cabracans and the cook, were in their quarters over the garage. Diana was in Sandy's rooms. She's moved out from her house and was staying there until she could find a suitable apartment or Roger takes her back on her terms."

I hadn't known that. So, Mimi didn't know everything.

I said, "Who else was there?"

"Rosemary. She quarreled with that thing called Kordik and moved to my house. She said she had no place else to go, and I wasn't going to kick out my granddaughter."

"I can reactivate the security cameras in the hallway. They were turned off because your son and daughter-in-law said they were expensive to run. I'll see to it that they're operating again. The ultraviolet lights and film will be activated again, too. If someone turns off the hall lights, the cameras will still be able to film the intruder. And you should change the lock to your rooms.

"Now, I need your authorization to fly to Florida and interview a woman who might be able to shed some light on Diana's life. It could be a waste of money, but I really believe it's a necessary part of the investigation."

"Whatever you want. I trust you. Here's the key to my house."

25

The Reverend Mrs. Angela Boomall, though she rambled while she talked, had made sense. Her mind had been tethered to this earth. But, for the last ten minutes, it was out there somewhere else, perhaps flying toward the Pearly Gates. All I could do was to wait for it to come home.

Mrs. Boomall, a nurse's aide named Jim Sutos, and I sat in her tiny living room in her tiny suite, sixth floor, Glory Gardens. Sutos was supposed to keep an eye on the old woman and on me. But he was already snoring, his head lolling to one side. I wasn't surprised. It had been obvious that he was on some tranquilizing or stupefying drug.

The rest home occupied the upper six stories of a ten-story building just off the beach. There may once have been gardens or flower displays around or in the building. There were none now. The structure didn't look old enough to me to be condemned. But it was to be torn down and a twenty-story-high condominium and shopping complex built in its place. A number of the residents had been moved out; the rest were scheduled to be gone within four weeks.

Mrs. Boomall sat in a rocking chair her grandfather had made. She was in a long cloth robe of some faded material, a thin nightgown hanging below that, and frayed blue slippers. Wide stretches of her scalp shone through straight, sparse, and white hair. The blue eyes behind thick horn-rimmed spectacles were as frayed as her slippers. Old age had thinned and sharpened her long nose. A huge mole with a vague resemblance to a legless and antennaeless cockroach was near the left corner of her mouth.

The chair faced a large plateglass window through which she could see the Atlantic Ocean. On the other side of the water was Africa, but that was not what her inner eye saw. I don't know what she was visualizing, but it certainly was not in this universe. Not at that moment, anyway.

Her husband, the Reverend Heber Boomall, pastor of the Descent-of-Doves Pentecostal Church, had died of a heart attack in this very room ten years ago. His large photograph, hanging on the wall, showed a gaunt, clean-shaven, and stern-faced man with a scar on his right cheek. It almost matched mine. His widow said it had been made by a knife in a tavern brawl in those sinful days before Heber saw the Light and accepted the Lord as his Savior. The Boomalls could afford this relatively expensive rest home because they'd inherited money from her wealthy brother, who'd taken Christ to his bosom on his deathbed.

"Just in time, too," she'd said. "One more minute, and my brother'd gone straight to Hell and its eternal torments. Heber had striven mightily with him all that night, quoting Scripture and painting the hellfire of eternal damnation and the joys of eternal life in Paradise, and, just before dawn, my brother said that he believed, truly believed, that Jesus had died for his sins and that he really appreciated it and when he got to the land of Beulah up there he'd lie down with the lion and the lamb and hope he and the lamb would get up again, though just what he meant by that I don't know. He no sooner said that than his soul went up to meet its Maker. Praise the Lord, from whom all blessings flow."

My Louisville colleague, Murchmassey, had found out that the Boomalls had wandered through the midwest and the southwest for twenty years as revivalists. He'd given me the data over the phone while I was on the airliner to Florida.

"I found this out when I tried again in Ballard County. I found Mrs. Boomall's aged cousin, who'd corresponded with Mrs. Boomall while she was on the road. She told me the Boomalls lived in a trailer and usually pitched a tent for their revival meetings. But they did settle down in San Bernardino, California, for several years, probably because of this child, Angela. She seems to have popped into their lives and then popped out. The cousin was never told where Angela had come from or what eventually happened to her.

"She might've been some runaway orphan they picked up, but the orphanages aren't going to give you any information."

I'd checked out with Mrs. Boomall most of what Murchmassey had told me. I was holding back the inquiry about Angela because I hoped that Mrs. Boomall would mention her voluntarily. Now, I'd decided to mention Angela as soon as the old woman became lucid again. I hoped she would.

". . . that Regaltin was the biggest crook alive," Mrs. Boomall said. "He gave all us honest God-fearing ministers of the Lord a bad name. Can you imagine? During his sermons he sold pieces of salt he swore to high heaven came from Lot's wife's body. He also . . ."

She stopped talking, and her eyes seemed to focus on me. Then she said, "What was it you asked me?"

"Nothing important," I said. "I would like to ask you about Angela."

"Angela? That's *my* name!"

"The child Angela," I said. "Your daughter."

Mrs. Boomall smiled, and she said, "We named her Angela—after my mother and me. She was a gift from the Lord. Heber and I had prayed to Him every day and night to be blessed with a child, and we'd striven mightily to conceive one. He was a very virile man, Heber, especially after the meetings, when the tents were brimming with the juice of the Holy Spirit, but his seed was weak. The Lord denied us a child. Maybe it was because of Heber's sinful youth."

"How did the child come into your lives?" I said.

"It was in Quartzsite, Arizona, where some godly folks lived but not enough to pay our expenses. I don't know how she found us, that child so far, so very far from home, her saintly mother dead, her wicked father taking up with that evil woman who hated her, no one to protect her against her lecherous ungodly father. But she came in that hot evening, so hot even Satan would've hated it. The poor little thing, so thin and hungry and ragged. I asked her how in the world she'd ever found us, and then . . ."

"Mrs. Boomall!"

"The Great Whore of Babylon, the Scarlet Woman, the nine-headed dragon of the last days . . . I warn ye, O ye evil generation and fermenters of sour evil wickedness . . ."

I sighed with frustration. But she surprised me by coming out of the clouds almost at once.

"And then . . . what was I saying?"

"The child Angela," I said. "You said you and your husband called her Angela. But what was her real name?"

"Angela? That was her real name. Heber and I named her, and that makes her name her real name."

I had trouble hiding my impatience. But I spoke smoothly and as if not very concerned.

"I mean . . . what was her name before she was Angela?"

"Oh, that. Harly came to us as if the Lord God Hisself had

sent her, and she was our joy and delight, the child we couldn't have—"

"Harly!" I said.

She didn't hear me. I don't think she saw me, either. She smiled and rose, shaking, and spread her arms wide, her gaze on something far to the east.

"At last!" she shouted. "At last! The glory! The glory! I see the Lamb in all His glory! O, Lord Jesus, I see You! I see the Light and the one hundred and forty-four thousand who have the name of the Lamb and of the Father written on their foreheads! Take me, take me!"

I had to turn around and look toward the east. I saw only the ocean and the ten o'clock sun and white birds wheeling and diving. But she was so convincing that I felt something, some Presence. My skin got cold; the hairs on my head stood up.

And then she cried out, "I'm coming! I'm coming! O God, I'm coming!"

The aide opened his eyes and reared up out of his chair. "Wha . . . ? Wha . . . ?"

Mrs. Boomall fell back into the chair, and the chair rocked a few times and then was as still as the woman who sprawled in it.

Her death was dramatic, so much so that God or a novelist might have arranged it. However, as it turned out, she was not yet dead. Mrs. Boomall had had a stroke, a completely paralyzing stroke. I'm sure she would have preferred death, anyone in his right mind would, but there she was. I hoped that she was still envisioning the the glory she'd seen and that she'd be locked into it until the real death came to her.

In the meantime, I was trying to remember where I'd heard the name of Harly. It seemed to me that it should not be hard to remember. Yet, I couldn't bring it up from the vasty deep— love that phrase—of my unconscious.

At the moment, I was on the plane from Fort Lauderdale to Chicago. Coach class, sucking hind tit, of course. My clients, no matter how rich or how friendly to me, never authorized first-class fare.

However, use of the phone on an airliner was OK if it wasn't personal business. I called Mert Plateburn, the Chicago PI, to find out how the watch on Mordoy was doing. He didn't even say hello to me. "Bad news!" he blurted. "The Mordoy woman has disappeared!"

I said, "What do you mean, disappeared?" Then I said, "Never mind, Mert. That was a stupid question, sheer reflex. Give me the story."

Plateburn and his two best operatives had dogged her for three days. This was relatively easy because she was part of a team staking out a mansion in Evanston on an insurance fraud case. Plateburn was sure that she wasn't aware she was being shadowed.

"And then, this morning, she just up and vanished!" Plateburn said. "As far as I can tell, it has nothing to do with the case she was on. Here's what happened.

"At seven this morning, Mordoy, instead of going to Evanston to relieve the man on duty there, drove to an area a block west of Michigan Avenue and close to downtown Chicago. She went into the Ruffler's Nest Hotel, an old building with a sidewalk café in front of it. She found a parking place on nearby Cedar, not easy to do, then walked down to and around the corner and crossed the street to the hotel and went into the lobby, if you can call it that, and—"

"I know the place," I said. "Most of its guests are permanent. Some people think it's a hangout for male and female whores and petty crooks, but that's probably not true. Anyway, the owners run a tight ship. I tried to get into it once to follow a woman from Peoria her rich husband thought, rightly, was cheating on him. I offered the desk clerk two hundred dollars for the name of the man she was meeting and his room number. But the bouncer hustled me on out."

"Things've changed since then," Plateburn said. "Well, Mordoy didn't come out of the hotel for four hours. I figured her car'd be hung with overtime parking notices. Whatever she was doing, she must think it was worth paying those fines. Then I got to wondering about the car. I couldn't leave my post, so I called the agency and got a operative who was nearby to check on the car. It was long gone!"

He paused. I said, "She'd left by the rear door?"

"No. Apparently, she'd slipped out of a ground floor window. I'd swear she hadn't detected me, but I was wrong. Or someone tipped her off. Anyway, I banged on the glass door, waved a wad of money at the desk clerk, and got buzzed in. This guy musta been a different one from the guy you encountered or he'd finally got wise to all those opportunities he'd lost in this land of plenty or you didn't offer enough dough.

"I gave him plenty for him and the bouncer. He showed me the room number of the couple Mordoy'd visited more'n once. He said I could go up and look around since the couple had checked out three hours ago. That kinda upset me, you know. So I got him to describe the couple. Damn! I'd seen them coming out, each with a big suitcase, but thought nothing of it. A black male, down in the register as Lemangelo Elseed, and a white woman, Artemis Moondeer, believe those monickers or not. In their middle thirties, born in the middle 1960s, yet dressed like flower children. Born far too late but living in a time they never knew. I'm having their backgrounds checked out even as we speak. You know, Tom, I didn't think nothing of it when they came out the door. I didn't know about any connection to Mordoy. Why should I?"

"Right," I said. "No blame there. Go on."

"I went up to the second story. The stink of Lysol, soap, water, vagina juices, sperm fluid, tobacco, dirty toilet bowls, and unwashed bodies got stronger. I felt like tossing my hot-dogs and beer."

"Mert," I said, "I know you're writing a PI novel. But I'm not an editor who might buy your manuscript."

He laughed, and said, "Yeah, sorry. Get carried away. You got the picture. Anyway, the room was empty. And where was Mordoy? The clerk got alarmed because he knew she hadn't come out the front way, and the alarm to the back door wasn't off. I told him it didn't matter. I already knew she flew the coop.

"We checked out her agency. They said she'd resigned that morning, would pick up her check later—I doubt she'll do that—and left no forwarding address. We checked out her apartment. Same story. Gone. Left the furniture and most of her personal possessions. No forwarding address. Must've been in a hell of a hurry. But I checked, and the police don't want her for anything."

So, what would Mordoy do now? She wasn't a woman who'd easily give anything up, and she was dangerous. Like a wounded African buffalo in the tall grass, I thought. She'd hunt the hunter. If she wasn't in Peoria by now, she was on her way to it.

I thanked Plateburn and said that, as of now, he was off the job. Send me the bill. But I might be using him again soon. Then I called Faith Alliger and told her what I'd learned from Mrs. Boomall. It wasn't, I admitted, much. But it had given me an avenue to explore.

Then I asked her if anything more suspicious had happened. As, for instance, anything missing from her suite or her purse or anything to indicate an intruder. She said that she'd not noticed anything out of the way.

I told her that the operative I'd hired to check on the film in the hallway monitors had reported that they showed nothing unusual.

"Keep alert," I said. "Just in case. Meanwhile, anything happened there I should know about? Like . . ."

"Yes!" she said. She sounded angry. "That Kordik scum . . . he beat Rosemary up!"

"Oh?" I said. "How badly is she injured?"

"She's home, I mean, here with me. She has a black eye and a bruised cheek, but she's not confined to bed. She says they quarreled about money, but I think she's lying. The police are looking for him."

"Don't let your guard down," I said. "Good-bye, Mrs. Alliger." I heard her phone click off. I started to hang my phone up. Something clicked on, not in the phone but in my mind.

I remembered where I'd heard the name of Harly.

26

"Harly!" I said loudly.

The few people on the sidewalk in front of Mocha Joe's Beanery looked curiously at me.

Diana Alliger, her back to me, carrying a shopping bag, had been walking westward from the coffee store. Hearing me, she stiffened and broke her stride, though almost imperceptibly. Then, not turning her head in the slightest, she picked up her brisk pace again. Her low heels clattered on the cement sidewalk.

I said, even more loudly, "Harly! I want to talk to you!"

Her shoulders came back a trifle more, but she forged ahead, neither slowing nor speeding her pace. I hurried after her and caught her elbow just as she turned to go into a store. She turned, and snarled, "How dare you?"

I don't think she remembered my voice. After all, she'd heard it only once and that briefly and in an emotionally charged situation. But I lifted my sunglasses, and I could tell from her expression that she recognized my face. I was the man who'd been present when Simon Alliger had forbidden her and several others to enter the house. It wasn't long ago, though it seemed so to me.

"We have to talk, Harly," I said. I let loose of her elbow.

She opened her mouth as if to deny that that was her name or perhaps to threaten to call the cops. But something in my manner or perhaps a sense of the inevitable stopped her.

"There's Maid-Rite there," she said. "They play loud music. I doubt anyone'll overhear us."

Side by side, neither speaking, we walked across the square to the restaurant. The eleven o'clock sun was beginning to heat the city, but Diana looked cool and fresh in her long print summer dress. I'd followed her car that morning from the Alliger mansion to this shopping plaza. When the moment seemed right, I'd struck.

Now, we'd see what would happen. I really didn't have much to bluff with, but it could be enough.

We took a small table away from the other tables. Diana removed her sunglasses. I looked across the table into those marvelous blue eyes. I thought, This could be Heaven. But there's an old proverb that says that Satan has blue eyes. It also goes on to say that one of those blue eyes is just under his tail.

She said nothing. It was up to me to set the tone of the dialogue—if there was going to be one.

"Do you know who I am?" I said.

She nodded, and then, as if remembering that the dark shades would hide her eyes, put them back on.

"You're Thomas Gresham Corbie, a private detective my father-in-law hired to investigate me."

I thought, She's so beautiful. If it weren't for just the shadow of a hint of wrinkles around the neck (and she's so young, too!), she'd be flawless. Well, there was also the hint of lines emerging from the corners of her nose to the corners of her mouth. And her eyes were just a trifle too close together.

"You don't know as much about me as you might think," I said. "And I know a lot about you that your husband and his grandmother don't know. I don't plan to use that against you. I am not your enemy even if I was first hired by Simon Alliger. Keep that in mind. I am not your enemy. I am not a blackmailer. But there are some things . . . I need to know the truth. . . ."

"You called me Harly?" she said. "What do you mean by that? Who do you think I am?"

She had me there. Though I had certain suspicions and speculations, I didn't have enough nailed-down facts to steamroll over her. I had a theory about who she was and where she came from before she was in Pasadena. But my theory was seriously flawed. Only she, as far as I knew, could supply the bridge between speculation and fact. It was up to me to somehow get it out of her.

I decided to navigate by dead reckoning and to be frank, or, at least, to seem to be frank. I'd appear to know much more than I actually did know. That would be dangerous, but it might work.

I said, "I don't think that William R. Rolanski and Myrna Groat Rolanski were your biological parents."

I paused. Her face kept its lack of expression. But she paled a little.

"You're the child of a man named Deak Mobard," I said. "He had a brother named Almond. Until recently, they lived at Goofy Ridge."

She didn't flinch, and she got no paler.

"Your mother was Mary Groat."

She laughed. I don't know how she did it since she must have felt numb inside her. But her laughter sounded merry and carefree, not at all put on. I reminded myself that she was an actress.

"After your mother died, you ran away from home, maybe

because your father raped you or tried to rape you. Anyway, you did go to California where your aunt, your mother's sister, lived. First, though, you were adopted by a couple named Boomall."

She said, "What proof do you have for those ridiculous statements? Where did you pull those names from?"

I didn't see any need to tell her that I'd recently followed what I can only describe as a hunch. Whatever a hunch is. I hadn't really expected to find the marriage license of the lawless Deak Mobard in the Illinois State records. There certainly wasn't any for his marriage to Milly Jane Foushee. Of course, if she married both Deak and his brother, Almond, it would have been illegal.

But the computer search turned Deak up immediately. And I had no trouble getting a copy of the license of his first marriage. His bride's Christian name was Mary. Her surname was Eldins.

I had hoped that it would be Groat. But it wasn't. Usually, my hunches lead to success. This one, however, was a flop.

In spite of that, I had a hunch about my hunch. I decided to dig deeper. So, I ran the name of Mary Eldins through the ghostly jungle of the computer system. Hallelujah! The Mary Eldins I was seeking turned out to have been married to a Job Eldins. This was in Mound City, Illinois. The small community, noted for its Indian mounds, was on the Ohio River. From there you could swim across to Ballard County, Kentucky.

When I found this out, I came close to baying out loud like a hound on the trail of a fox.

Mrs. Mary Eldins' birth name was Mary Groat!

I delved deeper, but I could find nothing that would prove that Mary Groat was Myrna Groat, Mr. William R. Rolanski's wife. Nevertheless, I was certain that Mary was Myrna's sister.

I had expected Diana Alliger to shatter into pieces when I announced that her real mother was Mary Groat, the late wife of Deak Mobard. But she was not fazed. Not outwardly, anyway.

So, I brought up my big guns and laid down an enveloping artillery barrage.

I said, "Lorna Mordoy!"

She did blink, and she did flinch, and she did lose more color. But none of this lasted more than three seconds. She laughed again, and she said, "Who?"

Coconuts didn't have harder shells.

I was defeated — unless I tried an even bigger gamble. I didn't want to do it. I might be way off. On the other hand, something working in me, an intelligence report from my mind, a message I hadn't quite decoded yet, told me that there could be a connection. So, I got ready to send in the cavalry.

"You know who," I said.

"You tell me."

The waitress came then and took our orders, a big diet coke for her and a mug of coffee, as hot and as black as hell, for me. I ordered that to show her how cool I was. She didn't seem to be impressed.

After the waitress left, I leaned over close to Diana — her perfume was delicate and at the same time with the hint of an odor like a tiger in ambush; I'd have to get a bottle for Glinna — and I said, "Listen carefully. Then you'll understand how much I know about this mess. I'll give you two names, but the woman's name is not the one she was born with."

I paused, then said, "They're living in Chicago now. But at one time the couple lived in California. One was Lemangelo Elseed. His first name is pronounced Luh-MAHN-juh-lo, but I've been told it was originally spelled L-E-M-O-N-J-E-L-L-O. His woman companion calls herself Artemis Moondeer. Artemis was the ancient Greek goddess of the moon, of wild animals, and of the hunt."

I stopped briefly and stared into her eyes. She was fighting hard to keep control of herself.

I said, "Diana was the ancient Roman equivalent of the Greek Artemis. Get it? This Artemis in Chicago was once named Diana!"

Her body quivered. Her face looked as if it was about to crumple. But if this woman had been an army, she'd have been almost undefeatable. She rallied swiftly, and she charged back.

"What kind of fool are you? And what kind of idiot ninny do you think I am? Flinging names around that mean nothing to me! What do you expect me to do, confess? Confess to what?"

She stood up, not slowly, and glared down at me. "Don't bother me anymore, little man, or I'll have my lawyers all over you!"

I stayed in my chair. "You couldn't stand the publicity. You sure as hell don't want the police to get curious about you. Sit down, Diana. We'll get everything clear, straighten it all out. This Mordoy woman is very dangerous. Let me tell you . . ."

But she'd picked up her handbag and was gone.

I put the money for the drinks and for the tip on the table though the drinks hadn't arrived yet, and I followed her. Halfway to her parked car, I caught up with her. I said, "I talked to Angela Boomall a few days ago, the Reverend Mrs. Boomall!"

She didn't stop, though she did open her mouth. Perhaps that was a reflex, a response to her natural desire to ask about the woman. But she closed her lips firmly together and kept them tight while she drove away.

I went to my own car. No use bugging her anymore just now. She was my lobster. I'd supplied the pot, the water in the pot, and the fire under it. I'd dropped her into the pot. Now she could boil herself in it with worry and fear. When she was tender enough, she'd be ready for the cracking.

Meantime, I'd better find what I needed to validate my suspicions. That wasn't going to be easy to do.

I phoned Faith Alliger. She answered after three rings.

"Tom Corbie," I said. "If you have time to talk a minute, would you tell me if the police have found Kordik yet?"

"Tom, they're not looking for him. That fool Rosemary told the police she didn't want to press charges against him. But he still hasn't dared show his face here."

"Mrs. Alliger . . ."

"Call me Faith, please."

"OK, Faith, it is. I'm not prying into your affairs, but I need to know something about your will. Mainly, who gets the money and the house if you should die, God forbid."

"Because you worry that there might have been an intruder the other night? That may have just been the imagination of a very old woman."

"Yes, but I can't assume that. I have other reasons, too."

"Simon's and Sandy's deaths?" she said. "You think . . . ?"

"I have to consider the possibility they were murdered," I said.

I didn't get the reaction I'd expected.

"You really think it's possible? How exciting! That brightens up my otherwise very dull life. If only Bobbie were here to share this . . . she'd say so many funny things . . . anyway, the will. The house and the bulk of the stocks, bonds, and shares in the many businesses go to Roger or his heirs. I'm leaving four million to various charities, ten million to Bradley University, other relatively small bequests to various persons."

"Rosemary?"

"She gets a million—if she can prove she's drug-free at the time of my death and if she has gotten rid of Kordik or any other scumsponge parasites she's picked up and if she goes back to college full-time. The money is in trust and will be parceled out as the trustees think she needs it. If she quits college or associates with drug addicts or other criminals, the money goes to charity. She gets nothing."

"I suppose Roger's will gives Diana most of his fortune? Or has he changed it since they separated?"

"His will did give her most of his wealth," she said, "but the situation, as you know, has changed. I don't think he's changed his will yet. But my will . . . Roger gets most of my money, as I told you. But I didn't tell you . . ."

She paused for perhaps ten seconds, then spoke in a low voice. "I should've told you that I set terms for Roger, too. I hated doing it, but I'm not going to let him throw away what many generations of Alligers worked to accumulate even though I don't approve of all of their methods in getting it."

Again, she paused. I waited. Then she said, "The money he inherits from me will be in a trust and paid out in installments, though they'll be much more generous than Rosemary's. However . . . for five years, he, too, has to keep proving he's drug-free."

By the time I was through talking to Faith Alliger, I was at the apartment building. There, I used my home phone to call Mert Plateburn.

He said, "Where Mordoy is is anybody's guess. We can't get the police in on the search since she's committed no crime. Or has she?"

"I wish I could tell you she has," I said. "How about Elseed and Moondeer?"

"They might as well be on the moon. Now, you asked me to check them out. Far as I know, they have no relatives, and nobody at the Ruffler's Nest'll admit to knowing them, let alone being their friend. Neither one has an Illinois driver's license or ever had one. Not under their names, anyway. There're no Illinois birth certificates for either, no tax records, no bank records, no police record, no gun license, no work record, nothing under those names. You want me to start a search?"

"Just the LA area, including Pasadena, especially Pasadena. Whatever you can get by computer."

"You got a reason for that area?"

"When it jells, I'll tell you. Call me if you find something."

After I hung up the phone, I sat thinking. I was glad that Glinna was not here and would be gone for a week. She was attending a national convention of wiccas in Los Angeles. I'd be in danger. Hence, she would be, too, if she were here.

Elseed and Moondeer were part of this blackmail of Diana. But if they were arrested or tried to act on their own, they'd be a danger to Mordoy. So, Mordoy got them to run, too, probably by telling them that they were close to being exposed as collaborators in the murders of the Alligers. But where had she hidden them? How about under six feet of earth?

Whatever had really happened, I was convinced that Mordoy was going to try to eliminate me. Very soon. I would have tried to eliminate her long ago, but the only way to do that was to kill her. I couldn't do that—except in self-defense. And, if I told the authorities what she'd done so they'd arrest her, I'd be in jail, too.

Maybe, I thought, I should do just that. Whatever the consequences, I'd have to take them like a man.

No, I just couldn't do it.

But I hated myself because I couldn't.

And, ever the optimist, I hoped that all would in the end be well.

27

The phone rang. I awoke so swiftly I must've been cruising just below sleep's surface. For some nights now, the thing that knits up the raveled sleeve of care had been taking too many coffee breaks. My dreams were troubling, yet they were not about anything I could describe when I woke up. Mostly, they seemed to involve mixed metaphors.

I got up on one elbow and looked at the digits on the luminous screen of the caller ID. It was 11:32 P.M. The call was from Simon Alliger's office. Ice coated my neck hairs. A dead man was calling me.

I picked up the receiver. "Corbie speaking."

The voice was loud and shrill. "Mister Corbie! It's Rosemary! Rosemary Alliger! I need to talk to you! Right now! Can you come out now? I'll turn the alarm off and let you in through the front door!"

I paused for two beats, then said, "That depends on why you want me there. What do you want to talk about?"

She waited for three beats, then said, "It's what's been going on! All about what's been going on! I've kept quiet so far! I shouldn't have, but I couldn't help myself! I was afraid, so afraid! And so ashamed!"

"That sounds intriguing," I said. "But it doesn't tell me a thing about what's troubling you."

There was a silence for a few seconds before I said, "Who are you afraid of?"

"I really don't want to tell you over the phone. This line may be tapped."

"Who'd do that?"

"I can't say! I really can't!"

"Then I won't come. I don't know what you're up to."

"This is for real!" she said. "Please come! Please! Please! Believe me, once you get here, you'll understand!"

"Is your grandmother OK?"

"What? Why, yes, of course!"

"Is she involved in this?" I said. "I mean . . . is she in any danger?"

"She could be," Rosemary said. "Will you . . . ?"

"Who else is in the house?"

"What? What's the difference?"

"I have to know."

"Oh, grandmother's in her room, and Diana's in hers, as far as I know. That's all. Please, no more questions! Get over here! Please! If only I could tell you why! But I can't! Not over the phone! It's too dangerous! If you don't come now, I may have to leave this room and try to call you from another! But I'm not sure . . ."

"Not sure what Burt Kordik might do to you?" I said.

She gasped, then said, "I don't know how . . . OK, I am afraid of him. But he's not the only one. Now . . . are you coming over? Oh, I'm sorry! I forgot to tell you where I am. I . . ."

"Stop!" I said. "Don't say it! I know exactly where you are. Are you armed?"

"Yes, I have a pistol I got from Father's guncase."

"Stay there until you get my next call. I'll be there in fifteen minutes or less, then I'll call again. For God's sake, don't shoot anybody unless you're absolutely sure you're in danger."

I replaced the receiver. Then I left a message for Mimi Rootwell on the machine in the Tanglewood office. I told Mimi what time it was and that I was leaving to see Rosemary Alliger, who seemed to be very alarmed but was vague about why she was calling me. If anything happened to me tonight, Mimi would start digging into the why and the how, and she'd not stop until she had the answers.

Rosemary might really be as scared as she claimed to be. Or Lorna Mordoy might have put her up to luring me to the mansion. In either event, I couldn't ask the agency for backup, not if I wanted my part in this affair to be a secret. For the same reason, I couldn't call in the police, especially since I didn't even know if they'd be needed tonight.

I dressed quickly, though I took the time to put on a shoulder holster holding a .32 revolver with a four-inch-long barrel and an ankle holster holding a .22 revolver with a three-inch-long barrel. If there was going to be shooting, which I doubted, it'd be close-range work. Extra clips for the .32 were in my jacket pocket. I also stuck an ice pick into the narrow sheath on the other side of the ankle holster. And I took along a small flashlight and a pocket-size kit of picks and other locksmith tools.

I wore dark-blue socks and running shoes, dark-blue slacks and a dark-blue shirt, no necktie, and a dark-blue jacket. I wore the jacket only to conceal the shoulder holster and the pistol. Mordoy's plastic eye parts were, of course, in my jacket pocket.

When I went into the front room, I didn't turn on the lights. Instead, I stood at the French windows for a while and studied the cars in the parking lot, which was bright silvery under an almost full moon. No strange cars were in the lot.

Within sixty seconds, I was headed for the Alliger house. This time, however, I took a different route to it. I drove east on War Memorial Drive and, just before reaching the McClugage Bridge, left the road and took the route to the lower end of Grand View Drive. The car went through what used to be called the Devil's Hollow and on up the steep and winding road to the top of the bluff. At my right, far down, the Illinois River shimmered in the moonlight. To my left were trees and houses.

I came upon the Alliger driveway from the south, and I entered it where I usually exited. I'd seen no cars parked along the big road, no possible trailers or ambushers. Just before I turned onto the driveway, I cut off the headlights. Though the overhanging tree limbs made the road dark, the moonlight filtering down through the branches paled the blackness. I could see well enough to drive slowly, and I didn't want any watcher in the house or the woods to be warned I was coming. Though I felt somewhat foolish because of these precautions, I'd rather be embarrassed than dead.

It was 11:51 when I entered the driveway.

Patches of black and light from the branches and the moon lay on the tar road before me and ran through the windshield. I'd turned off the air-conditioning and lowered the window by my side. The air was very warm, though it would not have made me sweat if I hadn't worn my jacket.

When I got to the bend in the driveway and could see the entire house, I stopped the car. There were woods to my left and right. The line of garages with the servants' apartments above them were to my left, westward. The bend in the road was where the car would be parked while I went to the house on foot. All the windows in the mansion were dark. But

Simon's office was in the rear of the house. I wouldn't be able to see any light in it.

I called the phone in Simon's office. It rang once before the receiver was lifted. "Yes?" Rosemary said.

"Corbie," I said, though my voice should have identified me. "I'll be at the front door in a minute."

I hung up the receiver and quietly got out of the car and softly closed the door. I'd made sure the interior lights wouldn't come on when I opened the door. The car keys were in my shirt pocket.

Ten seconds after I'd called, a lamp blazed out from the front room windows, illuminating part of the porch.

Even if Rosemary had run at top speed, she could not have gotten down from Simon's office to the front door in ten seconds.

I suppose the confederate, standing by the front door in the dark, had been listening in to us with a cellular phone. But he or she had been too nervous or too impatient to wait until Rosemary was at his side. Or, much more likely, Rosemary's colleague was too stoned to use his intelligence — if he had any such thing.

Whatever had happened, I had stepped off the road and into the woods on its left. And I was moving as swiftly and as quietly as I could for the back of the garages. It wasn't far to go, perhaps sixty feet or seventy feet. Before I was more than twenty feet into the woods, however, headlights brightened the tunnel formed by trees. Then a car raced up and stopped, brakes squealing, just behind my car. And two other headlights swept from around the bend in the other direction. The second car stopped. My vehicle was between the two. I would've been trapped if I'd not taken off so fast.

I hadn't seen those two cars waiting for me up the road, waiting for me to pass them. But they hadn't seen me because

I was taking a route they hadn't expected me to take. By the time they'd changed their plan of action, and it hadn't taken them long, I was gone.

I didn't stop to look at them until I was behind the garage. Then I crouched low and stuck my head out from the corner. By then, the headlights were off, and the people who'd been in the cars were on the road. They were talking in low voices because they didn't want to wake up the servants in the quarters above the garages. The front room and porch lights of the house had also been turned off. The moon was bright enough for me to see two figures coming down the porch steps. The short small one in a dark shirt and slacks was Rosemary. I could see her blackened eye and bruised cheek. The other was tall and thin and shambled when he walked and wore a white shirt and light-colored slacks. Easy to see at night. Kordik, of course. I was sure I'd guessed right about the confederate being stoned. Otherwise, he'd have worn dark clothes. Moonlight gleamed on the metal of the revolver in his hand. Rosemary seemed to be unarmed, but that didn't mean she was.

Three persons stood by the two cars. All were in dark clothes and wore dark hats or caps. One of them turned on a flashlight and probed the darkness with the beam. It didn't come near my corner of the garage. Then a woman said something in a sharp and commanding tone, and the flashlight was turned off.

Kordik and Rosemary joined the group then. There was a brief parley. The figure which I thought was Mordoy's seemed to be doing most of the talking. It seemed to me that she was smart enough to have figured out what they should do next. That was to get out of here as soon as possible. I was hiding, and to track me down would lead to gunplay. The servants and Faith Alliger would call the cops. Mordoy didn't want that any more than I did. She had figured out that I had to keep silent about this affair because I didn't want the cops involved either. But, if I was pushed hard enough, I'd have to bring them in. And then it'd be all over for her and her co-conspirators.

Unless they got me first, and I was sure they'd not be wasting any time trying for that. In fact, I might find them waiting for me along Grand View Drive or at my apartment building. Cutting my life line was the first item on their new schedule.

I left the back of the garage and went through the woods toward them. They'd be leaving very soon. But I needed to identify the two who'd gotten out of the car that had pulled up behind my car. I thought I knew who they were, but I had to be sure.

The woman whom I thought was Mordoy walked to the car that had stopped in front of mine. She opened the driver's door. Unlike me, she hadn't turned off the interior lights. I saw her well enough, though her long-billed cap helped conceal her features. Lorna Mordoy, no doubt of that.

Kordik got into her car on the front passenger side. She turned on the ignition and started backing her car down the driveway. She didn't turn on the headlights until the car was out of sight around the bend.

The other two, who had to be Elseed and Moondeer, were busy making sure I wouldn't drive my vehicle for a while. Elseed opened the hood, removed the distributor, and threw it into the woods. Moondeer had let the air out of two of my tires.

Meanwhile, Rosemary had walked back to the front door of the house and was now standing there and watching the others. I figured she must be panicked, her bones aching with despair. She'd soon head for her cache of crack or whatever she was on.

The other two, their work done with my car, opened the two front doors of their vehicle. The interior lights came on.

Elseed got into the driver's seat. The woman, sitting down beside him, removed her cap.

I sucked in air. I'd expected to see the man, a dark-skinned and bearded mulatto, Lemangelo Elseed. I'd not expected to see the face of a woman I'd thought was sleeping in the mansion. The face of the woman in the car was beautiful, and her dark-red hair was cut in a China chop. She was, no doubt about it, Diana Alliger.

Something exploded in me. I was furious. Though I'd strongly suspected her of murdering Roger's parents, I'd just not believed that she was guilty. Not deep down really. I suppose it was because she was not only so beautiful, though I knew beauty had nothing to do with goodness, but because she was courageous and ambitious and had had a hard life and fought her way against the current.

I'd admired her. Never mind what minor faults she might have. And now she'd betrayed me. Me! That's why I was taking this so personally, why I'd lost my temper and, with it, my good sense.

That's why, just as Elseed turned the motor on, I burst out of the woods and ran to the open window of the driver's door and grabbed his beard with my left hand and jerked his head around and slammed my fist against his temple.

I let loose of the beard. My left wrist shot pain throughout my arm, and my right hand hurt even more. He fell over against Diana. She screamed. I ran around the front of the car. Just as I was almost even with the right front fender, light blazed again from the porch. Demented though I was, I had enough self-control to pause. Whoever was stepping out of the front door might be armed and dangerous. Or, if it was Faith, she should be warned to get back inside the house.

The woman in pyjamas who came out onto the porch was Diana Alliger.

The false Diana!

28

I was shocked and a little confused. What the hell? I thought. Yet, I'd been expecting something unusual. Just what, I hadn't known.

That surprise slowed me down, but so briefly that an observer wouldn't have noticed it. As I'd intended, I went around the front of the car to the other side. The right front window was down. I jerked the door open with my left hand. Agony again ran from my wrist up to my elbow. Despite that, I grabbed the woman by her hair with my left hand and pulled her half out of the car. I was more vicious than I would otherwise have been if the two Dianas hadn't looked so much alike. I was so angry because I felt like an utter fool, a one-hundred-percent moron. I should not have felt that way. But I did.

She stopped screaming when I struck her jaw with my fist. I opened my left hand, and she fell unconscious onto the tarred road. The blow, though not as hard as the one that'd felled Elseed, hurt the hand even more. But I didn't have time to hop around yelping with pain.

I whirled around, facing the porch. Rosemary and the fake Diana were still standing there. Rosemary's eyes and mouth were wide open, and her right hand clutched her throat. Diana, the fake one, recovered much more swiftly. She said, loudly, "What's going on?"

Then, as if suddenly realizing that she might not like the answer to her question, she spun, shoved Rosemary to one side, and ran back into the house. I saw her in the window of the door as she locked the door. Then the porch and front room lights went out.

I doubted she'd be calling the police. Not as yet, anyway.

Rosemary had staggered into the side of the house and thus kept herself from falling. She reached into her handbag, which was hanging by a strap over her shoulder, and pulled out a key with her left hand. Then she reached in again and pulled out a small revolver with a two-inch barrel. She got the screen door open, unlocked the door, opened it, and went inside. This took some dexterity, what with holding the gun in one hand and the key in the other. But she managed it, and she locked the front door behind her.

It was evident that she was going after the Diana in the house. I didn't know what to do then. That Diana was in very real danger. If I read rightly what had just happened, I'd been wrong thinking she was guilty of murder. And she needed me right now. But I didn't want the two I'd punched out to recover consciousness and come up on me from behind.

I quickly checked out the Moondeer woman, a.k.a. Diana Groat Rolanski the original, with one hand. No weapons on her body. So I took her handbag, which felt heavy enough to contain a pistol, and hurled it into the woods. Then I pulled Elseed out onto the road with my good arm, which actually wasn't that good. I frisked him and found a clasp knife with a six-inch blade and a .45 Luger automatic. I put both weapons into my jacket pockets, and I ran toward the front porch. At the same time, I reached into my shirt pocket and took out the key to the Alliger house.

Just as I stepped onto the dark porch, bright lights flashed across the left side of the mansion. I turned. A car had come up the driveway and stopped behind the one that Elseed had driven. Though I couldn't see who was in it, I was certain that Mordoy and Kordik had returned. Mordoy, I supposed, had been waiting on Grand View Drive for Elseed and Moondeer. Now, she'd come in to find out what was holding them up.

I unlocked the front door, stepped inside, and relocked it. Though the lights were off, the moonlight through the windows did show furniture and other objects. I felt the wall by the door for the light switches. Something rustled behind me. I started to spin around. Something struck the side of my head.

The next I knew, my head ached sharply, a bright light was in my eyes, and my eyes began to focus. I was also slightly sick to my stomach. I saw a table in front of me. I realized I was sitting in a chair with my hands tied behind me and my legs bound to the chair legs. My mouth was jammed with something soft, maybe cotton, and—I assumed—tape sealed my lips. I also felt wetness in the hair on the left side of my head and a warm ribbon of blood running down the left side of my face and on my neck and shoulder.

Then everything became clearer. I was in the kitchen of the Alliger house. The two Dianas were sitting in chairs to my left. I could recognize the fake Diana at once because her hands were tied behind her, and her lips were covered with tape. The other Diana, the real one, held a gun.

On the table before me: my pistols and ice pick and the

Luger and knife I'd taken from Elseed. On the edge of the table opposite me, the two parts of a plastic eye glistened in the lights. Whoever had frisked me had found them in my inner jacket pocket. I was sure that Mordoy had ordered them placed where I could see them.

Kordik leaned against the wall near the door to the hallway which led to the front room. A Browning Hi-Power 9 mm. automatic pistol was stuck in the belt holding up his worn pair of jeans. Of course, he was sneering.

Rosemary sat in a kitchen chair on the other side of the door. She was holding a Colt Detective Special .38 revolver. Its butt end, I assumed, had knocked me out. She looked scared.

Elseed wasn't present unless he was standing behind me. Three seconds or so later, Mordoy entered through the door to the hallway. Stuck in her belt, the safety on, was a handgun I'd not seen for years, a Heckler & Koch VP70Z 9mm. Parabellum with an 18-shot magazine. Its four-and-a-half-inch-long barrel meant it wasn't any good at long distance. But I was sure Mordoy was no slouch at using it.

As soon as her co-conspirators saw her, they became fully alert, foxhounds eager to show their mistress how good they were.

The bright overhead lights made her face look much older than when I'd seen it in the Duck Inn. There, she'd seemed to be about thirty. Here, wrinkles and lines I hadn't seen before added a hard fifteen years to her face. But then everybody here looked haggard and older. My face must've been ghastly, what with the bloody wound on my head, the pain, the paleness from loss of blood, and the mental shock I was suffering.

This time, I thought, is different. I'm not dealing with the drunken and moronic Mobards. No hope for escape here. I'm done for. But, five seconds later, my spirits began to rise. Somehow, I told myself, somehow, I'll find a way out of this awful trap.

Mordoy must have seen the change in me. Maybe my eyes lost their dullness and sparkled.

"Forget it," she said. "Before you leave this room, you'll be wishing you were dead."

She took the Heckler & Koch from her belt, released the safety, and placed it on the edge of the table. It pointed at me.

"I'm going to take the tape off," she said. "Don't yell. Not that it'd do you any good. The old lady's asleep and can't hear you, and they can't hear you in the servants' quarters either. Anyway, I'll knock your ears off if you try to yell. Nod if you're going to keep quiet."

When I nodded, my head hurt even more. She motioned to Kordik. He came around behind me and yanked the tape off. It hurt, though not very much. He pulled out most of the cotton with two fingers. I opened my mouth to ask her a question, but she spoke first.

"Elseed's dead," she said. She was smiling. "You killed him, crushed in his temple."

Diana, the original Diana, a.k.a. Artemis Moondeer, gasped, and she paled a little. But she said nothing.

"I wasn't trying to kill him," I said. "But I'm not sorry. Except for what it's doing to my knuckles."

They felt as if they were swelling up, and they still hurt.

"You'll be sorry. I guarantee that. You've fucked me up too many times for me not to make sure you're sorry."

I coughed for a moment. Cotton strands flew out from my mouth. When I'd recovered, I said, "OK. I figured on that. But, before you do whatever you're going to do, how about answering some questions? Just a couple, the big ones?"

She smiled, and said, "Maybe. But, first, you have to answer a couple of my questions. Deal?"

"Deal. But how about taking off Diana's tape? It's very uncomfortable."

"Let her suffer. Now, who knows about me, my part in this? Aside from having worked for Simon Alliger, I mean?"

"There's me, of course," I said. "You, Kordik, the — "

"You're playing for time. You know I don't mean the obvious people. Who knows? The grandmother, your boss? Who else? The police?"

I didn't know how much she knew. She was probably testing me to see if I was telling the truth. So, I told her the truth as I knew it. I ending by saying, "You know I'm in no position to bring in the cops."

"Yes, I worked that out. How'd you find out about the tie-in between Mrs. Roger Alliger, born as Harly Mobard, and Diana Rolanski, born in Pasadena, the original one?"

"I figured out that the Diana Rolanski who married Roger Alliger was not the original Diana, the child of Myrna Groat and William Rolanski. Shortly after William Rolanski died in Pasadena, or maybe before, his daughter Diana ran off with a man. I don't know who he was, maybe it was Elseed. He'd come from Chicago, and he and Diana ran off to Chicago. She was only fourteen, barely fourteen, then."

I stopped, then said, "How'm I doing?"

"Just fine, so far."

"Then this Diana," I bent my head toward Mrs. Roger Alliger, "showed up. She was the same age, and she was a runaway, too, only they were going in different directions. The newcomer looked a lot like Diana Rolanski. Why not? She was her first cousin. Her mother — dead by then — was Mary Groat, Myrna Rolanski's sister. Mary was the newcomer's mother, and Deak Mobard was her father. The newcomer's real name, I believe, was Harly Mobard."

Mordoy laughed, then said, "Harly for short. Harlequin for real. After the harlequin, the Maine duck, the most beautiful of ducks. Deak named all of his children after ducks. Teal, Wood, Drake, so forth."

I nodded, though doing that sent sharp-ended pulses through my brain. "Yes. Harly, I believe, was also named Angela, Angela Boomall. But that was for a relatively short time before she came to Los Angeles."

Mordoy looked surprised. She said, "You did your detecting."

I continued, "I just don't know exactly how Harly talked Mrs. Rolanski into passing her off as her daughter or why she would do it. Of course, moving from Pasadena to Los Angeles enabled them to pull it off."

"You knew that Myrna Groat Rolanski had a history of mental ailments? That she was in a sanitorium for six months with a nervous breakdown? That Myrna Rolanski hated her daughter because she was hooked on drugs and was fucking everything with pants, including a black man?"

"What I didn't know, I guessed. I assumed that Harly Mobard showed up shortly after Diana had run off with a man, maybe with Elseed. My operative, Garry Deb, couldn't find any record of Mrs. Rolanski's reporting it to the police or hiring a PI to track her down. She just accepted Harly as her daughter, a replacement for the girl she hated. After a while — I'm guessing — the half-crazed woman thought that Harly *was* her daughter."

Mordoy jerked a thumb at Harly Mobard. Harly tried to say something through the tape.

"After her real mother died in Goofy Ridge, no one protected her from her father when he tried to rape her. She fought him off twice, and the second time she gashed his face with a knife and knocked him out. Then she took off for California and her aunt, but she lived for a while with the Boomalls, who called her Angela. You know the rest."

"No, I don't," I said. "I admit I was wrong. I had Diana—
Harly—pegged as the murderer. But I wasn't sure. Now, I
know—too late. But how did you kill Simon and Alexandra
Alliger? And who actually did the killing? How were you and
these others going to benefit?"

She laughed loud and long, tilting her head up, her false eye
glinting now and then. Kordik and Moondeer—that is, the
real Diana Rolanski—also laughed. Rosemary, however,
looked sick.

When she was through laughing, Mordoy said, "We don't
know for sure who killed Alexandra, though Simon hated
his wife enough to do it, and I believe he did. None of us
did it, and who else could have loaded the bottle of wine
with all those drugs and then tried to wash out all traces of
them?

"As for Simon, the bees he was running away from when he
fell down the stairs . . . well . . . Rosemary released those. She
didn't, of course, catch them on the grounds and so take a
chance of being observed. No, we caught them, and she
brought them into the house in her handbag. A modern ancient Greek drama. Daughter slays father. Not with a knife but
with bees."

I looked at Rosemary but could not read whatever it was
that was twisting her face and paling her skin. Guilt? Shame?
The rending teeth of conscience?

"Just to make sure about certain items," I said. "When Harly
was being blackmailed by her father, she called you in to help
her? Right? And then you blackmailed her? And you got Rosemary and Kordik to help you? You promised them a big share
of the money Diana . . . Harly . . . would inherit? To do that,
though, you were also planning to eliminate Roger after waiting for a while so the police wouldn't get suspicious about so
many deaths in the family in such a short time.

"Let me make a guess. Roger was going to die of an over-dose. But Diana . . . Harly . . . didn't know about that. All she knew was that you were cutting yourself—and Rosemary and her bugshit boyfriend—in for a lot of money."

"Right."

"They're not very bright," I said. "Can't they figure out what you'll do to them when enough time has gone by and you have an opportunity to knock them off, too?"

"They're quite happy with our deal. Anything else?"

"A couple of things. How'd you find out about the Diana Rolanski, the real one, born in Pasadena, and Elseed?"

"They were involved in a scam I broke open in Chicago. Elseed and Moondeer got off, no charges against them. But when I was hired by Simon Alliger to investigate Mrs. Roger Alliger and then when the Mobards tried to blackmail Harly, I got to thinking. Artemis Moondeer looked very much like Harly, though they don't resemble each other as much as iden-tical twins do. But it seemed to me that Moondeer could be Harly's runaway cousin. I investigated, got Moondeer to open up to me, and it wasn't hard getting her to work with me. She'd been on drugs and booze and living like a skid-row bum ever since she ran off with Elseed."

"I got one more thing," I said. "Your plans were upset when Harly tried to call it quits. I'm guessing that she told Roger about her past, everything except your blackmailing her and Rosemary's part in it and that her father was Deak Mobard, the river-rat poacher and small-time criminal. She couldn't bear for him to know about her real family and her up-bringing."

"Right," Mordoy said.

"And you got desperate when Harly told you to go screw yourself. But here we are. Elseed's dead. You have to get rid of his body. You're going to kill me, right? There's my body to get rid of and the police inquiry about it. You can't dodge that. And if you kill Harly, your whole plan is snafued. You're not stupid enough to try to pass off Diana as Harly. It'd never work. Also, you must know Rosemary's going to break. She's a weak vessel."

"It's all taken care of," Mordoy said. "For one thing, when Harly sees what I'm going to do with you before I kill you, she'll keep her mouth shut until the day she dies of old age. The old lady'll be dying soon, a natural death. I don't have to help her along—unless she lives too long. And then Roger will DOA in one way or another, and Harly will inherit. Rosemary, Kordik, and Moondeer'll be happy to live in Chicago or wherever and spend all the money they'll be getting."

She smiled, then said, "Your curiosity satisfied?"

"Not as long as I live," I said.

"Welllll," she drawled.

My neck hairs were once more encased in ice.

She nodded at Kordik, still standing behind me. He grabbed my hair and jerked my neck back. More and worse pain ran through me. He stuffed the cotton back into my mouth, slapped the tape over my lips, and then let loose of my hair.

Mordoy picked up the plastic sphere and held it high against the light. "You kept this so you could give it back to me," she said. "You thought it'd be a dramatic moment, perhaps a symbolic one. An eye for an eye. The good PI throws the bad PI's artificial orb onto the table in front of her. Here's your Plastic Eye, villainess! It's got more soul in it than you have in your whole body! Something like that, right?"

I nodded. Why not? Nothing I did was going to change what was going to happen to me, whatever that was.

She gestured at Moondeer. The woman got up and passed on my left and was out of my sight. A drawer squeaked as it opened. Silverware or knifeware rattled. Knifeware? No. It was a tablespoon that Moondeer put on the table.

The pain in my head was nothing to the pain I felt when Mordoy spooned out my left eyeball and tore it loose from the optic nerve.

"Tit for tat," she said.

I fainted.

When I came to, I still had the tape over my mouth and my hands-were tied behind me. But the ropes binding me to the chair had been untied. Kordik was lifting me up from the chair. The pain was unendurable, but I had to bear it unless I fainted again, and I wished I could. The weapons and the fake eye-assembly and the real eye were gone. Vaguely, I was aware that they were in a white plastic garbage sack held by Moondeer.

Then I was between Kordik and Rosemary. They were lifting me and dragging me at the same time.

The door to the hallway was wide enough for Kordik to haul me through. Moondeer waited in the hallway to resume assisting him. Harly, I was half-aware, was free of the chair but her mouth was still taped. Rosemary, sobbing, went first into the huge front room. Mordoy and Harly followed her. Both then stopped.

The room was dark except for the light from the driveway lamps and the moonlight coming in from the windows. Mordoy turned on her flashlight and pointed the beam toward the front door. We were supposed to precede her to it.

I'd closed my left eyelid to shut out the air hitting the nerves on the inside of the socket, but that didn't ease the agony one bit. Phlegm was filling my throat. I could feel the hot vomit in my stomach getting ready to propel itself upward and fill my throat and mouth.

I was going to throw up and then choke and die unless the

cotton stuffing was taken out of my mouth and the tape was removed from my lips.

I let my legs go dead. It was easy to do because they were half-dead anyway. Kordik cursed. Moondeer said, "Did he faint?"

They laid me down on the floor in a patch of light. Mordoy came out of the darkness and leaned over me. She said, "He's either faking it to gain time or he's really passed out. Never mind. You two, grab a leg each and drag him."

Then the lights in the room came on.

I couldn't see anything except the ceiling and part of the gallery running alongside the second floor. Someone was crouched behind the railing of the gallery. Whoever it was, he or she was poking a rifle out between two of the verticals. I couldn't see it well. But it looked like its caliber was .30-06. I couldn't really tell.

The person up there never said a word. The rifle boomed. A click followed. Ah, I thought, bolt action. Then Mordoy fell onto my chest. I blacked out, though I knew somehow as I passed out that the vomit was finally coming.

I did hear other shots, though. Two. Some man was screaming. A woman was screaming. And my senses slipped away from me.

When I awoke, I was being carried out on a gurney. The tape was gone from my mouth, but the bitter taste of vomit was in my mouth. I saw uniformed policemen, two of whom I knew, standing near me in the big room. And then a familiar voice told the ambulance men to stop the gurney. Faith's wrinkled face, looking grave, appeared above me. She was wearing thick shell-rimmed spectacles.

"You poor thing!" she said. She bent down and kissed me on the forehead. Then she straightened up. "I'm old, but I can still shoot straight."

I think the attendants had given me a shot of pain killer.

But, though I was fading away, I said, maybe murmured, "You were the . . . rifle . . . ?"

"Yes, my dear."

It wasn't until next morning that I thought, dully, of course, because I was so sedated, Here I am, the big, strong, tricky, and steel-nerved private dick who's saved from death . . . from the villains . . . by . . . face it, admit it . . . a ninety-two-year-old woman.

month later, I was almost used to the plastic ball which had been inserted into my eye socket. Muscles had been sewn around it, and a shield looking like my good blue eye had been inserted in front of the ball and under the eyelids. Perhaps, thirty thousand years from now, long after my coffin and body have become dust, erosion will reveal the ball and the shield to some nomadic tribe. Those descendants of a perished civilization will declare they're the long-sought two-part eye of the god Lawngtaymnosee, and worship them.

Thus, I will, after many millennia of dusty obscurity, attain my natural and rightful status as a god. It's nice to think so.

As for the present, I'd gotten off much better than I deserved. I didn't come up out of the mess smelling like cherry pie, but I was not in disgrace and not in jail. However, I was still in trouble, since Glinna was still somewhat reproachful toward me.

It wasn't until the pain-dulling drugs had worn off that I found out what had brought Faith Alliger to the gallery just as

Harly and I were being taken away from the house. A very vivid dream in which I played a prominent part had awakened Faith. (She never did tell me what the dream was about, but she blushed when she mentioned it.) Then, she thought she heard a noise in the next room. She'd investigated but found no one. However, she was so convinced that someone was prowling around that she'd gone out into the hall and then to Simon's office to get a rifle from the gun cabinet.

There she found the lights on, the cabinet door open, and a pistol missing. She did not know, of course, that Rosemary had been there to arm herself before phoning me. But Faith took a rifle and loaded it with ammunition from a box on a lower shelf. Then she called the police and, instead of going back to her room, as the police advised, went down to the gallery. Shortly afterward, Harly and I were conducted from the kitchen.

The old lady could see that Harly and I were being abducted and that I was in very bad shape. (Later on, she told the police that she'd ordered the abductors to throw down their weapons and put their hands up. But Faith was protecting herself with the fake story. No fool, she did not give the criminals a chance to shoot at her.) She put a bullet in Mordoy's brain, killing her instantly, and wounded Kordik in the shoulder. He'd dropped his gun, and, with Rosemary and the original Diana Rolanski, had fled in Mordoy's car. They had headed down the steep winding drive to Galena Road, two police cars, lights flashing, sirens wailing, in close pursuit.

Near the bottom, the car had soared off the road, gone over the side of the hill, rolled over three times, hit a tree, and burst into flames. All its occupants were charred to the bone.

Diana Alliger, born as Harly Mobard, and Faith Alliger had been taken at once to the nearest hospital for observation. Roger and his lawyer, Jack Crotal, arrived at the hospital twelve minutes later. Crotal managed to confer with the women before the police questioned them and to advise them what story they should tell the police.

Roger, I was told later, seemed to be as much in shock as the women. I think that it wasn't so much from the events as that he was half-stoned on drugs and booze. I hear that he's still shooting heroin and sniffing coke. It won't be long before Roger does to himself what Mordoy'd planned for him. And then Harly, the ragged river rat waif who'd lived in a shack with a dirt floor and in a leaky houseboat, will become mistress of the Alliger fortune.

As soon as I recovered enough to think clearly, I was advised by Crotal to get myself a lawyer. Which I did, hiring John Garm of Lamia, Garm, Rusalka, and Jones, a firm regarded by many as ravening monsters. Garm then arranged for my story to coincide with Diana's. As far as the police were concerned, she was indeed the daughter of Mr. and Mrs. William Rolanski, and what was in the public records was the truth.

I told the police that I'd been hired by Faith Alliger to investigate Mordoy. Why had Mordoy attacked me and Diana? Because, I said, and Diana backed me up, Mordoy and the others in the plot had decided to abduct Diana and to murder her. Then Rosemary would be in line for the inheritance. I suggested that Roger would have been murdered next, after a suitable time. Rosemary would get the Alliger fortune. But Mordoy wouldn't care to keep sharing the money with Moondeer and Kordik. So, they'd have to go. And I had to be eliminated, too, because I knew too much about Mordoy. Hence, Rosemary's phone call to me. The story Diana, a.k.a. Harly, and I told was a mixture of truth and fiction but was accepted as all true by the police.

What had really happened was this: Harly had balked at

killing me. Then Mordoy, desperate, on the run, perhaps not thinking as coolly as usual, had threatened to kill Harly if she didn't co-operate. Mordoy had ripped out my eye to show Harly what'd be done to her if she crossed Mordoy.

I'd killed Elseed, and I admitted it to the police. But it seemed evident to the authorities that I'd acted in self-defense. (I hadn't, really. Not technically, anyway. But who was there to contradict my story? And isn't attack the best method of defense?)

As the first step to starting a new life now that the old one had been erased (in a manner of speaking), I'd decided to declare to the IRS the money I'd taken from the Mobards in Goofy Ridge. It was the only honest thing to do. It was also, in a way, part of my repayment for the unethical, if not downright unlawful, things I'd done as a private investigator. But I'd made full payment for my sins when I'd lost my eye. That kind of thinking might seem peculiar to some people. Not to me. I had absolved my guilt, done high expiation, with the sacrifice of my eye.

From now on, my life was going to be conducted strictly on logic and common sense. No more would I give in to foolish impulses which would hurl me into a bottomless mire. No more would I be ruled by greed. I'd learned my lesson. I'd traded an eye for wisdom.

One thing remained to be dealt with. Actually, that had nothing to do with the Alliger case, and I'd just as soon have let it go. But Sheridan Mutts wouldn't cut it loose. He'd phoned me three times since I'd gotten out of the hospital. The third time, he interrupted me while I was reading a book on Peoria Indian myths and legends. At the moment the phone call came, I was immersed in a tale wherein Withiha the trickster, the Great White Hare, had been challenged by a giant, Stone Head, to a duel to the death.

"You're not going to weasel out of this, you coward!" Mutts bellowed. "Not unless you apologize and admit you're a yellow-bellied shit-eating skunk and get down on your knees and kiss my big bare hairy ass in a public place!"

The first two times he'd called, I'd reminded him that the restraining order on him forbade phone calls to me. But I knew I was wasting my time attempting to talk good sense into his brain. I might as well try to toilet train a bird.

"Lily-livered craven!"

In a way, he was delightful and refreshing. I don't think there was another person in Peoria who used such old-fashioned phrases. Yellow-bellied? Lily-livered craven? I almost liked him.

"OK," I said. "I'm sick of you and your moronic drivel. I'm still not well, and I'm one-eyed and don't have the full strength in my left hand. But I can knock you ass-over-appetite six different ways on a Sunday and not work up a sweat."

I talked that way because I wanted to show him that he wasn't the only one who could spout clichés.

"Next Saturday night, 10:00 P.M., at The Last Stand, we tangle. Weapons: garbage can lids. No fists, no head butts, no kicking. Lids only. First man to be knocked down, he loses. And he kisses the winner's disgusting ass. Rhino Bill'll be the referee. Anybody breaks the rules gets whatever Rhino Bill decrees is the punishment. He also agrees to get out of town as soon as possible if he loses. He goes at least a hundred miles away, and he never comes to Peoria again. Also, if, no matter what the reason, he fails to show up for the fight or backs out of it, he abides by the same rules. Agreed?"

Mutts seemed taken aback for a moment. Then he said, "Garbage can lids? Get out of town, move to a place at least a hundred miles away? Well . . . OK. Agreed. Get ready . . ."

"Be there," I said.

As soon as I hung up, I was deep in doubt and anxiety. If I did lose, how would I explain to Glinna that we had to give up our jobs and find a place to live in another town?

Answer: I'd be leaving without her. She'd be angry enough to put a spell on me, turn me into a toad or a televangelist. I wouldn't blame her.

I picked up the phone and called a man and a woman, both of whom worked in The Last Stand and owed me for favors I'd done for them when I used to be a regular patron there. Since they detested Mutts, they weren't reluctant to help me.

Four days later, Saturday evening, 9:45 P.M., I drove to The Last Stand. Glinna was in Chicago attending a meeting of the Illinois chapter of the Covenant of the Goddess. I was wearing the summer uniform of Last Stand customers—workboots, jeans, a big belt, and a T-shirt.

The tavern was near that section of Galena Road that ran just below the foot of the high bluffs along the western side of the river not very far north of the city limits. I turned onto a dirt road that went east to the river's edge. After I passed through a woods, I came to a large sand-and-dirt parking lot. Tonight, it was packed with cars. Beyond, on high upright logs and partly built out over the river, was a long one-story red cedar plank building with a high-pitched roof. The outside was lit by large electric lamps, around which fluttered a storm of insects. A big sign, white with black letters, hung down over the main entrance. THE LAST STAND.

When I entered, the roar of voices and jukebox country-western music and a cloud of tobacco smoke and the odor of tobacco, beer, whiskey, sweat, belches, farts, fried hamburgers, fried onions, french fries, and a hint of vomit and urine smote me.

Above the entrance was a big sign: NO WEAPONS, CHILDREN, OR PURITANS ALLOWED. Flanking that, but on the walls at eye level, were two identical signs.

LIST OF FORBIDDEN WORDS
The following are slurs, politically incorrect words, obscenities, and blasphemies the management will not tolerate under any circumstances:

Below each warning was a large blank space.

I stepped inside this refuge for the genuine macho and the fake macho, a tavern perhaps not quite like any other in the world, though the Peoria Chamber of Commerce never mentions it. My eye smarted, and my nostrils cringed. But I'd soon get used to it. Through the swirling blue clouds I could see, though dimly, to the other end of the huge room.

Behind the bar there were four bartenders. One of them was the man I'd telephoned. Sam "Queer Keg" Tomavii. A tall very black and kinky-haired man whose parents had been cannibals. His teeth were filed to points, and he sometimes wore a pointed bone in his nose. Since he was born and raised in the high misty mountains of the great island of New Guinea, six thousand miles east of Africa, he objected fiercely to being called an African-American.

However, Sam liked to tell his customers that his name was Queequeg (hence, altered by the customers into Queer Keg) and that he was a native of the South Pacific island of Kokovoko. Before he came to Peoria, he said, he'd been a harpooner on a whaling ship.

A customer once said to him, "I looked for Kokovoko in an atlas, couldn't find it."

Queer Keg: "It's not down in the map; true places never are."

His reply was a quotation from *Moby Dick*. Behind that black cannibal face with the filed teeth was a scholar. Also, he enjoyed a joke, especially practical ones, and he disliked Mutts.

I made my way toward the bar across the sawdust-strewn floor around the round wooden tables and the customers in their chairs and the spittoons. On the way, I greeted some old habitués, men and women I used to see a lot before I got married. They shouted words of encouragement. "Kick the shit out a 'at windbag, Tom!" was the mildest. But I also had to endure comments about my ass having been saved by a little old lady.

The walls all around were hung with paintings, prints, and posters. There was, of course, the famous but historically incorrect Budweiser painting of Custer's Last Stand. There were old movie stills and posters advertising once-great western stars Tom Mix, Buck Jones, and Ken Maynard. Real men, giants, unlike the narrow-chested punies in the era following them, especially the flabby Gene Autry, who couldn't punch his way out of a paper bag or act or sing his way out of one, either. There were blowups of John Wayne (a worthy successor of Tom Mix) as U.S. Marshal Rooster Cogburn, Clint Eastwood as Dirty Harry Callahan, Janet Leigh nude from the waist up in the shower scene from *Psycho* (this must have been from Alfred Hitchcock's collection), the calendar Marilyn Monroe, Betty Page, and many other undressed females. But this was the age of equality, so there were also posters of a nude Burt Reynolds (a white movie actor), Dennis Rodman (a black basketball player), and a gargantually endowed but now-dead white porno star.

Hanging horizontally above the bar was a dried blue whale's pizzle at least ten feet long. No wonder Glinna hated this place.

I ordered a beer. While sipping it, I looked around. I spotted Rhino Bill, the owner of the tavern. Then I saw Mutts, his live-in Cindi Wickling, two male cronies, and their bouffant-hairstyle bleached-blond good-time women at a table. A waitress, one of those who owed me, was serving them schooners of jalapeno beer, a specialty of a local microbrewery. According to what she'd later tell me, Mutts and party had come in at eight on the dot and had been drinking steadily since then, though they'd wolfed down lots of beer nuts and a specialty of the house, raw mountain oysters (that is, bull or pig testicles).

The young, lithe, slender, and fresh-looking but squint-eyed blonde serving them was Deirdre Harmos. She was usually on the same shift as fortyish, blond chunky, beat-up, and lame Ruthie Omohundro, the woman who owed me a favor. They wore only white T-shirts, shorts, and sandals. On the back and fronts of the shirts were the legend: NOLI ME TANGERE. Latin for Don't Touch Me (Mark 20:17).

Rhino Bill didn't allow his customers, male or female, to harass his waitresses.

Customers: "You Noli?"

Waitresses, flashing weary smiles: "No, me Tangere."

I waited until Harmos held up her hand with the thumb and forefinger forming an O and Queer Keg also signaled to me. Then, I tapped Rhino Bill on the shoulder, and I said, "I'm ready."

He gestured at Rooster Wooster, the bouncer, to turn the jukebox off. A few seconds after the music had died, Rhino Bill yelled, "OK! The battle starts in three minutes! Anybody wants to see it, out on the dock now!"

Chairs scraped as they were shoved back, boots clomped on the sawdust-strewn floor, and a loud chattering arose. I walked out to the dock behind Rhino Bill, who was carrying an electric cattle prod. He used this to punish fighters who broke the rules or refused to stop battling when he thought they should. Though macho, he worried about lawsuits and losing his liquor license. He tried to make sure that nobody was badly hurt.

There were about sixty people out on the big dock behind the tavern. They opened up to let me and Mutts through. Inside the cleared space, he and I were each handed a used garbage can lid. He was swaying a little, and his face was very red in the lights of the big kliegs on the dock. It was showing the first signs of internal distress.

When Rhino Bill had finished bellowing the rules for the fight, he shook the prod as if it were a marshal's baton, and shouted, "Go to it! May the best man win!"

I could hear the gurgling in Mutts's bowels over the noise of the crowd. Nevertheless, he stepped forward boldly and swung his garbage can lid, edge horizontal, at me. I blocked it by using my lid as a shield. The clanging was loud. A shock ran down through my arm, but I did not drop the lid. He stepped back, breathed deeply, and then, snarling, stepped forward again.

But he dropped the lid, bent over, and clutched his paunch. "Goddammit! I'm sick!"

Then he got down on all fours, groaned loudly, and filled his pants with some of the foulest stuff I've ever smelled, and I've smelled a rotting human corpse floating in a sewage tunnel. No one doubted then that he was truly sick. But they didn't stay to commiserate with him.

I was declared winner. Mutts refused to kiss my bare ass. But he knew that he couldn't evade moving out of town at least a hundred miles away. That made a big problem for him since his bail bond terms prohibited him from leaving the metropolitan area.

I grinned all the way home. The taste of the castor oil which Queer Keg had put in the beer had been disguised by the strong jalapeno flavor. And Deirdre Harmos had made sure that Mutts was the only one to get the doctored-up beer.

30

Two weeks later, at 9:48 in the evening, the phone rang in my bedroom. I was sure that something bad had happened because the caller ID displayed the number of the phone in Faith Alliger's bedroom. She'd been in failing health, and I'd twice visited her. Though I dreaded to pick up the receiver, I did what had to be done.

Diana Alliger spoke in a very low voice. "Mr. Corbie, she's asking for you again. This time . . . I'll only say you should hurry."

Glinna, who usually went to bed early, was sleeping soundly. After I dressed, I wrote a note for her and left it on my bedside table. Twelve minutes later, Juan Cabracan conducted me to Faith's suite. Both Roger and Diana Alliger greeted me, she warmly, he coldly. But he sat down in an easy chair in the outer room, and she led me into the bedroom.

Its lights were low, and two tall candles burned with flickering flames on a small table to the left of the bed and by the north wall. Above them was a large framed painting of a young woman, a flapper of the early 1920s, Bobbie Gerichter.

On my first visit to this room, I'd expected to find a portrait of her long-dead lover, Avram Gessner. But it'd become evident during our talks that Avram had faded away and Bobbie dominated Faith's memory of the past. After all, Avram had been very serious, and Bobbie had been so much fun and had been Faith's companion since kindergarten.

The windows behind the bed were open. The wind was mild, fresh, and cool and lacked the heavy wetness it had been carrying for the past week. There was no odor of medicines or of approaching death. Nor was there the usual paraphernalia of the hospital, the oxygen tube, the IV drip, the urine catheter, the beeping monitors, nothing sticking out of her. She had opted to die at home and opted not to put off the end for a few weeks.

The old lady was on her back in the bed, two large pillows under her head. She opened her eyes when Diana said, "Faith! Tom Corbie's here!" She smiled slightly, and she held out a skeletal hand. Her eyes were deep-sunken and ringed with black. I took her hand; it was very cold.

She murmured, "Bend down, Tom. I'm too weak to . . ."

I did so. Now, I could smell death, though the odor was not strong. Or, maybe, it was my imagination.

She said, very softly, "Tom, I'll sum up the essence of the world as I perceive it, if you're interested."

I said, "You know I'm much more than just interested."

"Very well. It's mostly bullshit. However, despite how I feel about this world, I've had some good times, great times. I'd rather have been born than not born, rather lived to an old age instead of dying young. Still . . ."

She was silent for several seconds. I squeezed her hand gently, and I hoped my expression transmitted to her just how I felt about her. I really liked the old woman. And I'm sure she really liked me. It wasn't a sexual feeling, though, if we'd been the same age, it would have been. No question of that.

She said, "O wanderer and gatherer of wisdom, tell me a wondrous tale, a tale to light my way into the darkness prepared for me by the Sunderer of Delights. A tale that will completely surprise me and fill me with wonder."

I didn't know why she was talking like a character out of the *Arabian Nights*. But I nodded. And then I looked over my shoulder. Roger was not in sight, but Diana was standing in the doorway. I said, "We need complete privacy, Diana."

She turned and walked away. I bent down again and spoke softly. "You must promise me that you will never tell anyone else this story, nor will you allow what I tell you to change what you've planned for a certain person in this tale. It is a true tale."

She whispered, "I promise."

I said, "Once upon a time, there was a daughter born into a very poor family who lived in a shack or, sometimes, in a houseboat on the river." And I told her what Diana's true name was and where she was born and how she had happened to become Diana Rolanski. I told her everything, including my meeting Mordoy, the shootout at Lakeside Cemetery, my captivity by the Mobards, my escape, and how I had killed Deak and his son, Teal. When I'd ended, I said, "Is that a tale to light your way, Faith?"

Her eyes had been wide open and shining throughout my revelation. Now, she said, very weakly, "Thank you, Tom. That was a truly wondrous story, a story of an errant or perhaps erring knight and a Cinderella. Still, you had to play all sorts of tricks, deceive many people, lie a lot. I don't doubt your intentions were good, but the road to hell . . ."

". . . is paved with good inventions," I said.

She said, "What? Oh, you . . . !"

Then she laughed so loudly and so long that Roger and Diana came to the doorway. But the laughing became a bubbling sound as of phlegm rushing into her throat. Then came a long rattling sound, and she died.

I suppose that was a pun to make many choke, but I'd not expected that it would kill her.

Diana and Roger ran into the room then. Diana started weeping and saying that she should have been there for Faith's last moments. Roger asked me what I'd said to her. I think he believed that I'd somehow brought about her death, but he was too conscious of slander suits to accuse me.

I waited until the ambulance people came, told Diana that I felt as bad as she did, and then left. Roger was not backward about telling me to leave the family with its grief. I repressed the impulse to tell him that he was far more a stranger to her than I was. I got home at 11:03 P.M. but didn't go straight to bed. What delayed me was the mess Glinna'd left in the front room. I'd noticed on the way out an open book face down on the sofa, a sandal on the floor by the sofa, and a crumpled piece of tissue paper on the rug by the French windows.

After replacing the book on a shelf and picking up the sandal, I went to the tissue and started to bend down to get it. At that moment, a pane of glass in the French window shattered. I heard the bullet whee just over my head. And I heard it spang off the tachyon emitter, knocking it over and denting it, ricochet again, this time off of the bronze statuette of the Cretan snake goddess, denting it and rocking it in its high niche on the wall. For the second time, a glass pane broke. The bullet had ricocheted out of the French window. And, as I discovered after I'd called the police and waited until I was sure the would-be killer was gone and then looked cautiously out of the window, the bullet had gone at a downward angle.

There, lying on his back in the bushes along the edge of the parking lot, the bright moonlight on his face, the rifle by his side, was Sheridan Mutts. The bullet he'd fired at me and that might have hit me if I hadn't bent down to pick up the tissue paper, that bullet had ricocheted back out of the window at just the right angle to hit Mutts in the forehead almost between his eyes. Of course, by then it had lost much of its original energy. But it had enough to knock him out.

The cops arrived, and it was midnight before I got to bed. Glinna slept through everything. I didn't awaken her because she'd have been angry at being dragged out of her abysmally deep sleep. But I might as well have. She became furious in the morning when I told her what had happened, and she chewed me out for an hour. But, as I knew would occur, she suddenly realized I might've been killed, and she began weeping and then laughing, and all was well.

Some people still don't believe this story about the ricocheting bullet and my luck in not getting hit. But I tell them about what happened to my father's father when he was living in Chicago. He was at that time a drunk and a skidrow bum and had a false name because the police wanted him for embezzlement.

One day, drunk and walking on the tracks of the elevated, he was hit by a southbound train. It should have hurt him badly or killed him. Instead, it lifted him up and over to the northbound track. The train coming along there caught him in mid-air and threw him back to the southbound track. And another train there caught him and curved him back into the air and then down to the ground.

He was bruised somewhat, and his leg was broken. Those were his only injuries.

After his encounter with the trains, he was convinced that God was looking out for him and had indeed performed a miracle to save him. He got religion, quit drinking, turned himself into the police, was acquitted at the trial, and returned to his law practice.

The wonder of this tale shone in the eyes of my hearers—

in those who believed it, anyway—and I'm sure they were better men and women for it. I saw no reason to tell them that my grandfather later on backslid, started drinking again, and, once more, became a skidrow bum. But that was his choice. No one forced him to take that road.

Recently, while drinking coffee at Mocha Joe's with my father, I said, "Even though I've lived through some very bad times and have lost an eye, I'm still an optimist."

He said, "You're an idiot!"

I didn't reply.

Then—did I detect a smokecurl of wistfulness?—he said, "But you're a happy idiot."

I smiled. No need for words.

Nothing burns in hell, except self-will.

—*Anonymous German medieval monk*

The Americans—a moral people except when it comes to murder and so on.

—*Trader Horn*

Jesus's act bombed in Peoria. He no sooner stepped off the bus from Chicago than he was given the keys to the city. He stuck these up the mayor's major attribute. Then things got worse. What kind of Socialist crap is that about the rich and hellfire, the camel and the eye of the needle?

—*Memoirs of Orson Bunhanger*

My heartfelt thanks for data provided me by the following:

Rick Baker, Mary Kay Berjohn, Terry Bibo, Lynn and Julia Carl, Richard Corley, M.D., Bette Andre Farmer, Bob Hinman, Bill Knight, Gloria LaHood, George T. McWhorter, Don Oberle, Patrick Rhode, M.D., Charles and Janet Roth, Ralph Sawyer, Lil Schindler, Dede Weil, and Gary Wolfe. All were very helpful and saved me much time and sweat.